ROAD OF BONES

Christopher Golden

TITAN BOOKS

Road of Bones
Print edition ISBN: 9781803361475
E-book edition ISBN: 9781803361482

Published by Titan Books
A division of Titan Publishing Group Ltd
144 Southwark Street, London SE1 0UP
www.titanbooks.com

First Titan edition: November 2022
10 9 8 7 6 5 4 3 2 1

This is a work of fiction. All of the characters, organizations, and events portrayed in this novel are either products of the author's imagination or are used fictitiously. Any resemblance to actual persons, living or dead (except for satirical purposes), is entirely coincidental.

A CIP catalogue record for this title is available from the British Library.

Printed and bound in the United Kingdom by CPI Group Ltd.

Praise for *Road of Bones*

"Golden, an economical writer, creates a mother lode of terror in just over 200 pages… Shamans and spirits, the undead and the feral, the creatures of the Kolyma Highway and the unimaginable horrors of its history make for riveting reading."

The New York Times Book Review

"Christopher Golden's *Road of Bones* is tightly wound, atmospheric, and creepy as hell. It will take you to a place you've never been before, and the trip will scare the hell out of you. I loved it."

Stephen King

"Two men willing to risk their lives for a last-chance reality TV pitch find themselves on a white-knuckle hell ride on Siberia's infamous Kolyma Highway. *Road Bones* is unrelenting and will chill you to your core."

Paul Tremblay

he road is long, the night is cold, and there's terror t every pullout, nothing but dread between. Just try and put this book down, I dare you."

Stephen Graham Jones

"A masterclass in mind-set and setting; I've never felt the temperature of a book so firmly. I've also never been so afraid to step outside. In some ways a quick story (the central events span much less than 24 hours), in other ways enormous: the emotional stakes could not be higher. A breathtaking experience, a glacial gust of a book, Christopher Golden's best yet."

Josh Malerman

"*Road of Bones* is wonderful! The frozen waste is so vividly rendered, I felt the biting cold in my own bones and drew breath with the characters as they fought for survival against the vastness of nature. Gripping, eerie and ultimately beautiful. It's a breakneck speed adventure, with so much soul at its heart."

Catriona Ward

"I don't know how else to say it. This book is scary as f***. Do not read alone in the dark."

Catherynne M. Valente

"This book is legit great. Golden is the master of what I think of as 'adventure horror.' People in strange places and extreme situations meeting terror at the edges of the world. *Road of Bones* is scary as hell and does not fuck around."

Chuck Wendig

"Golden is writing at the top of his game."

Publishers Weekly (starred)

For John McIlveen and Tony Tremblay,
the nicest guys in horror

1

Teig snapped awake behind the wheel and hit the brakes, but the tires found only ice. Prentiss screamed as they slid across rutted permafrost. Teig turned into the skid and tapped the accelerator, heart thundering as he tried to get the treads to grip the road. He looked past the guardrail at snow-caked treetops, mountains in the distance. The drop off the edge would kill them, but at least it would be faster than freezing to death on the Kolyma Highway.

The tires caught. Teig gave the wheel a nudge, turned away from the drop, but momentum slammed them into the guardrail. With a crump of broken metal, the truck broke through, tilted toward the drop, and Teig bellowed in fear as he floored it. Metal shrieked as the broken guardrail dug into the UAZ's side panel, but the truck leapt forward.

Veins pulsed at his temples as he pumped the brake. He dropped the UAZ into park, killed the engine, and stumbled out of the truck on an adrenaline high that made him want to roar. Instead he dropped to his knees and leaned over the guardrail, sucking in breath after breath of frigid air. The view might have been spectacular, but the drop would have killed them. Thirty feet to his left a small section of the guardrail had been punched through, and another dozen feet of it was now bent and mangled, all from the impact of the truck. How he had kept them on the road, he had no idea. Teig took another deep breath, mostly to prevent himself from puking up the sugudai he'd had for lunch.

A door slammed. Boots crunched on the snow. Teig heard his name being called but he hadn't finished combating his nausea quite yet. The cold helped. Icy air seared his lungs and stung his exposed skin. His breath fogged in front of him. The only sounds were the wind and his pounding heart and the ticking of the rapidly cooling engine.

And that voice. Prentiss.

"—fuck are you doing?" he barely heard.

Prentiss shoved him with a boot, shouted his name. Teig grabbed the guardrail to keep from toppling sideways onto the snow, his head clearing at last. He turned to glare at Prentiss, saw the fury and fear on his friend's face, and knew he had to get on his feet.

"Keys, Teig!" Prentiss snapped. "Give me the goddamn keys!"

Just past him, Teig saw the side of the once-orange UAZ Expedition, now dented and scraped, the metal perforated in two spots, as if the broken guardrail had clawed at the truck. The thing might be a barebones model, but it had been enough to keep them alive.

"Teig!" Prentiss barked. He thrust out his hand, palm up.

At last, the word *keys* registered in his brain. Teig launched himself from the ground, rushing to the open driver's door. He'd left the keys in the ignition but Prentiss had naturally assumed otherwise. Teig reached in, turned the key, and the engine hummed and clicked, groaning. Trying to turn over.

The cold had seeped in already.

"Fuck!"

Prentiss grabbed Teig's jacket from behind and shunted him aside. He climbed into the driver's seat, tapped the accelerator, foot on the brake, and tried the ignition himself. It coughed but didn't catch.

From behind the steering wheel, Prentiss turned to stare at Teig, eyes wide. "Felix, what the fuck did you do?"

Teig wanted to pitch him over the guardrail. Most days he and Prentiss were close friends, maybe best friends, but as colleagues they spent a lot of time virtually on top of one another, often in close spaces or on dangerous terrain. Prentiss might be a much larger man, but Teig had never let himself be bullied. Not by anyone.

Of course, most of the time he didn't have it coming. Today, maybe he did.

"Try it again!"

"I don't want to flood it," Prentiss said. He might be angry, but his eyes were bright with the fear of a dog in the lights of an oncoming car.

"Start the fucking truck!"

Prentiss turned the key. The engine coughed again, started to grind, and the floor dropped out of Teig's stomach. He loved his work, but he didn't want to die for it.

The engine caught, growled to life, and left Teig and Prentiss staring at each other, relieved but still amped up.

"You fell asleep behind the wheel," Prentiss said, his voice only a rasp above the rumble of the engine.

Teig exhaled, his body finally registering just how cold he was. Even with all his layers, he felt it in his bones. His exposed face stung as if with sunburn, but he knew this feeling, understood it was just the brutal cold. Clouds hid what passed for daylight in Siberia in the winter. The display in the truck had read thirty below zero, Celsius, and it would get much colder in midafternoon, when the sun went down. Even now, that sting would turn into frostbite in ten minutes or so, if they stayed out there on the road and he left his face uncovered. He reminded himself not to face the elements without pulling on his balaclava. Growing up, he just called those things "ski masks," but Prentiss always corrected him. Seventies bank robbers wore ski masks, apparently, while secret agents and assassins wore balaclavas. As if he needed Jack Prentiss to teach him how to be cool.

Okay, maybe he did.

"Hey," Prentiss said, reaching out of the truck with his boot and nudging Teig with it. "You *fell asleep* behind the wheel."

Teig couldn't deny it. He'd almost killed them—twice. First hitting the guardrail, then turning off the engine.

"I'm wide awake now," he said.

"You think I'm going to let you drive after that?" Prentiss asked. He rubbed a glove across his graying beard. "Jesus Christ, how did you convince me to come here?"

Teig ignored the second question. "Look at the road and tell me you want to drive, and I'll happily take a nap in the passenger seat."

Prentiss exhaled. He turned up the heat, staring out the windshield at the road ahead of them. After a moment, he slid over without a word and Teig climbed up into the driver's seat. He yanked the door shut, put the UAZ in drive, and started once more along the Road of Bones.

"Don't fall asleep," Prentiss said.

Teig forced a smile. "Don't bore me to death and I'll stay awake."

They'd started the journey in Magadan, a port city on the Sea of Okhotsk, in northeast Siberia. The city's population hung just below ninety thousand and kept declining as the elderly passed on and young people departed. Migration tended to only happen in one direction out here, which shouldn't have surprised anyone. Nobody picked up their lives and decided to seek a fresh start in Siberia.

Teig had done plenty of reading about the treacherous weather, especially up the Kolyma Highway, but he only began to really understand after the first two hundred miles, when his gaze kept shifting between the gas gauge and the roadside. There were gas stations every hundred and fifty miles or so, but with the wind and snow, the crunch of tires on permafrost, and the white silence that stretched out around them, the idea of those gas stations began to seem like dreams of a desert oasis. If you ran out of gas on the Kolyma Highway in winter, you stood a fair chance of freezing to death.

They'd departed Magadan with a full gas tank at eight o'clock the previous morning, an hour before dawn, and managed a little more than half the sixteen-hour drive before settling into the accommodations Teig had arranged. They slept at a lodge whose chief appeal was the presence of a garage where the truck's engine and fuel line wouldn't freeze overnight. The stopover was so small its name had already faded from memory, more a settlement built around a gas station than a proper town. The Kolyma Highway did not draw a lot of tourists, but the number was greater than zero. Even so, the old man running the lodge studied them with the curiosity of an anthropologist.

When they'd set out from the lodge this morning, heading northwest, the air had already been cold enough to kill. The temperature kept dropping and Teig had begun to wonder if this trip had been an exercise in abject stupidity. He hadn't shared that concern with Prentiss, who had only agreed to come on this trip out of friendship and because Teig owed him nearly eight thousand dollars. Prentiss knew Teig's grand plans were unlikely to pay off without help, so he had come along to protect his investment.

Teig told himself that Prentiss still had a little faith in him, even when nobody else did. Cold comfort, but a comfort nevertheless.

The truck rattled along the road. Teig sat up straight, determined not to be lulled back to sleep. Kolyma Highway ran twelve hundred miles through the frozen heart of Siberia, from Magadan all the way to the sprawling river port of Yakutsk. Fewer than three hundred miles from the Arctic Circle, the port city received the equivalent of only five hours of sunlight each day in the month of December, and most of those days the sun hid behind the clouds. With an average low winter temperature of forty below zero, not accounting for the windchill, no person in their right mind would ever want to live there. Yet Yakutsk had a population triple that of Magadan—nearly three hundred thousand people. It had museums and theaters and nightlife, a beacon of civilization in a frozen wasteland. Humans, it seemed, were like cockroaches. Determined enough, they could thrive anywhere.

Teig and Prentiss weren't going all the way to Yakutsk. They were going somewhere with far fewer people, somewhere even colder—the coldest inhabited place on earth, in fact.

"What the fuck is wrong with us?" Teig said with a laugh.

Prentiss sat up straight, shaking his head as if to clear it. "You awake?"

Teig flexed his fingers on the steering wheel. "One of us has to be."

Prentiss frowned, taking offense. "With the sky up here, it always feels like I should be in bed."

"At least it would be warmer."

Technically it was daytime, but all that meant up here was a kind of forever twilight, a gauze-filtered gray-blue sky. Even with the heat in the truck up full blast, Teig could feel the cold through his boots and two layers of socks. His toes ached. His hands felt numb on the wheel, despite the thermal lining of his gloves.

"It's not bedtime," Teig said. "It's basically *lunchtime*."

"When do you think we'll reach the next petrol station? We're supposed to pick up the guide in . . ." He glanced at the dashboard clock. "Half an hour."

"We'll be late," Teig said. "But only twenty minutes or so. It takes forever to go anywhere on this road."

Prentiss grumbled, but he settled into the seat like a bear in his den.

The Englishman wouldn't get an American football reference, but Teig always thought he looked like a retired offensive lineman. Six-foot-two, strong as hell, with a barrel chest and a proud beer belly. Both his hair and his bushy beard needed a trim, but such things were never Prentiss's concern.

"I don't need to look pretty," he'd say. "I'm never the one on camera."

They'd met four years earlier. Prentiss had proved himself to be grumpy, brutally honest, and diligent about his work. What clinched their friendship, however, was Teig's realization that he'd found a tolerable traveling companion. Neither of them went out of their way to feign good cheer on dark days. The two men shared a philosophy that made room for mood swings, and that philosophy bound them to one another.

What bound them even more tightly, however, was the seven thousand, eight hundred, and forty-two dollars that Teig owed his friend. Prentiss wasn't the only person walking around with an IOU from Felix Teigland, but the debt to him was certainly the largest. Teig was a fast talker, always with a scheme he would trumpet with unfettered enthusiasm—a feature documentary from a fourteen-year-old director out of Argentina, salvage rights to a Spanish galleon, a TV series about World War II comic book artists who were secretly spies, a mock-umentary in which the history of Scooby-Doo and his gang would be investigated as if they'd existed in real life.

Teig had come up through the ranks. He'd started the summer before his senior year in college working as a grip with the crew of *Ghost Sellers,* a reality documentary series about a trio of paranormal investigators whose schtick was to "officially" verify properties that advertised themselves as haunted. Mostly they were hotels and bed-and-breakfasts that used their ghostly reputations as a lure for tourists, but some of the episodes were about homes and other buildings for sale, where the owners thought being haunted was a selling point. Teig had worked on that crew for two seasons before the series was canceled, and he'd been extremely dissatisfied with the supposed hauntings and the so-called investigators. He had reason to want to find ghosts, but he'd never seen evidence of one, despite the show confirming twenty-seven "official" hauntings while he'd worked with them.

Still, it had started him in television. Since then, he'd worked his way up in various jobs. He'd been a research assistant, a PA, and occasionally an on-screen "talent." Seven years ago, he'd founded his own company, Teigland POV, and after a wild four-year ride, he had established solid contacts with executives at Discovery and NatGeo. In quick succession he had sold a pair of documentaries and two series, the latest of which, *Public Service,* traced the history of sex work around the globe.

When the last of the execs he'd befriended left Discovery and only one ally remained at National Geographic, he started to sweat. He needed something great, a show that he could pitch to anyone, not just those who already felt favorably toward him. What he wanted was his own *Wicked Tuna* or *Ice Road Truckers* or, God forbid, *Duck Dynasty.* A breakout show, something quirky but commercial. Something that would run for years and keep his company afloat. Without a home run, his career would hit the TV scrap heap in a matter of months.

Teig's successes had made him enough money to keep the company going and to pay off most of the people who had gambled on their faith in him and lost. One by one, he made them whole. But there were still those he owed, and things were getting lean again, and Teig had started to worry.

He thought he'd found his home run idea with the Kolyma Highway, but he wasn't going to sell it without some proof-of-concept video, something to bring into pitch meetings with him so he could say he'd been there, tell them what it felt like to be in a place so cold that a single mistake or one bad twist of fate might kill you.

So, here they were. Teig and Prentiss on the Road of Bones. What were friends for, if not to risk their lives together?

It wasn't the desolation or the darkness or even the climate that had persuaded him to invest in this trip. It was that name, the Road of Bones. Official maps referred to it as R504. It wasn't much of a road. The pavement started at both ends but not long thereafter the pavement gave way to packed gravel, which had been laid down over the permafrost for most of the Kolyma Highway's length. In many places, the road was barely wide enough for two cars to scrape the paint off each other as they passed. The landscape consisted of snow, skeletal trees, mountains, and the occasional guardrail, as well as settlements that were considered urban but many of which were made up of a few dozen buildings and the hardy souls who went along with them.

In the days when Stalin had built the Soviet Union, massive deposits of gold and uranium had been discovered, which meant there was a lot of money to be made. Teig understood why people would have migrated into the region at that point—money was always a great motivator—but there had been people here for centuries before that, and their motives were a mystery. The Yakuts had come along in the thirteenth century, by which time there were indigenous tribes already living in the region.

He understood those settlers might have arrived in summer, but at the first winter night when the temperature dropped cold enough to freeze a man's eyeballs in his head, most rational beings would have considered heading south.

The ones who'd had a choice, anyway.

"You're dwelling on it again," Prentiss said.

Teig exhaled. Usually he denied it, but this time he nodded. "Can't help myself."

"This is the show you want to make, man. If you're going to let it get under your skin like this, why come all this way? I could be somewhere warm, with some*one* warm."

"I know. You're right."

Prentiss snorted. "I'm always right, Felix."

"You know I hate that name."

"It's *your* name! I'm not the one who gave it to you. Call your mother and shout at her if you like."

Teig shot him a sidelong glance. "All right, John."

"Only my gran calls me John, and that's because I don't have the heart to knock her teeth in."

"Don't sell yourself short, brother. You absolutely strike me as a guy who wouldn't hesitate to knock his granny's teeth in."

Prentiss batted his eyelashes. "You say the sweetest things."

The truck shuddered as Teig followed a curve in the road, tires grinding over the frozen ground. The engine noise had been like a drill in his skull for the first hour or so, but he had grown used to it. Those ruts in the road, though, the way the truck rattled over them . . . Teig wouldn't ever get used to that.

"You're right. It's all I can think about," he said. "The bones."

Prentiss exhaled. "I knew you were bloody dwelling on it again."

Teig had spent his junior year of college in bed with a girl named Miranda, whose two favorite things were ghost stories and his tongue, in that order.

Out of necessity, he had watched what felt like hundreds of episodes of shows about tense-looking ghost hunters pretending to hear strange sounds or feel temperature changes in old houses. He'd been a determined skeptic at that point, though his time with Miranda would be the thing that later led him to *Ghost Sellers*. While Teig had kept his mouth shut about his doubts, Miranda had held him tightly while watching all of those shows, covered her eyes, jumped in all the right places. Teig never expressed his opinion, partly to avoid insulting her, but mostly because he did not want to have to explain the burning resentment he felt toward those shameless pretenders.

What would he have said?

I waited for my sister's ghost, and she never came.

He would have given anything for just a glimpse of Olivia's ghost, to know that somehow, somewhere, her laughter lived on.

Teig had been twelve years old when the silver minivan had slowed to a stop at the corner by their house, a frantic, cinnamon-furred puppy yipping happily by the partly open driver's window. Eight-year-old Olivia had clapped her hands in excitement, beaming with joy as she started toward the van. The driver, in a dark hoodie and sunglasses, had left the van running as he moved into the back and racked the side door open, the puppy in his hands.

The goddamned puppy.

It had been Teig's job to watch her that day. Their mom had been in the hospital, dad working in his office at home. Olivia had always pulled his hair and tried to boss him around plenty, but she'd also made him laugh the way nobody else ever had. She'd been a daring little kid, jumping from swing sets and searching for new ways to crash her scooter. Anytime one of their parents had said "you're gonna kill yourself one of these days," Olivia would narrow her eyes with a sly grin. "If I do, I'm gonna come back and haunt Felix every day forever!"

The van had been found behind an abandoned strip mall, black and twisted from fire.

Olivia had been found two months later in the same condition.

Teig had waited years for her promised ghost to appear, but it never had. By the time he got to Miranda's college dorm-room bed and her obsession with ghost hunters, all hope for an afterlife had been burned away.

But after an entire school year with Miranda, watching those shows got him doing research on hauntings, and he began to wonder. Teig told himself it wasn't hope, that he had zero expectation of Olivia's ghost making a sudden appearance in his dorm room or on some episode of *Haunting America,* but a little spark of something had returned to him during that year, and it had never quite gone away. One day while working on *Ghost Sellers,* he'd been tasked with driving Deja Madison, one of the show's stars, to the latest "haunting." Teig had taken the opportunity to ask her, point-blank, if she believed in any of what they did on the show. He'd expected her to be angry, maybe even fire him, or to take him into her confidence and admit that it was all a sham. What Teig hadn't anticipated was the way her eyes had lit up and the fervor of her confirmation. Yes, she'd said, at least ninety percent of what they put on television was pure theater, all bullshit to make audiences and the network happy.

"But that ten percent," Deja had said. "That's the sweet spot."

She'd begun telling him stories about places she'd been, things she had seen and heard and felt, that were so unsettling Teig caught himself holding his breath a couple of times. They passed two hours in the car and Deja never tired of his questions, nor of talking passionately about the ghosts she believed she had encountered. Teig had ended that day not quite convinced, but not so determined in his skepticism.

He wanted to believe.

He'd always wanted to believe.

If one could be haunted, if ghosts might appear, then one day Olivia might keep her promise and come back to him, and Teig might finally be able to tell her how sorry he was for what had happened to her. He might finally be able to beg her forgiveness.

Years passed. Business took him on a ride. Success and failure chewed him up and now were getting ready to spit him out. He had given up searching for ghosts years ago, but if he was honest with himself, he'd never given up completely. When he first read about the Road of Bones, it woke something inside him, some little bit of fear and dread. He'd never been anywhere with a history as dark and sad as this place.

Despite the time he'd spent working with so-called paranormal investigators, he had never been anywhere that felt as haunted as this.

Teig shivered, and not from the cold.

He rubbed his eyes. "Shouldn't be much farther. Once we pick up the guide, you should probably drive for a while."

Prentiss shifted on the creaking seat. "You all right?"

"It's a lot to take in. This place," Teig admitted. "Reading about it is one thing. You see the word 'gulag' in print and you have a vague idea of what it is, but then you come up here and realize those prison camps were *here*."

He glanced out his window, watched the dead trees passing by, the landscape so desolate it might as well have been another planet. But this was earth, all right, the world of human beings whose cruelty knew no bounds.

"I don't like to think about that stuff," Prentiss said, looking out his own window. "But you know, if you get this project off the ground, we're going to be doing nothing *but* thinking about it for a long time."

Teig exhaled. "People should know. The ugliest parts of history are the most important parts to remember."

Prentiss nodded, and then the two of them let the rumble of the engine speak for a while. Teig meant what he had said. It felt important to him not to let the horrors of this place be forgotten. He'd lived all his life without ever hearing about the building of the Kolyma Highway, and when he'd asked amongst trusted friends, none of them could recall ever hearing the story.

There had already been a web of concentration camps in Siberia—gulags—but when the Soviets discovered gold and uranium deposits, Stalin wanted a road built between Magadan and Yakutsk. At least eighty new camps were constructed along the route to supply a readily available workforce. Political prisoners, criminals, unfortunate innocents, men who'd dared look at the wives of Soviet officials—they all fed the gulags. Hundreds of thousands were put to work building the Kolyma Highway. Over the years, as many as six hundred thousand people died while constructing the road, most by freezing to death.

Their bodies were buried where they fell, plowed under the permafrost.

Hundreds of thousands of frozen corpses lay beneath the Road of Bones. They were driving across potholed, rutted, icy graves—had been since they'd begun the trip—and there were hundreds of miles to go.

2

The station had no sign, but nobody passing by would have needed one. There were three rusting pumps beside a chain-link fence, beyond which stood a quartet of massive gasoline tanks. Elsewhere those tanks would have been underground, but whoever owned this faded fixture at the world's end had decided against burying them in the permafrost.

Teig frowned as he pulled the truck up to the pump, staring at a squat little building that must have been the cashier's office. It looked more like a bomb shelter, a century after whatever war it had been built for. Someone had spray-painted a few Cyrillic letters that caused Teig to rethink his assumption that the station had no sign. It might've said "gas station" or "cash only" or "biohazard" for all he knew, but it meant something to someone.

He put the truck in park. The engine ticked and rumbled. Prentiss looked as if he'd fallen asleep, but the man snored like a grizzly with a deviated septum and right now he looked too peaceful to be anything but pretending.

"Cut the crap," Teig said. "Go in and get the guide. And see if we're supposed to pump our own gas."

Prentiss opened his eyes, put on a pitiful face. "It's awful cold out there."

"I've got to keep the engine running. Besides, we both know you have to piss. You always have to piss."

With a heavy sigh, Prentiss shoved open his door. The cold swept in, shocking and brutal. "You know I don't like new people, Teig. That's why you're the producer and I'm the guy behind the camera. You wanted me to take the wheel anyway, so I'll do that. You can handle our encounters with the locals."

Prentiss leveraged himself out of the truck without waiting for a reply and swung the door shut. He marched around front and crossed through the headlights, the icy air casting his features in a strange light. He'd spoken the words in typical curmudgeonly good humor, but Teig knew he meant them. There were certain keys to being a good friend, chief among them loyalty, shared philosophy, and willing sacrifice, but Teig had learned that the most appreciated trait in a friend was knowing when to speak up and when to keep silent. Often, he failed in that regard, but he strove to learn and that had to count for something.

He gave the engine a little gas, listened to it roar, then climbed out and let Prentiss lumber into the driver's seat.

Prentiss gave him a mischievous smirk. "If they sell snacks, get some."

Teig barked laughter. "Look at this place. It's like the zombie uprising has come and gone. I doubt they have those Flamin' Hot Cheetos you love."

"If they have anything resembling a Cheeto, I'll be happy. Beggars can't be choosers."

Teig trotted to the bunker, frowning at the spray-painted graffiti. The single window was filthy with what looked like decades of grime. Someone had used a finger to scrawl the word OPEN in English, and Teig wondered if that had been meant for him.

He pushed through the door and stepped into a cloud of acrid cigarette smoke. Most of the ceiling lights were burned out, but four bulbs provided enough illumination to see the two people in that square box of a room. A heavyset woman in wool trousers and a thick, stained sweater slouched in a plush purple chair, stroking the pelt of a sleek-furred Russian Spaniel. The dog sniffed in Teig's direction and looked away, elegant and aloof, like a prince who'd found himself cast down to live amongst the peasantry. The woman raised an eyebrow in his direction, puffed a stinking Turkish cigarette, then turned to her human companion.

"This must be your American," she said in tortured English, and smirked as if simply speaking his language showed her disdain for Teig, like she knew he couldn't return the favor and wanted to remind him. She was right.

The man she'd addressed sat on a stool behind a small counter that sagged beneath the burden of a cash register. On a shelf behind him were displayed a variety of bags of chips and other snacks, but they could have been dried, shaved fish or nacho crisps for all he knew. Not a Cheeto in site. Cans of Coca-Cola lined the lowest shelf. Prentiss would be pleased.

"You're late, Mr. Teigland," said the man behind the counter.

"All the more reason I need a guide. I assume you're Kaskil?"

The guide inclined his head in something approximating a bow and slid off the stool to emerge from behind the counter. Teig had spoken to him via email and once on Zoom, but in person he seemed jarringly out of place. Kaskil's thick reindeer boots were old and scuffed and had clearly seen him through many a year, but his heavy sweater was crisp and new, vividly red. His trousers also looked new and when he reached for his coat and long, heavy scarf, they also seemed not only fresh off the rack but stylish. There were no boutiques or department stores on the Kolyma Highway, but Kaskil dressed like a man with money and taste. Tall and slim, he had his hair and mustache trimmed so he looked like a 1940s Hollywood actor, or he would have if not for the black spider tattooed on his neck, facing downward. Teig knew the tattoo meant something, possibly something criminal, even prison-related.

Kaskil saw him looking. "You have a question?"

"I'm going to have a lot of questions, but not the one you're thinking of."

The guide nodded once. "We should get along very well." Kaskil gestured toward the door. "I presume you need gas."

"And the bathroom," Teig said. "And some of those snacks for my cameraman."

Kaskil rattled off instructions to the big woman in something that wasn't Russian—Teig assumed Yakut—and then plucked the Turkish cigarette from the woman's fingers and put it to his lips. He took a long drag and handed it back, after which the woman rose, kissed his cheek, and went to pack up snacks from behind the counter.

Teig blinked in surprise.

Kaskil smiled. "My grandmother." He zipped his coat and wrapped the scarf around his throat, covering that spider. "Come on. I'll fill your gas tank and show you how to find the toilet. Then I'll take you to the coldest place on earth."

An hour later, Kaskil seemed less amiable than he had at the gas station. Now at the steering wheel, Prentiss had banned him from smoking his putrid Turkish cigarettes in the truck. Teig didn't much care either way, but since he'd be saying at least a temporary goodbye to Kaskil in a day or two and intended to keep working with Prentiss for years, he knew whose side he had to land on.

Prentiss had the Dead Kennedys playing through the speakers. He kept the volume down, which only served to turn the music into a low, thumping drone, a punishment to the skull. In the backseat, Kaskil sighed dramatically. Teig stifled a laugh. The guide seemed to have zero filter, which should make for good company, as long as Prentiss didn't murder him.

"That was about me, wasn't it?" Prentiss said, turning to glare at Teig.

"I imagine so. You tend to exasperate people."

"Fuck you, Felix."

In the backseat, Kaskil muttered something in his own language, but it blended with the quiet jackhammer of the music.

Prentiss shot a blazing glare at the rearview mirror. "Anytime you want to stop and take a cigarette break, let me know and I'll pull over."

Kaskil showed his teeth but Teig doubted anyone would have interpreted that look as a smile. In the gray light inside the car, Kaskil sat in a bubble of potential, radiating the energy of twin promises—one of aggression and the other joviality. Teig thought of his uncle Frank, who had always been ready with unsolicited advice while Teig was growing up. "Whatever people give you, give it back to them times ten," Uncle Frank had said. "Be ready, always, to take everything to the next level. Someone's nice to you, make it your job to improve their day, give them a laugh or a pat on the back. But someone comes at you with attitude, or looking for a fight, you drop the fuckin' sky on their heads. Be ready either way, every day."

The energy that radiated off Kaskil was what Teig thought of as "Uncle Frank energy." If Teig didn't know any better, he'd have thought Kaskil must be his long-lost cousin.

Now the guide shifted quietly in the shadows of the backseat.

"Mr. Teigland," Kaskil said, "your friend is less charming than he thinks."

Prentiss grunted in amusement. "Don't worry, mate, I know exactly how little charm I have. I'm not bothered."

Teig turned and smiled back at Kaskil. "He's really not. If you're seeking charm on this trip, I'm afraid I'll be the best you can hope for."

"I live in Akhust, my friend. Charm is in short supply."

Teig blinked in surprise. "Wait, you live in Akhust?"

"My family are reindeer herders. I grew up taking care of the beasts."

"You don't look like a reindeer herder," Prentiss said.

Kaskil laughed softly, all the tension vanishing. "I suppose not. I've traveled here and there, but I'm home to stay now."

"And now you're herding tourists," Teig said.

"Reindeer are easier," Kaskil replied. "We don't have many tourists, but those who do come like to have someone to guide them. We get curious people, adventurers who want to explore and learn. Mostly in the summer, of course. It can be muddy, ugly terrain, but at least it isn't trying to kill you."

"And when there aren't any tourists?" Teig asked.

Kaskil smiled. "Ah, well . . . the reindeer are at least more charming than Mr. Prentiss."

Even Prentiss laughed at that, but Teig was still focused on Kaskil. The lowest recorded temperature in Akhust was just a hair shy of one hundred degrees below zero. He hadn't been able to avoid preconceptions about the people he would encounter along the Kolyma Highway. Kaskil was not what he imagined, though the man's grandmother filled the role nicely.

"We'll want to interview you on camera," Teig said. "Your family, too."

Kaskil seemed not to hear. Prentiss drove through a series of deep potholes, jouncing all three of them in their seats, but Kaskil didn't blink. Teig looked out to discover what had him so mesmerized and saw a concrete wall fifty feet from the road, topped by barbed wire. Beyond it were the roofs of industrial buildings, bleached white by decades of summer sun, almost blending with the snowy mountains in the background. They were ugly boxes with long rows of small windows, and Teig felt a swirl of nausea in his gut as he realized he was looking at a gulag.

The three men rode in silence until the abandoned prison camp vanished from view. The truck rumbled over more deep ruts in the road, and Teig pictured bones beneath their tires. Human skulls. Some of them might have been members of Kaskil's family, a couple of generations back. Not long ago at all, really.

A few miles farther on they passed an abandoned church on the other side of the road. Half its stone face had collapsed into a tumble of rocks that the guardrail kept from spilling into their path. He wondered if the church had been built for the workers to pray for release from their suffering, or for their overseers to pray for forgiveness.

Teig glanced into the backseat. The gloom outside the windows seemed to have infiltrated the truck, the shadows to have deepened. Only the guide's scarf seemed bright in the darkness there.

"Do you think they had funerals for the workers who died on the road?"

Kaskil's eyes shone in the dark. Glistened. "The prisoners would have remembered their dead. There would have been prayers said, memorials if nothing else."

He sounded more hopeful than certain, as if he refused to imagine otherwise.

Prentiss leaned toward the glass, peered down at the road beneath their wheels. The truck swerved a bit before he gripped the wheel a bit tighter and straightened them out.

"I hate thinking of all those people, just plowed under the road," the big man said. "It's not exactly holy ground."

Teig fought the urge to roll his eyes. Prentiss had a superstitious side thanks to a religious upbringing that didn't come out often. Horrifying as this place might be, Teig wasn't worried about whether the dead had been buried in holy ground. He'd visited enough haunted places that he knew not to expect phantoms. The lives of those who'd died here were awful enough without adding the afterlife into the mix. But it would make for excellent and eerie television.

"Actually, some of the road *has* been blessed," Kaskil said. "If you believe the stories."

Teig perked up. "What stories?"

Still mostly in shadows back there, Kaskil turned to look out the window. "You must've done *some* research before you came. There are always ghost stories out here, but Ludmilla's ghost has been very popular the past few years. She wanders the road, speaking prayers for the dead, hoping such blessings will allow their spirits to find peace. You will certainly want to devote an episode of your show to Ludmilla."

Despite the hot air blowing from the heating vents, Teig shivered. He didn't believe, but he wanted to. That little spark inside him, the hope that he'd see Olivia again someday, still burned. He saw Prentiss stiffen behind the wheel, and Teig couldn't deny that he felt colder, that the little hairs stood up on the back of his neck.

"Are you saying you believe this story? *You* believe in this ghost?"

Kaskil leaned forward. The dashboard lights cast a blue pall over his features as he smiled. "Believe in her? I've seen her, my friend. I wouldn't be at all surprised if you see her, too."

3

Teig had been hoping for a nap once Prentiss took over the driving, but having Kaskil in the backseat erased any chance of that. Narrating their journey came with the job of being a guide, but Kaskil didn't just talk about the culture of Yakutia. Thus far, he had regaled them with tales of his father's flatulence problem, his grandmother's obsession with Japanese samurai movies, and his prison cellmate's suicide. All of that paled, however, in comparison to the adventures of Kaskil's brother-in-law, Aldyn. The husband of his older sister, Tuyaara, Aldyn left the house every day to pretend to work, but instead went to a small cottage just outside the town to bed an old woman who paid for the pleasure. The whole family knew—hell, the whole town—but he brought the money home and helped support the household, so nobody said a word. The widow had been through three husbands, two of whom she was suspected of murdering, but Kaskil thought as long as his brother-in-law wasn't married to the merry widow, he was safe.

His mother had died more than a decade earlier in an accident involving a snowmobile and a northern deer. Teig might have thought this a work of fiction if not for the genuine pain in Kaskil's eyes as he related the story. He knew it sounded ridiculous, even smiled as he said it, but the pain shone through. In the aftermath of his mother's death he had grown closer to his sister. Tuyaara and Aldyn had a nine-year-old daughter Kaskil called his little sunshine girl. He said it first in Yakut and then in English, but Teig didn't attempt it in the local tongue. He knew he'd be hopeless at it.

Kaskil directed this stream-of-consciousness babble at Teig as if Prentiss were invisible and the truck were driving itself. The big Englishman kept his hands on the wheel and his eyes on what passed for a road. Occasionally he sighed, but he said nothing, grateful that he wasn't the intended audience.

Teig's skull thrummed and his neck ached with the bobble caused by the road. He vacillated between being amused by Kaskil and wanting to murder him, but Prentiss ran out of patience before Teig did.

"I've got to piss," he growled, glancing at Kaskil in the backseat. "Anywhere I can do that without my bollocks turning to ice?"

Kaskil pointed at Prentiss. "I've got you covered. Another fifteen minutes or so and you'll see lights off to the left."

"A town?" Teig asked.

"I wouldn't call Olonkho's a town. Not even by Kolyma standards. But you will find a bathroom there. And a bar, if you'd like a burger or a vodka."

Teig wanted both.

Prentiss glanced back at Kaskil. "Excellent. Now then, you seem a pleasant enough lad, but do me the favor of shutting up entirely until we get there? I'd like a bit of quiet."

Teig shot a sidelong glance at his cameraman. What the fuck was Prentiss thinking? He might not have seen the spider tattoo on Kaskil's neck, but hadn't he just heard the guy talking about his prison cellmate? Despite the air of unpredictability around the guide, Teig had decided to like him, but they didn't know Kaskil well enough to push his buttons.

In the backseat, the guide raised both hands in surrender. "Shutting up."

They trundled through the strange gray daylight, the silence broken only by the engine and the wheels bumping over the road. Up a hill, in the deeper shadows beyond the tree line, he spotted several dark figures running low to the ground as if trying to keep pace with them. *Wolves*, he thought, watching them dart among the trees, strong and lithe and without a sound. He shuddered to think the wolves might actually be turning a predatory eye upon a passing vehicle, but then he saw an elk burst from the tree line fifty yards ahead.

Prentiss swore and tapped the brake as the elk bounded through two feet of snow, leapt the bank, and hurtled across the road. The tires skidded, but only a bit. The treads gripped the road, the truck bounced to a halt, and they sat in quiet awe as the wolves streamed across the road in pursuit.

The elk made it into the trees on the other side of the road with its lead cut in half. It would not escape its pursuers, and the knowledge caused a weight to settle on Teig's chest. They were creatures of the wild, of course, and this was simply nature, but the elk had nowhere to run.

"Ah, here we go," Prentiss said. "Thank God. I'm about to burst."

They came to a narrow, plowed road on the left. It curved away from Kolyma Highway and into the trees, then up a low hill, where a handful of lights beckoned.

Kaskil's hesitation to call it a town proved wise. Little more than a truck stop, the place had no name, so locals had taken to referring to it by the name of the bar—Olonkho's. Neon glittered in the windows, but there were a dozen or so structures in addition to the bar, including a big ugly parking garage and smaller buildings that might have been residences or workshops. The main feature besides the bar was some kind of auto repair shop with a single gas pump outside.

"Should we top off our petrol?" Prentiss asked.

He glanced at Kaskil, who smiled and raised his hands the way he'd done before, then picked up just as if he'd never stopped talking.

"The next station is still a hundred miles, so it certainly wouldn't hurt. Once you've filled the tank, you can park in the garage. It's not heated, exactly, but it's not so cold as out here. You won't need to leave the truck running to get it started afterward."

Prentiss let them out and drove off to fill the tank. The cold hit Teig hard. In the truck, riding in the passenger seat, it had settled like a permanent ache in his bones, but now that he'd stepped outside again, the warmth inside the truck seemed a tropical memory. His breath plumed in front of his face and he used thickly gloved hands to pull his scarf up over his mouth and nose. He remembered his earlier vow to put on his balaclava, but they were only walking from the truck to the bar. Despite the cold, he smiled behind his scarf.

A burger and a shot of vodka seemed like just the prescription for what ailed him.

"I can't believe you live here," he said, thinking aloud.

Kaskil laughed. "I hear that from all my clients. I don't suppose they realize how insulting it is."

Teig blinked, stung by the words and by their accuracy. "I'm sorry. You're right," he said, shivering. "It's just impossible for me to imagine this being an ordinary life."

"Mr. Teigland," Kaskil said, as if admonishing a small child, "you wouldn't want to make television about us if we led what you think of as ordinary lives."

They hurried toward the bar. With the truck's engine noise vanished inside the garage, Teig could hear the crack of the snow shifting, like someone knocking on driftwood. Above that, he heard voices raised in song. Music from inside the bar, he assumed, until he heard Kaskil clapping his thick gloves together and looked beyond the bar to a snowy field where four men in furry parkas moved in a classic dance number, like some kind of Yakut boy band. Music rang out, pumped from someone's phone or speakers. One of them wore a bright green jacket and thick fur pants. The others all looked like hunters, but they danced in perfect sync while a fifth person, maybe a young woman given her long black hair, used her phone to film their routine. The music was familiar, some recent pop hit, but the lyrics weren't in English.

"What the hell are they doing?"

"Making a music video," Kaskil said.

"They'll freeze to death."

Kaskil looked at him with what looked like pity. "They're having fun. Did you think we were all like my grandmother?"

The guide pushed open the door and vanished into the bar without another word, leaving Teig to feel like an asshole yet again. If he was going to make a series about life along the Kolyma Highway, he needed to try his best not to alienate the people who lived here.

But first he needed a drink.

He followed Kaskil into the bar. When he saw the bright decor and the smiling faces inside, he was no longer surprised. To him, it seemed like these people lived in a haunted, frozen hell.

To them . . . it was just home.

The owner—a big scruffy guy named Timir—stood behind the stained wooden bar counter, surveying the warmth and laughter inside the little kingdom he'd created for himself. The guy radiated a sense of pride, Teig thought, before realizing the gleam in Timir's eyes seemed more like simple contentment. His cheeks and forehead were lined with folds instead of wrinkles, like leather that had been soaked and then left to dry in the dark.

"It's embarrassing," Teig told him, draining the last of the beer he'd ordered.

"I think it must be," Timir agreed with a hearty nod.

Teig gave a quiet laugh. It wasn't only the language and customs that were strange to him here, but the way people thought. In the U.S. or the U.K., if he'd expressed discomfort or shame about the fact that he knew only a few words in the local language while so many of the locals could speak at least a little English, the response would have been to let him off the hook. *Ah, you're all right. Nobody can learn everything. American education.* Americans or Brits would have come up with excuses on his behalf or let him know they'd no expectations of him. But in Yakutia, they agreed that he ought to be embarrassed.

Timir picked up his beer glass and began to refill it from the tap, tilting carefully to be sure the foam did not overflow the rim. The moment Teig and Kaskil had entered the bar, Teig had begun to warm up. The smell of meat on the grill, of spices in a pot, rejuvenated him immediately, so that he no longer wanted vodka. Whatever smelled so delicious on the grill, he had wanted a beer with it. But he hadn't intended to have a second one.

Not that he declined.

The smell from the grill had turned out to be reindeer burger, hand-ground and mixed with crumbled bacon ends, and he'd ordered one based solely on the way the aroma made his mouth water. Timir served it smothered in cheddar made in Sizaya, a distant Siberian village, and with an imported truffle aioli. Teig could see the man didn't want to talk about himself, but it seemed clear he'd talk about his food or about the vodka his brother made for as many hours as a customer might be willing to give him.

Teig took another bite of his burger, relishing the flavors on his tongue. Every bite continued to erase the assumptions he'd made when planning his trip along the Kolyma Highway. Guy Fieri would have loved this place, he thought. Remote, almost a lost world, only discoverable if you were traveling the Road of Bones and hadn't topped off your gas tank at the last station, or if you had the urgent need for a toilet. And yet here was, quite possibly, the greatest burger he'd ever tasted.

Reindeer. His childhood self cringed at the thought. But it tasted so fucking good.

Timir set his beer glass on the counter. Teig swallowed the next bite of burger and gestured his thanks.

"You say you want to make TV here," Timir said. They'd already discussed Teig doing an episode of the show about the bar. "It's sort of funny."

"Funny?" Teig asked.

The owner grinned. "Americans come sometimes. Always surprised, Americans, when I speak English to them. I know they think the whole world learns English because we admire your country, or we want to live there, or some other stupid thing." He snorted a bit and swung his head side to side. "Of course you think that. But most of those people, they don't want to live in America. They learn English from the movies, or from TV shows. You make so many great movies. I learned most of my English from *Baywatch*. You know *Baywatch*? David Hasselhoff?"

Teig sipped his beer, nearly choked on it. "Yeah," he said, laughing. "I know *Baywatch*. I hope you have better American TV than that."

"Of course. My favorite is *Breaking Bad*. My wife likes the *Real Housewives*. That's what you should do, mister. *Real Housewives of Yakutia*."

Teig picked up his burger. "Stranger things have happened."

"Oh, *Stranger Things*. I like that one, too."

Someone down the bar called to Timir and the man went to serve him, calling out in Yakut, leaving Teig to ponder the bar owner's words. Millions of people around the world learned to speak English as a second or third language, or sixth, and fluently. He'd always thought they envied his country, maybe wanted to live there, but now he wondered if they just liked English-language movies and TV shows. And maybe, just maybe, they learned English because most English speakers were too lazy or arrogant to become proficient in other languages.

Teig supposed if Yakutia had a thriving TV industry, he might have learned some of the local language already, at least by Timir's logic. *Man, we suck,* he thought. *But at least we make good entertainment.*

He chuckled at his own small-mindedness and took another bite of his burger.

He heard a grunt over his left shoulder and then Prentiss slumped onto the stool, gazing in open lust at the half-eaten reindeer burger in Teig's hands.

"Tell me you ordered me one of those."

"I've got you covered, my friend. Should be out in a minute."

"Where did our guide get off to?"

Teig gestured toward the back of the bar, where Kaskil spoke animatedly to several people. It would have been easy to assume they were old friends by the way Kaskil addressed them, but the young man had a certain way about him that made Teig realize it was possible they'd been complete strangers fifteen minutes ago.

"Man, that kid can talk," Prentiss grumbled.

Timir slid a plate onto the bar and Prentiss eyed it with a foreigner's suspicion.

"Go on. Eat your burger," Teig told him. "It'll change your life."

Prentiss hoisted the burger and took a bite. He made an audible groan of pleasure and Teig watched as all the tension went out of his friend's shoulders.

"I'm going to be searching for a reindeer burger to match this one for the rest of my days," Teig said.

Prentiss grunted his agreement around his second mouthful. They had both needed this stop, particularly as it would be the last one before they reached Kaskil's hometown and faced the weather there. Teig couldn't imagine anywhere colder than where they were right now, but they'd be there soon enough.

Teig looked over at the fire blazing in the hearth in the corner of the barroom and felt the warmth spreading inside him from the food, the beer, the fire, the sound of cheerful voices, and he wondered if it would have been better to stay out in the cold. The longer they stayed inside, the less he looked forward to going back to the truck. Maybe that was the secret of making a life up here in the nothing part of nowhere. To adjust to the cold you had to live through the worst of it, learn to survive it.

Let it in, he thought. The idea coiled in his head, nesting there, a possible theme for his TV project. You couldn't defeat the cold and it would never be your friend, but maybe you could let it get down in your bones without fighting back, forget about the idea of getting warm again, accept the ice until it became part of you. Be cheerful like these folks, work hard, laugh a lot, be light of heart, because though the cold might kill you, it hadn't yet. Instead, it gave you what you needed to live.

Teig took the last two bites of his burger in quick succession, then wiped juice from his lips with a rough napkin. He washed it down with a big swig of beer, pleased with himself. This trip had been the right decision. He could feel that now. He needed a hit desperately, and felt the flutter of hope. No, more than hope. He felt certain he would find the hit he needed on the Kolyma Highway. There were lessons to be learned up here. The show wouldn't just be about the locals and their lifestyle, it would be about the philosophy of what it meant to be human. *What we really need as human beings to be happy.*

A burst of laughter floated across the bar. Teig glanced around to find its source and spotted a pair of women embracing. One was the waitress he had seen before, the one employee in the place besides the owner. He assumed this must be Timir's wife, whose name he'd said was Sayaara. The other woman wore knee-high mukluks and a fur hat with a colorful traditional band woven into it. Locks of hair dyed the deep red of black cherries had snuck loose from inside the hat, falling across her eyes. As she broke the embrace, she tucked her stray hair back beneath her hat, then slipped into a fur coat that made her look like a Yeti, still chattering to Sayaara as she buttoned up. Her smile faded abruptly, perhaps at something her friend had said, and she reached out to take the other woman's hand in what looked like gratitude.

Then she was off, striding toward the door.

"I'll never look at Rudolph the same way again," Prentiss said.

Teig laughed and glanced at him for a moment. When he looked back at the door, the woman had already left. An icy gust blasted through the bar, but he felt as if he must be the only one who noticed. Everyone else simply lived with it. This was Siberia.

"I hate the thought of going back outside," Prentiss added, taking another bite of his reindeer burger.

"I'm with you. But we can't bunk down here tonight," Teig replied.

"Well, I hope whatever sleeping arrangements our guide's made for us, we don't wake up looking like Jack Nicholson at the end of *The Shining*."

Teig picked up his beer glass but set it down again, deciding he'd had enough. "I have my doubts about our lodgings, but I suspect we won't freeze to death."

"Somehow that's not reassuring."

Teig adjusted the cuffs on the several layers of shirt and sweater he wore. "We've got the right gear for the terrain and the weather. We'll be okay. I just want to get there."

"All right. Go piss. Collect our young friend Kaskil. By then I'll be ready to roll."

The door swung open again, but only a foot or two. Frigid air blasted in but nobody entered. After a moment, a man got up from the nearest table and shoved the door shut, making sure the latch caught this time.

"Hey, Prentiss," Teig said gently. "Thank you, brother. For coming with me. For trusting me."

Prentiss wiped at his mouth with a napkin, staring at Teig a bit dubiously. He swallowed a bite of burger. "You know we're friends, Teig—"

"I've always—"

"Hang on," Prentiss said sharply, holding up a hand. "Don't interrupt. We're friends. I trust your intentions if not your word, and I do think you're smart and you've got talent. But I'm here because I've invested a lot of time in your adventures and they don't always pay off. You owe me a chunk of change. So, yeah, I want to help you make it happen, but not for you. For me. If you succeed, then I succeed."

Teig nodded. "A rising tide lifts all boats."

"The tide better bloody rise."

"It will, Prentiss. I know it will. You'll get what you're owed."

What sun there was in Siberia in December had slipped away while they were eating in the bar. The clock read 3:27 p.m. and the Road of Bones had turned pitch black. A crescent moon hung ghostly behind a thin veil of cloud cover, but it provided enough light for the snow on either side of the road to shimmer.

Teig sat behind the wheel, grateful for the reindeer burger that warmed him from the inside, but wishing he'd had a mug of tea or coffee instead of beer. Between the cold and the drone of the tires on the road and the beer, he felt sleepy but he knew better than to ask Prentiss to take over driving again. They'd gotten back onto the road not fifteen minutes ago and he wanted to do his share.

He gripped the wheel and sat up straighter. His thoughts shifted back to the bar and the people he'd seen there, from Timir to the young guys making their video in the parking lot. An image swam into his head of the woman with the black cherry hair and the colorful mukluks. He couldn't be certain where she lived, but if she came from one of the small towns along the highway, most of them barely villages, it made him wonder about her prospects for romance. She'd been beautiful in her own way, not the kind of stunning woman who might cause men to crash bicycles or cars just by walking by—which he'd once witnessed with his own eyes—but certainly attractive. And that black cherry hair suggested she cared about how she looked, even if only for her own satisfaction.

"Kaskil," Teig said, glancing in the rearview mirror. "Do you have a girlfriend?"

"I did when I was younger." His smile remained, but something in his eyes turned it sad. "She had an aunt who lived in Japan. The summer she turned nineteen she went to visit the aunt and never came home. Now she's a student at the university in Osaka. I miss her, but I know many people my age who don't have a boyfriend or girlfriend."

"Why is that?" Prentiss asked.

In the backseat, Kaskil shrugged. Beneath the layers of his clothing and his jacket, the motion made a shushing noise. "We grow up together, you understand? Play together, fight together, until you feel like brother and sister, and then one day you start to notice each other and sometimes it's too late. Too strange to think of sleeping with that person. The trouble is, there aren't many of us, so there isn't a . . . how would you say it? A wide variety of choices. And if you didn't grow up herding reindeer or living in a place like this, there isn't a lot to lure someone to settle here forever."

"At least your work gives you the opportunity to meet people from different parts of the world," Prentiss said. "Maybe you'll meet someone nice from the Caribbean and end up living on a tropical island somewhere."

Kaskil laughed. "I meet women in this work, yes. But none who want a great romantic fling with a reindeer herder or a man who has been to prison. Not to worry, though, I have no interest in living on a tropical island."

Teig looked out his window, watching the strange scaffolding of bare trees against the snow, and the white mountains in the distance. "I guess home is always what feels like home. I've only been in this part of the world a day and a night, and already I know I'll need a week in the tropics just to get some warmth back in my bones."

"And you, Mr. Teigland?" Kaskil asked. "A girlfriend? A wife, perhaps?"

Teig shook his head, focused again on the road ahead of them. "I hardly stay in one place long enough for a second date with anyone. Ask Mr. Prentiss about his love life instead."

Kaskil began to ask, but Prentiss pointed a stiff finger at the young man. "Don't you do it. I've had three wives. He just likes to get me riled up."

Teig laughed and glanced in the rearview mirror. "Two of them were beautiful."

"What about the third?" Kaskil asked.

Prentiss sighed, then punched Teig in the arm. "Fucker."

Teig swerved, just a bit. The tires rumbled but did not slip. "Asshole," he said, rubbing at his biceps. "Gonna fucking crash us again."

"Me?" Prentiss said, but he didn't bother reminding Teig who had nodded off behind the wheel earlier today.

"Go on, Prentiss," Teig said. "Our guide asked you a question."

Even Kaskil had a smile on his face now.

Prentiss snickered, laughing at himself. "My third wife. She's beautiful, too, just a bit more country-girl than the first two. Ruthie loved me like nobody ever has, and I guess you could say when I met her I realized I'd never really understood what people meant by 'in love' before that. She's smart as hell, and funny, knows what she wants and goes after it."

Now Kaskil sat forward. "You were both so in love? Why is she your ex-wife?"

Prentiss looked wistful. "She loved another man more than she loved me."

"Oh, no. I'm so sorry." Kaskil looked crestfallen.

"Don't be, kid," Prentiss grumbled. "When Jesus gets his hooks in deep, there's no competing with that guy."

Teig laughed softly, watching the headlights explore the road as if the darkness fled before them. "She still loves you, brother."

"That's why she asked the church for an annulment," Prentiss said.

Teig heard a little noise in the backseat, a small "oh" as Kaskil worked out what the hell Prentiss was talking about. Prentiss had been a bit brusque with the young man at first, but now the three of them settled in comfortably together for the trip. They'd shared a story and a laugh, and that had been Teig's intention. Prentiss could be standoffish with new people and it helped to break the ice. His wife Ruthie had been wonderful at coaxing him into social gatherings and conversations with acquaintances. She'd even managed to get him to engage in occasional small talk, but Prentiss and Ruthie were done now. God had seen to that. Which left it up to Teig to remind Prentiss that being a little friendly wouldn't kill him. Out here in the cold, it wasn't just pleasant to have a friend, it felt necessary.

Teig sure as hell wouldn't want to be out on this road alone.

Not for anything.

4

For more than an hour, they drove without seeing another vehicle. Darkness fell so early that time seemed to blur, as if the night had marched out to meet them. By the time the dashboard clock ticked toward the dinner hour, it felt to Prentiss as if the whole world had already gone to bed and only sleepwalkers and sinners would still be up. Even Kaskil succumbed to the lullaby of the engine and the wheels on the road, first falling quiet and then drifting off to sleep in the backseat.

Prentiss glanced over his shoulder. "Kid's sleeping like a baby back there. Must be nice."

"You don't think you could fall asleep out here, all quiet like this?" Teig asked.

Prentiss glanced out the window so Teig wouldn't see his eyeroll. He had taken a nap earlier and Teig knew that, but this was about something else. *Yes, Felix,* he wanted to say, *I've forgiven you for falling asleep behind the wheel.* For all his enthusiasm and occasional brilliance, and despite the genuine kindness in his heart, Teig could be monumentally irritating. Prentiss considered him a brother, always wanted to give him the benefit of the doubt, but he engaged in some passive-aggressive behavior that made Prentiss seesaw between frustration and amusement.

"If you're sleepy, I can drive again," Prentiss floated.

"I'm fine. Just another hour or so, I think," Teig said. "Then food, coffee, a bed."

"Good. The road is rattling my skull," Prentiss said.

Whatever they were looking for up here in the wilderness, he hoped like hell they found it, for Teig's sake—and his own. Prentiss could still remember the day they'd met, on the first day of shooting promo footage for *Gold Salvage*, one of the projects that Teig had set up at Discovery only to have the plug pulled the day before contracts were to be signed. Financiers had dropped out, unpersuaded that there would really be gold aboard the Spanish galleon on the Atlantic sea floor, no matter how much "evidence" Teig presented. Five thousand of the nearly eight grand Teig owed Prentiss came from that job. Ironically, that debt had been the reason they'd become friends. Teig kept insisting he would find the money to pay Prentiss back eventually, but in the meantime, he would find him more work . . . and he had. Most of it had paid, but occasionally promised money wouldn't come through, projects would fall apart.

Several times, when they'd been drinking and Prentiss felt the strength of the bond between them, he'd offered to let Teig off the hook, but Teig wouldn't hear of it. That was the way Felix Teigland worked. He had enough enthusiasm to get everyone around him excited, often enough to get them to work for free or for payments promised at some future date. He never let people down intentionally—it just happened. One by one, the people he'd disappointed got fed up with the unpaid debts and broken promises, and the charm of Teig's well-meaning enthusiasm lost its sparkle. They grew angry with themselves as much as they did with Teig.

Prentiss understood all of that. He'd gone weeks at a time without speaking to Teig, blocked him on his phone, deleted emails unread.

But he missed his friend and kept coming back, making excuses for Teig the same way he did for his ex-wife Ruthie.

"This is gonna be different, man. I swear," Teig had said, begging Prentiss to come to Siberia with him. The same promise he'd broken half a dozen times before.

But what the fuck, right? Prentiss needed the money, and the friendship, and being with Teig always made him feel better because at least there was one person in his life with his shit *less* together than Prentiss himself. It also didn't hurt that Prentiss's most recent gig had fallen through, he had few other friends, no capital, and his wife was now married to Jesus. Siberia? Why the hell not? It wasn't as if he had anywhere else to be.

He turned to look out his window again. "I thought I saw something out there in the trees a little while ago."

"What do you mean 'something'?"

Prentiss offered a hollow chuckle. "You'll give me a ton of shit."

"I'll do that anyway." Teig glanced at him. "You know there's all sorts of wildlife up here, even with the cold. Might've been a bear. Reindeer. Moose."

Prentiss kept peering out the window. "Are tigers nocturnal?"

Teig laughed. "What the hell are you saying?"

"See? I told you."

"A tiger? You think you saw a tiger?"

Seconds of quiet ticked past.

"I need music," Prentiss said, glancing over his shoulder at the slumbering Kaskil again. "But I don't want to wake the kid."

"It's barely six p.m. Go ahead and wake him."

"That's not nice. Obviously I'm the good parent," Prentiss said, scratching at his beard before he reached for the volume control on the dash.

"He's not our son."

Prentiss turned the volume up but found only static. He shot Teig a stricken glance. "You monster, denying your responsibilities to our cherished boy. I demand a paternity test."

"How do I know where else your camera has been?"

They shared a quiet laugh. Prentiss tried for a minute to find a radio station but it was a fruitless effort, and he began to try to sync his phone to the truck's Bluetooth. In the absence of the radio static, he heard a rustling in the backseat.

"I'm not a child," Kaskil said. He spoke politely, the words crisp, but there was no mistaking the anger simmering there.

Prentiss shifted his bulk sideways in his seat so he could give Kaskil his full attention. "Hey, man, I'm sorry. I meant no disrespect. You're obviously good at your job. I just tend to think of anyone under thirty as a kid."

The glow from the dashboard cast a mask of shadow across Kaskil's face.

"I hunt. I help my family to survive. I care for my niece when her parents are irresponsible," the guide said. "I'm not a child."

"We meant nothing by it," Teig assured him. "It won't happen again."

Kaskil settled back into the seat and closed his eyes. "Also, they are rare, but there is such a thing as a Siberian tiger."

Prentiss glanced at Teig and a silent understanding passed between them. Not only did Kaskil know the region intimately, he was a part of its culture, had been born and raised here, and his powers of persuasion might be the difference between them convincing locals to cooperate with the TV series or being laughed out of Siberia. They needed the kid.

No, not the kid. Kaskil.

"Told you I saw a tiger," Prentiss said quietly.

He got his music playing, some old-school punk he knew Teig

could barely endure, but it served to break the awkward moment. The music drove the darkness back a bit, and it surprised him to see Teig nodding along to the Buzzcocks. Wonders never ceased.

He'd drawn a breath to express his astonishment when Teig hit the brakes. Prentiss turned to peer out at the darkness. In the road ahead, the headlights reflected off a red SUV, its front end halfway into a snowbank. A woman stood in their path, waving her arms, and Prentiss recognized her immediately. They'd noticed her in the bar. Colorful mukluks, fancy fur hat, hair a red so dark it verged on black.

"Pull over," Kaskil said. "Quickly, Mr. Teigland. Stop the—"

"He's stopping, mate," Prentiss grumbled.

Kaskil threw the rear passenger door open before the truck shuddered to a halt and rushed to the woman's side. He put one arm around her, ignoring the SUV as if it were invisible. In seconds, he'd hustled her to the door he'd left open and began bundling her into the backseat of the truck. Prentiss did not speak the language of these two, but he had no difficulty interpreting the urgent tone in Kaskil's voice, and there could be no mistaking the way the woman trembled as she slid across the seat. She took little sucking breaths between her teeth and curled into an upright fetal position.

"What happened?" Prentiss asked, studying the woman. He could see only her eyes, but then she tugged the scarf away from her face and he saw that her skin had turned an ashen, bloodless gray. "Asleep at the wheel?"

Kaskil yanked the door shut, ignoring them as he spoke with their freezing passenger. Prentiss had more questions. Had the car broken down? Had she crashed it into the snow? Could they use cables to give her engine a jump?

At length, Kaskil removed the woman's gloves and inspected her fingers for frostbite. He blew on them and studied them more closely before beginning to rub warmth back into her hands.

"Just engine trouble," he said at last. "She tried to get it started again while it was still rolling and ended up in the snow. The engine's dead—"

"But we have cables," Prentiss reminded him.

Teig shook his head. "Nah, brother. She's been here a while. Fuel lines are frozen now."

"Exactly," Kaskil said. "We can get someone to tow it to a repair shop tomorrow. Tonight the best we can do is get her to Akhust and keep her warm."

Prentiss watched the woman blowing into her own hands. She glanced at him, locked eyes, and she nodded grim thanks.

"She have a name?" Teig asked.

"Her name is Nariyaana," the woman replied. She tucked her black cherry hair up into her hat and sighed. "Nari, please. English have trouble with my name. So, Nari is better."

Prentiss blinked in surprise. "Your English is good."

"His is better," she said, pointing at Kaskil. Fussing with a lock of hair, she pulled off her hat instead, then gestured at Teig. "Make it more hot, please."

"Hotter," Teig said, turning up the heat.

Prentiss doubted Nari was in the mood for grammar lessons, but he wasn't going to argue the point. "What would've happened if we hadn't come by? Even sitting in her car, she had to be freezing."

"Yes," Kaskil agreed. "To death."

Nari seemed untroubled by this prospect. "I have my phone, but . . ." she waved a hand in the air. "No signal."

Prentiss stared at this woman, her eyes alight with intelligence, and realized they had saved her life just by coming along when they had. Nari seemed unfazed and unimpressed, as if dying from engine trouble was no more worrisome a road hazard than a flat tire.

A flat tire would have killed her just as surely, Prentiss thought.

"I'm glad to help," he said, fascinated by Nari and her embrace of the peril of life along the Kolyma Highway.

Teig put the truck into gear and accelerated slowly, watching the red SUV as they passed it on the road. Prentiss appreciated the caution. He found himself more fearful of car trouble than he'd ever been in his life. Whenever he felt anxious or awkward, he found that the fastest way to calm himself was to rely on his camera. If he took some photos or video, he could put some distance between himself and the real world, give himself some perspective.

In the driver's seat, Teig muttered something.

"What's that?"

"The title, I think," Teig replied.

"Which title is this? Number thirty-seven?"

Teig nodded slowly, studying the road ahead. "Just popped into my head. But I think this one's going to stick. I want to call it *Life and Death on the Road of Bones*."

Prentiss glanced into the backseat again. "That's actually a great fucking title."

He looked at his camera display. He decided to get some film of Nari, and chided himself for not filming her crashed truck. He raised his camera and aimed it at the backseat, but Teig caught his wrist and gently pushed his arm down.

"Give her some space."

Prentiss stared at him. "You remember why we're here, yeah?"

Teig kept his gaze straight ahead. "I brought you along, so yeah, I remember. Doesn't mean we have to be assholes."

Heat prickled at Prentiss's cheeks and the back of his neck. He flushed when angry, and he knew he must have been bright red just then.

He lowered his voice, faced forward so that the two locals chatting in the backseat wouldn't hear him over the engine. "Listen, mate.

No fucking about now. You sweet-talked me into the trip not with your honeyed voice and your dimples but the promise of money. The money you owe me, and plenty more besides. I know you mean every word when you make a promise, but we both know how often you manage not to keep them. So if I see something I think will add value when we present this show to buyers, I'm going to film it, your sudden ethical epiphany notwithstanding."

Prentiss waited for Teig to climb onto a high horse and give him some kind of lecture about who was in charge, or about treating their subjects with sensitivity, but he must have realized how completely full-of-shit hypocritical he'd have sounded, because he closed his mouth with a clack of teeth.

Good, Prentiss thought.

The seat crumpled beneath him as he turned and began to film Kaskil and Nari talking quietly, the latter still pale, hugging herself as if she could restore the heat her body had lost. If she had any complications from exposure, she didn't let on. They kept talking, but Prentiss saw the flicker in their peripheral vision that said they noticed the camera. He'd been filming for a minute or two when Nari turned her full face toward him and smiled as if they'd known one another for years.

"Are you going to make me famous, mister?" she asked.

Prentiss clicked off his camera, lowered it, and smiled. "It's a strange world. Anything can happen."

It had been one of the longest days of Prentiss's life. All he wanted now was to be out of the truck and inside someplace with four walls, a bed, and a furnace. Teig had chosen this trip, and a lot depended on it, but Prentiss wished they were already home.

For now, Akhust would have to do. They'd be there soon. Out of the cold and the dark.

They'd be safe.

5

The sky had cleared by the time Teig drove through the outskirts of Akhust. In the pale glow of the quarter moon, he could make out a variety of buildings, all of them frosted with snow and framed in ice. They passed an Orthodox church so caked with white it seemed to have been sculpted in snow.

"It's so quiet," Prentiss said.

"Nearly always," Kaskil replied. "After dark, at least."

The truck rumbled past a small playground—built for the summer months—where an outdoor thermometer showed the temperature at fifty-three degrees below zero. Teig figured that was Celsius, but when it was this cold there seemed no point in converting to Fahrenheit.

At the top of the thermometer post was a metal weathervane of the Soviet-era hammer-and-sickle. They really had entered another world.

"Prentiss, get the camera out. Let's mark our arrival."

The strange history of the place unfolded around them as Teig drove along what he presumed was the main street. There were a couple of gray buildings of the old Soviet model, concrete rectangles with no aesthetic value, but the rest of the town consisted of small homes and a few shops and offices, as well as a little school and several truck and auto repair places, garages, and squat buildings that might've been a slaughterhouse or a lumberyard.

A thread of pain wriggled in behind his left eye like the thinnest of worms. Teig scrunched that one eye closed and a quiet grunt escaped his lips. Prentiss must have heard, for he shot Teig an inquisitive look, which Teig waved off. "Bit of a headache," he said, which was no surprise after the journey that had brought them here.

But it wasn't just his head, was it? Another worm wriggled in his gut, only this one wasn't pain but something closer to nausea.

Teig flushed with that clammy heat so peculiar to the moment just before your body is overcome with the panting, feverish need to empty itself. The moment it's too late. The moment you go rigid, and the rush of sour bile comes up fast as a scream.

His foot came off the pedal. He took a shuddering breath, feeling a sheen of sweat on his forehead. And then it passed.

"Teig?" Prentiss asked.

He braked, slowing the truck, and blinked to clear his vision. "I'm okay. Just had a moment . . . I felt like I was going to be sick. Just a flash."

All three of his passengers were silent, watching him, as if bracing themselves for the torrent of vomit they feared might splash the steering wheel in the next few seconds. But to his surprise, the feeling really had passed. Teig took several deep breaths, clearing his head. The engine coughed a few times, reminding him that he did not want it to die out here in the open, where they might not be able to get it started again.

"Are you all right, Mr. Teigland?" Kaskil asked, polite as you please. As if he'd never been in prison at all.

Teig nodded, but he took steady, even breaths, not wanting to risk unsettling his stomach.

"Shit," Prentiss said. "I hope it wasn't your reindeer burger. I ate the same thing."

Teig wanted to tease him about being selfish, but Prentiss was right. It would be bad for one of them to become ill, but if both of them were down with some kind of virus, the project would stall, possibly die. No matter what, Teig didn't want to be sick so far from his own bed.

"I'm okay," he said, holding the wheel and starting to accelerate through town again. The windows they passed seemed darker, and the squiggle of nausea lingered just enough to keep him on edge.

The place didn't feel right. Cold as it was, and after dark, it made sense that the people would be huddled inside their homes to keep warm, isolated only with those closest to them. But Akhust's emptiness made the town feel even more desolate. Teig had been lonely all his life, ever since the van took Olivia away. Nowhere had felt like home after that, not even for a day. But he had never felt so far away from anything resembling home until now.

"How many people live here again?" Prentiss asked, raising his camera to film through the windshield.

"Four hundred," Teig replied, crouched over the steering wheel, taking in the strange, unearthly stillness. Snow covered everything, as if a storm had just blown through, caked onto every surface, but he knew the last real snowfall might have been a month ago and it had never gotten warm enough to start melting.

"That's wrong," Kaskil said. "My father says they're at five-hundred-thirty-two people now. Though that's counting me, and I don't live here full-time."

Nari had been almost silent for half an hour or more as they made the final part of their journey to Akhust. Teig had assumed she was lost in her own thoughts, trying to sort out how much of a pain in the ass this detour would be for her. Now, though, she leaned her head against the window, looking out at the distance.

"It feels like . . ." she began, reaching for the right words in English. "Forever." Dissatisfied, she pressed her fingers to the glass, indicating the trees and the white mountains that reflected back the moon. “Like the last stop before forever.”

Teig flinched at the startling echo of his own thoughts.

Kaskil switched to Yakut, perhaps trying to get her to elaborate, but Teig thought she had said it perfectly. He bent over the dash and looked out at those same mountains, at the wilderness beyond the edge of the town, and he understood. Here in this little scattering of human structures they could still convince themselves they were in the world of people, but once they passed into the woods, it would have been impossible to pretend they had control or authority over anything. Hunters and herders went into those woods or up that mountain from Akhust, and when they did they were surrendering to the primal nature of the world. Akhust stood as a stark reminder of how small a thing it was to be a human being.

Teig appreciated the fact of it, the aesthetics, and the opportunity to market the feeling he had right then in his chest, to give viewers a little taste of it. He just hoped they wouldn’t feel as unsettled by this place as he did, or nobody would watch a second episode.

Unless they do, he thought. *Unless they love feeling like this.*

If audiences loved this feeling, Teig thought he might make a shitload of money.

“This is right,” he muttered under his breath. “This is going to work.”

Prentiss turned the camera on him. “It better.”

It will, Teig thought. But he didn’t say the words aloud. Not on film. Instead, he tapped the brake to slow down and turned to face the camera. “After a drive that felt like another world, some kind of winter planet, we’re finally pulling into Akhust . . .” He glanced into the backseat at Kaskil. “If I’m saying that correctly.”

“It’s Akhust,” Kaskil replied.

“Isn’t that what I said? Akhust.”

"Akhust," Kaskil corrected him again.

Teig glanced out the windshield, smiling sheepishly. "Well, I'll get it eventually. Folks, we've made some friends along the way, and in fairly frightening circumstances. But then again, just stepping outside can be frightening up here. For now, we're going to get something to eat, get settled for the night, and in the morning we'll start our real exploration of what it's like to live in the coldest place on earth."

Prentiss took the unspoken cue and clicked off the camera.

The moment he did, Kaskil leaned forward. "That was the turn back there on the right. I didn't want to interrupt your shot."

Teig smiled, thanked him, and hit the brakes. Their guide might talk a bit too much, but if he had the sense to not ruin a take when Prentiss was filming, he would end up being even more useful to the show than Teig had hoped.

As he did a three-point turn, Teig felt a tap on his shoulder. In the rearview mirror he saw Nari watching him.

"Thank you for the ride," she said. "I think I would have died in my car if you had not appeared."

Teig turned down the wide, sparsely settled street Kaskil had pointed out to him. "It's our pleasure, Nari. I get the feeling people up here have to rely on each other a lot, and there's something pretty wonderful about that. I'm really happy we were able to help."

He would have said the same to anyone, and he would have meant it, but his gaze ticked up to the rearview mirror for another glance at her. Nari would be out of the truck in minutes. In the morning, or even tonight, she'd be gone and they would never see one another again. Teig considered that a shame. Yes, she was attractive, but more than that, she bristled with a kind of unsettled energy that intrigued him. It really was a shame that they would be saying goodbye so soon after saying hello.

Kaskil leaned forward and pointed to a small house, little more than a cabin, with a single light burning inside. "That's where you'll be staying. It isn't much, but it will keep you warm."

"Whose house is that?" Prentiss asked.

"It was my uncle's. He's dead now and my cousins left years ago. I stay there when I visit, so you might say that it's my house. But really, I think it is nobody's house. There are many like it. Houses full of nobody. But while you stay here, it will be yours."

"Perfect," Teig said, pulling the truck up in front of the little house. The deeper snow crunched under the tires. He kept the engine running for now; it wouldn't be safe to shut it off until he'd pulled it into the nearby parking structure. He stared out the window at the house and that single warm light burning in the window. "Thank you, Kaskil. Truly. I'm not sure we could pull this off without you."

Kaskil clapped his hands together. "Please remember you said that when I ask for a raise."

Prentiss laughed. "People really are alike all over."

Teig looked back at his guide. "I won't forget, my friend. I promise you that."

Electric radiators ran along the baseboard but the windows in the little house rattled with every gust of wind and the cold slithered in. Teig had slept in houses and inns by the ocean many times and left windows open, soothed by the ever-present whisper of the surf. In this little house, the wind provided that constant soundtrack, sometimes a whisper and other times a banshee wail. The house groaned and creaked like a hammer teasing a rusty nail out of old wood.

Teig unzipped his suitcase. Prentiss had gone into the kitchen to see if Kaskil had provided some way to make coffee or tea, anything warm, and Teig relished having a moment to himself. He opened his suitcase and dug out his travel kit. He wanted to wash his face and brush his teeth, put on a clean shirt and sweater.

What he didn't want to do was keep focusing on the wind. When it gusted hard, if he paused to listen, the whistles and wails sounded as if there were voices inside them.

"Success!" Prentiss declared as he stepped into the room.

Teig's heart jumped in his chest. "Don't do that!"

Prentiss laughed. "Sorry, mate. When did you get so easy to spook?"

"Since we arrived at the edge of forever, just like Nari said, and you decided to start sneaking up on me in the dark."

Prentiss plopped himself down in the one sprawling, comfortable chair. The room had a single bed but also a futon-style mat that Kaskil had unrolled on the floor. They hadn't argued yet about which one of them would get the bed.

"I won't lie," Prentiss replied. "It's been a long, weird day. Entirely surreal. I just think I've run out of energy to worry about it."

Teig thought about Nari again. She'd gone off with Kaskil in search of someone to help her out.

"I wonder if they'll be able to tow her car in tonight and get it started," he said. "Dark and cold as it is, I wouldn't want to be the person setting out onto the road right now."

"Right?" Prentiss said. "I just feel like burrowing into a mound of blankets and waiting till daylight. Trouble is, there's so little of it up here this time of year."

Rooting around in his gear, Teig found a thick cotton sweater that had been washed recently and hung outdoors to dry, back at home. He brought it to his nose and inhaled deeply, glad of the fresh scent. When he lowered it, another scent filled the room and he turned to look at Prentiss.

"You're making coffee."

"They don't call me Miracle Jack for nothing."

"Nobody calls you that."

"Ah, well, you should've known my mum. Woman always thought I was her little miracle. And Ruthie . . ."

He blinked as if he'd lost his place in a book and was searching for the right paragraph. Teig saw the flicker of pain in his old friend's eyes and felt guilty about teasing him earlier.

"Prentiss—"

"No, I'm fine. Just hits me weird sometimes," Prentiss said. "I don't think I've ever been as far away from her as I am right now. If Ruthie knew what we were up to, she'd pray for us. She'd tell me she still has love for me, that God will guide us on our path, and that I should listen for his voice instead of doing stupid shit like following Felix Teigland to Siberia."

Seconds ticked by in the chilly room.

Teig smiled. "Ruthie always was the smart one."

Prentiss nodded slowly, pondering. "I've thought about going after her, believe it or not. Three wives in, you don't want to give up easily. Ruthie's the only one I never fell out of love with. Woman used to drink, used to laugh, used to cuss with the best of us. I know that old girl's still in there, Jesus or no Jesus."

He gave Teig a mischievous look. "You wouldn't believe some of the places we shagged. Airplane bathroom at forty thousand feet. Hiking trails. The deck of the boat on that Danube river cruise we took. Iceland, on a trek to see the northern lights."

"Unbelievable."

"I know," Prentiss said. "It's all about church and prayer now. She wants to go on a pilgrimage to the Holy Land. I figure there won't be any shagging at the bloody Wailing Wall."

"No, no," Teig replied. "I mean, yes, it's creepy as hell to hear you talking about shagging a woman who's a nun, but I meant it's unbelievable that you hike. Never mind that you can fit into an airplane restroom with a second person. How does that work?"

"You dirty bastard," Prentiss sneered. "I ought to pummel you. Only you're right, actually. The airplane bathroom, mile-high-club thing was a disaster. Went in, dropped my trousers, got things started. She rapped on the door and I unlocked it, Ruthie pushes in there with me, but we couldn't get the door to close completely and never managed to get it locked. Just got rolling when a flight attendant gave the door a bit of a shove and whispered through the opening."

Teig narrowed his eyes, entranced. "What'd she say?"

"Apparently my thigh hit the emergency 'call' button. She wanted to make sure we didn't actually need her help, and to remind us the captain had turned the seatbelt lights on and we should return to our seats."

Teig burst out laughing. "I'm so sorry, brother. Jesus stole your best wife ever."

With a wistful smile, Prentiss rose and went back to the kitchen. Teig chuckled, still thinking about the story, but his thoughts turned to his own life. Prentiss had been married three times, while Teig had never gotten within a hundred miles of an altar. They'd talked about it many times but he always brushed off the question. One day, he would say, a relationship would come along that changed his outlook. He'd meet a woman willing to share her life with someone like Teig, a guy whose big dreams sometimes came true, but who couldn't force himself to work a regular job, no matter how he tried. Teig knew he was a risk, and someday he'd find someone sincerely willing to take that risk.

Or he wouldn't.

"Ah, fuck," he whispered to himself. "You're getting maudlin again."

Prentiss came back in with two mugs of coffee, the air cold enough that thick clouds of steam plumed from each cup.

"Teig, my friend," he said, handing over a mug, "I had my doubts. I truly did. But I think we're onto something here. Might be you'll be able to pay me what you owe me after all."

With a sigh that cleared his head, Teig raised the mug in a toast. "Brother, you might end up with a lot more than what I already owe you. No reason you can't direct some of these episodes, maybe come on as an executive producer with me."

Prentiss stopped with his mug halfway to his lips, peered at Teig over the rim. "You'd do that?"

Teig felt the urge to swallow the next words that sprang into his head. He had never been great at sentiment, never focused enough on the people in his life that mattered. The next gig, the next dream, the next hustle always seemed more important. For once, he let the words come out.

"I roll the dice a lot. Sometimes I've done okay and sometimes I've gone bust, but I've never had a home run. I've let a lot of people down in my life, brother, and you're just about the only one who hasn't written me off. Maybe the reason you're here is you think it's your best chance of getting some of your money back, but even if that's the only reason, it means you've still got a sliver of faith in me. I'll take what I can get."

Prentiss clapped him on the shoulder. "Look at you, Felix, getting all soppy on me. Yes, I've got a little faith left, especially now we've seen this for ourselves. People are gonna be sitting cozy at home on their sofas and they're gonna see the giant fucking reindeer pulling sleds and abandoned gulags and watch us search for a spooky old woman the whole country thinks is a ghost, and they're gonna love it. We're going to do all right out of this, Felix. I know we are."

Teig put out his mug and Prentiss did the same. They toasted to their venture and to the future. A moment later, taking their first sips, they grimaced at one another. The coffee tasted like rusty sludge, but at least it was hot. Teig took another sip, found it just as awful as the first, and still went for a third.

Someone banged on the door.

Before Teig or Prentiss could move, they heard the clank of it opening and felt the shocking cold gust in around them.

Kaskil stumbled across the threshold with Nari at his heels. She gave him a little shove, making room so she could haul the door shut behind her. Kaskil wore his hat pulled down tightly, flaps partly hiding his face, scarf obscuring his mouth. He looked out from beneath the hat with bright, skittish eyes and his chest rose and fell in quick, shallow breaths.

Nari said his name, grabbed his arm, and he spun on her and let loose a furious stream of language Teig could not translate. But he didn't need a translator to understand the look on Kaskil's face.

"Hey, calm down," Prentiss said. "What's happened? What's going on?"

"Something . . . strange," Nari replied, frowning at the word, perhaps unsure it was the right one.

But this was more than strange. Teig shot a sidelong glance at Prentiss and the two of them approached Kaskil slowly. The guide rubbed a hand across his mouth like a drunk desperate for a bottle. He kept looking around at different spots on the floor, like he thought he might find answers there, and then he turned to stare at the door through which he and Nari had just entered.

"There's no one," he said.

Teig's spine straightened. The worm of nausea squiggled anew in his gut. "Explain that."

Kaskil went to the window. He stood beside the frame and edged carefully so he could peek through the frost-rimed glass, as if he feared being spotted.

"Just as I said," he muttered. "There's nobody here. Nobody at all."

"So what are you looking for?" Prentiss asked.

Kaskil turned on him, eyes narrowed. He sneered, muttered something in Yakut. "Did you not hear what I just said? They're gone. I went to the house my father shares with my aunt and uncle, and it is empty. Their neighbors as well. The doors are open but there is nobody inside. I went to the garage to find someone to tow Nari's car. The place is . . ." He squeezed his eyes shut, searching for the word, and found it. "Abandoned."

Yanking off his hat, Kaskil peered out the window again and then started to pace. He moved in silence, but Teig could see his mind racing.

"The police are also gone," Nari said. "There are only two of them, but the building is empty. I walked to the back. That door is also open."

"Some kind of gathering," Prentiss said, brushing it off. "You've both got to take a breath. It's all timing. Small town like this, and you only checked a few places. There's a birthday party or something, right, Teig?"

Kaskil shot him a withering glare. Prentiss must have been trying to make someone feel better, but Teig wasn't sure if the words were meant to comfort the guide or Prentiss himself. For his own part, he felt a frisson of something not quite fear and not quite excitement. All the time he'd spent on *Ghost Sellers* had made him jaded. When it came to weird shit, cynicism was his fallback. But he thought about the way he had been feeling since they arrived here, the twist in his gut and the ache in his head, and the quiet abandonment of this place. He searched Kaskil's eyes and saw not just worry for his family, but real fear. In all of those ghost hunting shows, he'd seen zealous belief and fanaticism, and he'd seen cunning fraud from charlatans. He'd seen people who were unnerved or a little spooked, and he'd seen people thrilled by the idea of a haunting. But he'd never seen fear like this.

Whatever Kaskil had come home to in Akhust had scared the hell out of him.

"Let's have a look," Teig said, reaching for his coat.

"Let's what, now?" Prentiss asked.

"Get your jacket," Teig said. "And your camera. Bundle up, balaclava and everything." He turned to find Nari and Kaskil both staring at him.

"Something is wrong," Nari said. "We should go away now. Far away."

Kaskil tugged his hat back on. "I can't go. I must check on my sister's house."

Nari stared at him. "You saw the other houses. You shouted for your family, for anyone to answer, but nobody did."

Kaskil ignored her, despite his fear. Turning up his collar against the wind, he opened the door and stepped out into the dreadful cold. Nari called after him in Yakut, practically spitting the words. Teig thought she must be cussing at him.

She turned to Teig. "The truck is yours. We should leave."

He zipped up his coat, started closing the buttons over the zipper. "If something's happened to his family—"

"It is not just his family." Nari turned an anxious glance toward the window. "This is not our town. We have no reason to stay."

"A bit heartless, isn't it?" Prentiss asked her. Though it was more a judgment than a question. "If something's happened in town, we ought to at least call the authorities. And we can't do that unless we know what's gone on here."

Nari swore again.

Teig had pulled on his balaclava and gloves. Now he went to the door. "Nari, just stay here. We'll be back soon. If we don't find someone with answers, and if you really feel it isn't safe, we'll leave."

She shook her head. "After you do . . . *that* . . ." With a scowl, she pointed at Prentiss's camera.

The implication rang clear and true. Teig and Prentiss needed thrilling footage from the whole region around the Road of Bones, and whatever crisis they'd walked into, they would have to be total fools not to get some of Kaskil's panic on film. And if people had gone out into this landscape and left their doors open, he probably did have something to panic about. Teig pushed away such thoughts. They made him feel callous and predatory. He didn't like that feeling, but he couldn't pretend he wasn't up here hunting for his future, for a change in circumstance that would propel him to the life he'd always wanted.

He also couldn't pretend the uncanny wasn't a lure for him. If he'd come all the way to the edge of civilization and found himself an actual mystery, he wasn't about to run away from it. On the surface, he told himself they would find answers—and the missing people. But down deep, he couldn't help but hope he had finally stumbled across something else.

Teig went out first, layered in frigid-weather gear. Prentiss followed him, and the cold clutched at them instantly. Even in the short time they'd been inside, he had managed to forget just how cold the night could be. It stole the air from his lungs, tightened every muscle, gripped him around the chest.

Nari stood inside the open door, unsure, as if she might bolt.

"You coming or you staying here?" Teig asked.

Cussing again, she bent against the wind and cold and left the house, slamming the door behind her. "We go together."

The people weren't gone—of course they weren't. Despite the haunted look in Kaskil's eyes and his own private hopes, Teig told himself they would find a quick explanation. He couldn't help wondering if maybe the whole thing might be a sham—a show for the showman. The past two days had been so surreal, as if a dream had been layered like gauzy cobweb on top of the ordinary world, that a part of him felt *of course the people in the town have vanished*. But the rational fragment of his brain objected vociferously. Logic insisted they were either here, and engaged in some sort of hijinks, or they were gathered in one spot for a church ceremony or shamanistic ritual.

A wedding, he thought. *Or some kind of party. Some old couple's fiftieth anniversary.*

Firm, logical thoughts.

On the other hand, there was Kaskil. Teig believed the look in the guy's eyes—nobody could fake that. The absence of his family had spooked him enough that the moment they went out into the street, he stormed along the road toward a boxy structure that looked like a barn and a warehouse had mated.

"Kaskil, hang on!" Prentiss called after him.

The words were visible in the air, the breath of each syllable puffed out of Prentiss's mouth before the wind whistled them away. Kaskil either hadn't heard or wasn't listening, as if now that he'd deposited Nari with them and thus handed off any responsibility he might feel toward her, the rest of them had ceased to exist.

"Go on after him," Teig said. "Get some video."

Prentiss blanched, looking at him. "This is fucked up, mate."

"No argument. Hurry up. He's quick. And put on your ski mask."

Prentiss muttered under his breath as he dug into his pocket and yanked out a balaclava, then tugged it on. His beard looked ridiculous under the fabric.

Kaskil had already covered thirty yards, and Prentiss cursed a blue streak as he turned to rush after the younger man. Though his beard and his size always put Teig in mind of a bear, Prentiss could lumber along at speed when he got up a good head of steam.

Teig turned to scan the few houses along the road.

Nari stepped up beside him. "This is not a good idea. We should all stay together."

He studied her face. Exhausted, unhappy about being out in the cold . . . maybe a little frightened. Or more than a little.

Teig nodded. "You're right. I'm not keen on being out here alone. You and me, okay?"

Nari nodded.

He glanced around this dark little town, deep in the heart of nothing. The snow creaked and popped. Teig knew there might be frost quakes, loud noises like gunshots that came from snow settling in extreme cold, but he hadn't been prepared for the consistent crunch and pop, as if someone approached them in the dark.

The cold compressed his chest. Seared his lungs. He and Prentiss had prepared for this exposure. They had the right clothing, the right layers, masks and furry hoods, only their eyes exposed for very long, but nothing could really have prepared them for cold like this. It made a mockery of the way he'd understood that word every prior day of his life. To talk about the cold in this little town in the Siberian winter was like talking about water when what you meant was the deepest ocean a thousand miles from shore, and you're unable to swim.

This cold, like the ocean depths, meant if you couldn't do something to save yourself, you were going to die. This cold was a predator, and they were at its mercy.

"This way," he said, because they needed to move or freeze. And because the longer he stood in the road wondering if all these houses were empty, the more sure he became that they would be, and that prompted questions.

Teig told himself he wanted the only mysteries here to be the ones he manufactured for a television audience. But that wasn't entirely true.

There were three other homes within easy distance. They had driven past these places on the way into town and each of them had lights burning inside. Nari followed him as he hustled down the road to a place more chalet than cabin. The window over the front door suggested it even had a second floor. Teig pounded on the door, urgency making him forget his manners. He wasn't going to freeze his balls off out of courtesy. Stamping his feet, he glanced at Nari and saw that she was paying no attention to this house. Instead she scanned the darkened street and the open stretch of snow that separated the property from the one behind it.

He hammered at the door. "Only five hundred people. Stands to reason some of these places are already empty."

Seconds passed. From a street or two away, he heard Kaskil calling out for friends and neighbors, maybe for his sister. Teig gave up. He nodded to Nari and they set off toward the next house. Someone would be home.

"Go to the back door," Nari said.

Teig took two more steps before she grabbed his arm.

"The back door."

He stopped himself from arguing. If there was a back door, he might learn something from looking inside. Nari fell into step beside him and they huddled together as they trudged through the snow. The wind whipped around them in gusts strong enough to make them fight for forward motion.

They had just turned the corner at the rear of the house when Teig saw the pool of light that poured out the back door of the little two-story home. The door hung wide open. Snow had blown over the threshold and begun to layer the floor and the small table and the boots that sat on a woven throw rug just inside.

Footprints led away through the snow. At least three pairs—two adult, one child—and the largest were those of a barefoot man.

Teig shivered. The wind cut at his face. His nose had gone numb.

The footprints led off toward the thick woods at the western edge of the tiny town, in the foothills of the mountains beyond.

With a glance at the worry in Nari's eyes, Teig began to follow.

6

Jack Prentiss had been eleven years old when his mum had taken him and his sister, Lucy, on holiday in Italy. Their dad had just left them and Mum had made herself a to-do list of all the things she'd held off doing because Dad never made the time. Not a bucket list, she was sure to tell Jack and Lucy. Bucket lists were for old people to do when they were worried about dying. Nah. Sarah Hughes Prentiss had made it crystal clear that her to-do list was about living.

They'd traveled all around Italy and Sicily on that trip. Gone to Capri and taken a little rowboat inside the Blue Grotto, jumped off and swum in the vivid blue water of that dark little cave, like taking a dip in a lake full of fairy magic. Lucy had never stopped talking about magic after that day, had seemed to live her life in the joy of that moment, and Prentiss envied his little sister even today, though she taught English literature to teenagers and he figured that would suck the joy and magic out of anyone eventually. Anyone but Lucy.

Mum had taken them to Verona and told them the tale of Romeo and Juliet as a bedtime story. They'd been to Rome, of course, and to see *David* in Florence. Prentiss and little Lucy had wished they could stay in Venice forever. In the depths of his mind, he could still hear the echoes in the dark as the gondoliers shouted warnings to one another while approaching a turn in the narrow, ancient canals. Their gondolier wore a frilly white shirt and spoke to Lucy as if he were her very own grandfather, while Mum drank champagne. She'd given her boy Jack a sip that night and Prentiss had never forgotten. They'd shared a secret then, and he'd loved her even more for it.

They'd eaten far too much chocolate in Modica and stopped at an agriturismo farmhouse where a family had fed them the freshest and most delicious food Prentiss could ever recall eating, and he'd been trying to replicate that for decades, hence the considerable extra girth he carried. The farmers' little boy had introduced the three Prentisses to his pet ostrich and thereafter issued a string of the foulest profanity Italy had to offer, some of which even young Jack understood. His mother had gone from wide-eyed shock to a fit of giggling that left her wiping tears from her eyes.

The vulgar little kid and his ostrich had stared at the Prentiss clan with equal fury and confusion, presumably insulted.

They'd watched glass being blown on the Venetian island of Murano and been as confused and wide-eyed as that ostrich when the glassblower had proposed marriage to their mother, apparently in earnest. They'd seen ruins all over, from Agrigento to Ostia Antica, but the thing that had remained with Prentiss forever, that still haunted his dreams, was Pompeii. Buried by the eruption of Mount Vesuvius in AD 79, Pompeii was remarkably preserved. Ever since Teig had first told him about the Road of Bones, Prentiss had felt the echo of that childhood visit and the shuddery memory of fear. People had been buried in ash, had suffocated and died and been cocooned there. The streets of Pompeii were fascinating, the homes as well. He'd learned a great deal that day. But he'd also seen one of the preserved cadavers on display and had nightmares on and off for the rest of their journey.

He'd been in all kinds of places, the man behind the camera, shooting footage of places people said were haunted. But none of them had ever felt haunted to him, not like Pompeii.

Not until now.

He did a slow turn with his camera, watching through the viewfinder to give himself a bit of distance from the eerie quality of the moment. Teig had seemed certain they would find people somewhere, and Kaskil—poor son of a bitch, desperation gleaming in his eyes—kept clutching at hope like it was rosary beads, waiting for God to intervene. Prentiss could do nothing but steady his breath, try to keep from getting frostbite, and do his job.

That was his mantra in anxious moments. *Do your job. Do your job. Do your job.* Even if Teig owed him money, even if the cold scared him almost as much as the abandoned little town, the only thing he could think of to combat his fear was to do his job. If Ruthie were there, she'd have been praying to God, believing wholeheartedly that he would come to her aid. All Prentiss had was his camera.

This is priceless footage, he told himself. And that kept him going. He didn't want to be mercenary and he didn't want to be a vulture or a ghoul if it turned out all these people had committed ritual suicide in a barn or something, but he knew the market. He knew that this footage alone would be enough to make some executives catch their breath.

His boots crunched on the snow. He adjusted the balaclava over his face, then traded his camera back and forth between hands so he could stretch his fingers, keep the blood flowing.

Kaskil beckoned to him from the entrance to a building across the street.

"What's that?" Prentiss called, the wind snatching the words and carrying them away.

"The library," Kaskil replied. He grabbed the door handle, twisted, and pushed inward.

Prentiss hurried after him, watching through the viewfinder, hoping his camera didn't freeze. He'd never have been able to afford the one he'd really wanted for this trip, but he had managed to persuade an old friend to loan it to him, and he'd done his research on shooting in subzero temperatures. He had backup batteries in his pocket, kept the camera inside its bag when he wasn't shooting, and otherwise just hoped for a little luck. Even equipment made for subzero environments had not been made for anywhere as cold as this.

Kaskil led the way into the library. Prentiss followed, camera ahead of him. Kaskil tried to click the lights on but like the rest of Akhust, it stayed dark.

Ten feet over the library's threshold, Kaskil called out to the gloom. Prentiss held his breath as they both waited for an answer. Long seconds passed before Kaskil turned to look at him. Maybe the kid didn't realize he was on camera, or maybe he didn't care, but he did not even try to hide his emotions.

"I thought they might have gathered here," Kaskil said. "There are town meetings sometimes. I already checked the school and that was empty, too. I thought . . . if there was trouble, where would they go?"

His gaze turned vacant, a little lost.

"You have a lot of family here?" Prentiss asked, because he felt like he had to say something. Interact. Kaskil needed that, and deserved it. He'd come off as funny and tough, with backbone and flair, and enough tamped-down rage to suggest prison had done more to scar him than the tattoos on his skin. Now he seemed like a kid again, young and afraid for his family.

"I told you. My father. My aunt and uncle," Kaskil said, glancing at the floor. "They share a house. I went there, but nobody's home."

"We need to check your sister's house," Prentiss remembered.

Kaskil kept staring at the ground, perhaps hesitant about what he expected to find at his sister's house. At length he nodded, blew out a breath, and then marched past Prentiss and out the door. As they hustled past two other buildings, Kaskil's head stayed on a swivel, glancing back and forth for any sign of life. Prentiss watched him, kept the camera rolling, but the little town felt so abandoned that he felt certain they were alone.

When they reached the house, Kaskil opened the door. No key necessary. Nobody locked their doors up here.

The first thing the camera saw upon entry was the back door. In the little house, the distance from front to back door couldn't have been more than forty feet. The door hung open, a bit of moonlight glowing outside, snow piled up inside where the wind had carried it. Prentiss should have been a little warmer there, out of the elements, but somehow it felt colder. He shifted the camera around, caught up with Kaskil, saw the guy standing by his sister's dining table, staring down at the bowls and glasses. Whatever had been in them—both the drinks and the stew the family had made for their dinner—had frozen solid.

Prentiss knew Kaskil didn't like him much. He couldn't blame the guy, knew he'd been rude. This kid—this man—probably did not want his sympathy or his support, but he needed it. Prentiss crossed the ten feet separating them, the floor creaking beneath him, and laid a hand on Kaskil's shoulder.

Kaskil turned and shouted into the empty house.

Empty, because even though they hadn't searched every inch of the little place, they hadn't found anyone else in this abandoned town. Besides, it *felt* empty.

No hope in his eyes, Kaskil shouted again, and again, no one replied.

"Hey, mate, listen," Prentiss said. "Don't let your imagination run away. We don't know what's happened. The whole town's empty, which makes me think they were evacuated. Wherever they are, everyone's gone together, which means your family are okay, yeah?"

Kaskil turned to lock eyes with him, unconvinced.

"There are open doors all over town," Kaskil said. "Where would they ever need to go so quickly that they would leave their doors open? That they would leave dinner on the table?"

Prentiss lowered the camera. "We'll find out when we catch up to them. They'll be all right. Wherever they are, they're together."

Kaskil deflated further, glancing about the living room and kitchen. Then he turned and started for the open back door, headed back out into a night without answers.

He stiffened. Turned to the left, toward a door to another part of the house. A door that stood open several inches, only darkness beyond it.

"I heard it, too," Prentiss said, and he saw the flicker of hope in Kaskil's face.

The sound whispered out through the slightly open door again, and both of them knew it wasn't the wind.

Kaskil reached out, opened the door a little further, and slipped through.

Nari hadn't been very interested in what the American and the Englishman had to say. She appreciated the kindness they'd shown in giving her a ride—she'd likely have died without their intervention—but she didn't plan to be with them long enough to make friends. Now she found herself in Akhust, freezing in the cold and dark, with only these new people for company. She watched as Teig's flashlight crept after the footprints in the snow. He swung the beam back and forth, tracking the three sets of prints that led, side by side, toward the forest and the mountain beyond.

"We should not be here," she said.

Teig nodded without looking at her. He continued to scan the snow ahead.

"I wish we weren't," Teig admitted. "But Kaskil's family lives here. I can't just say, 'thanks, pal, you're on your own,' and leave him behind."

Nari understood and reluctantly agreed. Her first instinct had been to persuade Teig and Prentiss to get back into their truck and keep heading north, and to hell with Kaskil and his town. Before tonight, she would have thought herself a better person than that, but her skin prickled with fear every moment she remained here. It felt as if she were breathing in that fear, as if she were infected by it. Nari had never wanted to run so badly in her life.

On the other hand, she would have killed her mother for a cup of coffee. The day had started with breakfast in a little spot on the road from Magadan where they served the most delicious pancakes. Nari had journeyed to Magadan for her brother-in-law's funeral, but that morning she had been wonderfully alone. Unmarried, disinterested in marriage, focused on her jewelry business and her dogs, she usually preferred to be on her own. Her sister's husband had been the only member of her family who seemed to accept her just as she was instead of finding fault. Nari hadn't expected to cry for him, and yet she'd wept openly at the funeral. She'd been dutifully sympathetic toward her sister, managed not to tell her mother to fuck off, stood patiently while dozens of people offered their condolences, and then watched while Bayan's casket was lowered into the ground, and then she'd gotten into her car and headed north. She lived far away from the rest of the family for a reason, and she couldn't wait to be free of the suffocation of her mother's narcissism, safe at home with her dogs and her books and her work.

But Nari had never wanted to be *this* alone.

Teig pointed off to the right. "Check it out."

Other footsteps had joined those they'd been following. He let the beam of his flashlight sweep out across the snowy field that separated the backs of buildings from the forest, and for the first time Nari realized how many footprints there were. How many people had walked out to the woods tonight?

She took a step backward and forgot all about Teig. The wind gusted, whipping at her coat. The hood flapped over to cover half her face but Nari didn't bother to push it away. All of her attention focused on the trees at the edge of the forest, at the footprints that vanished into the woods. At the way the trees swayed in the wind.

Only it wasn't the wind at all.

Twenty feet into the forest, spruce and pine trees shifted and swayed, but they did not strain in the same direction. As the wind let up, they continued to shudder as if something jostled them from within, brushing against their trunks and cracking their branches.

"Mister," Nari rasped, not bothering to glance at Teig as she took another step back.

She smelled something old and earthen, like rust and freshly turned soil.

Teig's flashlight illuminated a copse of bone white birch trees. Something cried out, there in the forest, and one of the birches cracked and fell over, branches snapping off on the way down. A wave of stink washed over her, the smell of mold and decay, and she recoiled, holding one arm up to press her scarf more tightly to her face.

Nari swore, low and ugly, something half profanity and half prayer. She spoke again, barely aware words were coming from her lips. The trees stopped their shaking and Teig seemed to exhale, but Nari only stared at the darkness, the darkness within darkness, which nothing could illuminate.

In the absence of light or sound or motion, something growled. She'd lived in Siberia her entire life and heard every kind of bear and wolf, and this was neither. Another birch cracked, and then all the trees began to shift, branches shaking, as something huge pushed them aside, whispering something between a snarl and a voice.

Teig whispered to her. "What the fuck is this?"

As if she knew. As if this must be a typical night in Siberia. Or anywhere, for that matter.

Wishing she could be anywhere else, even back in her car trying not to freeze to death, she tried to muster up enough words in English to reply. But then they heard the shouting. Prentiss called out for them, his bellow echoing off the buildings and the forest and the snow.

Nari turned and bolted in the direction of those shouts.

She heard the crunch of Teig's boots on the snow as the man followed, heard him huffing for breath, but her entire focus was on Prentiss now. Whatever had been in that forest where the footprints vanished into the trees, Nari would outrun it. No way would she die here in the middle of nowhere, with no one to feed her dogs, no one to tell her mother all the reasons they'd barely spoken in the past three years.

If anything really had been back there in the forest, and it came for them, she wanted to make sure she stayed a few steps ahead of Teig. He'd been kind to her, but they were still strangers. She didn't want to meet whatever had drawn those people into the forest. Not for Teig, or for anyone.

Prentiss shouted for them again.

Kaskil stared at the little girl in the room, ignoring the shouts from outside. She wore a sweater that her great-grandmother had made for her. The sleeves were too long and only the tips of her fingers poked out. Her unruly mess of black hair fell about her face as if she'd just been through a jungle, but Kaskil knew the girl simply hated to brush it. Her hair nearly always looked like this. He knew because they shared blood, Kaskil and this little girl. She was his niece, and she'd been here in the house alone.

Here in the town alone.

"Ariuna?" he said, kneeling beside her.

The girl's eyes gleamed in the darkness. A precocious nine years old, she normally spoke almost nonstop. At family dinners, her parents had to get Ariuna to slow down long enough to take a bite of food, sometimes even a breath. Kaskil had once seen her become light-headed because she'd been doing more talking than breathing.

Tonight she was silent.

"Una," he said. "Please. Where are your mother and father? Where is everyone?"

He removed a glove and touched the side of her face, felt her forehead. The back door still stood open and his niece was so cold. Kaskil bustled around the room and found her coat and boots and a hat. She never glanced his way, not even when he knelt beside her again and helped her struggle into the coat.

A voice behind him asked, "What's wrong with her?"

Kaskil jerked back from Ariuna, startled, and turned to glare at Prentiss. "Do you think I know the answer to that? Or to any of this?"

Prentiss gave a quick, apologetic nod, but Kaskil saw that his camera had come out again. He'd been filming before he'd spoken up, had caught the quiet, fearful panic of an uncle terrified for his niece. *Asshole,* Kaskil thought in English.

"This isn't your fucking reality show." He glared at Prentiss for a second before putting Una's hat on her head. It was like dressing a doll. She let him do it but did nothing to assist him.

"It's the job, mate," Prentiss said.

Kaskil ignored him. Held the girl by her shoulders. Spoke to her in Yakut again. "Una, where are they? What happened?" His chest ached and he cupped her chin in his hands, moving her face so they would have been eye to eye if she had seemed capable of focusing on him, or anything.

"Sweet girl," he said. "Are you in there?"

Footfalls shuffled behind him, he heard a muffled whisper, and even before he turned Kaskil realized that Teig and Nari were already inside the house. Of course they were. Prentiss had gone out to shout for them, to call for help, and they'd come inside with him when he'd returned. They had been outside the room, standing in the kitchen near the open back door, and had heard what he'd said to Prentiss.

That was good. Kaskil didn't want to have to say it again. Teig might be paying him for this, might have promised much more in the future, but a nightmare had come to life here in Akhust, and tonight Kaskil could not imagine any future at all.

"Una, please," he said, as he grabbed her boots from the corner and began to slip them onto her feet.

Her gaze did not waver. She stared at nothing, shoulders slumped. Kaskil began to look around the room, searching for some sign of struggle, some clue that might help explain what had happened here and where everyone else had gone.

"Prentiss, put the camera away," Teig said.

Kaskil exhaled. Sorrow flooded him, replacing his fear, but at least he didn't have to explain to Teig why this wasn't a moment for his fucking television show.

"Whatever this is," Prentiss rasped, "we need to document it."

"I know. But right now, you need to go out to the truck and make sure the engine turns over. Start it up and drive it over here. We need to shift some things to make room for the little girl."

Kaskil frowned, but didn't argue. Of course they had to leave. Wherever his family and the rest of the people in town had gone, they had left Una behind. Kaskil needed to get her somewhere safe, with other people and real heat. Somewhere they could contact the authorities and a search could begin for the people who'd vanished.

Prentiss didn't argue with Teig. He lumbered out the open back door, leaving Teig and Nari in the kitchen.

"She all right?" Teig asked, stepping into the room. "Does she know what happened?"

"I believe Una is in shock," Kaskil explained. "She hasn't said a word. But you're right. We have to get out of here, get somewhere safe."

Even as he said the words, he caught the fear in Nari's face. Still in the kitchen, she kept glancing over her shoulder, looking toward the open door where Prentiss had just left them. Something about that skittish look, the wide eyes, the way she twitched her head like a nervous bird, unnerved him even more than the vacant look on his niece's face.

Kaskil zipped Una's coat and lifted her in his arms. Teig stepped aside as Kaskil carried the girl into the kitchen. Nari had moved deeper into the house, farther from the open door.

"We have to go," Kaskil told her in Yakut.

The words made her snap around to stare at him, and then at Una in his arms. "Yes," she said, reaching out to adjust the girl's hat. "And quickly."

Nari looked up, met Kaskil's gaze for the first time. "If we are quick enough, we may get on the road before they come out of the woods."

Confused, Kaskil started to ask what she meant. What had frightened her so badly.

Nari hurried out into the cold and the dark without a look back. Kaskil glanced at Teig for answers, but the man ignored the look, and for the first time Kaskil saw that he, too, seemed haunted, on edge, fearful of whatever might be in his peripheral vision.

Teig ushered Kaskil out the door.

The wind slashed at them, cold blasting through the town, swirling along the streets.

Nari stood in the road, poised as if to bolt, staring toward the forest.

Something moved in the dark, a tree or a man, and for a moment Kaskil felt a flicker of hope.

Then Nari backed away with a stream of profanity and prayer, turned, and fled into the dark.

7

Prentiss turned the key again. The ignition coughed but didn't catch. He took his hand off the key and stared at the frost on the inside of the windshield. The only light inside the parking structure came from orange emergency lights that were running off a battery backup or generator somewhere, but it was enough for him to see ice crystals growing and spreading on the glass. The garage existed for no other reason than to keep vehicles warm enough to prevent fuel lines from freezing. This shouldn't be happening.

It hasn't even been that long.

He jiggled the key in the ignition. When he'd turned it before it had felt stiff, like the mechanism itself was on the verge of freezing up.

"God, I've never had any reason to think you're up there," he muttered, voice muffled by his balaclava. "If you've any interest in changing my mind, now'd be the time."

Prentiss took a deep breath, turned the key. The engine coughed, made a grinding noise that inspired profound dread, and then it caught. The truck roared to life. Ruthie would have been thrilled. Prentiss laughed and blew the horn a couple of times in celebration. He revved the engine—the truck clearing its throat, he'd have said—turned up the defrost as high as it would go, and dropped it into gear.

As he headed for the garage exit, he glanced heavenward. "Asshole.

I still think you're nothing but a fable. Get me home safe and warm and maybe I'll come around."

He pulled out of the garage. With the engine running, the dashboard lights aglow, he felt enveloped in a small pool of normalcy that brought into sharp focus just how weird and unsettling their arrival in Akhust had been. Where were the people, really? Evacuation did seem the most likely, but for what purpose? What danger had the villagers faced? Surely someone would have rung up their boy Kaskil and warned him.

The headlights washed across the others as they hurried down the street to meet him. Kaskil carried the little girl in his arms, wrapped in a heavy fur blanket. Teig jogged lightly behind them, but he kept craning his neck to one side, looking toward the trees. Prentiss didn't like the expression on his face, but even then it took him a moment to realize what else was wrong with this picture.

He parked the truck, left it running, and climbed out. Kaskil pushed past him, bundling the little girl into the backseat, speaking soft assurances.

Prentiss stood in Teig's path. "What's going on, Felix? Where's our hitcher?"

Their hitcher. The woman, Nari.

"Watch them," Teig said, eyes locked with his. "I've gotta find her." He started off into the dark between houses, headed for the woods.

"Find *her*?" Prentiss grumbled, calling after him. "She's the one who said we shouldn't split up, and now she's—"

Screaming.

Screaming, and running toward them out of the dark.

She looked to Teig like something out of a dream. In his imagination he could still see the cherry hue of her hair, but in the dark it turned black. Nari swept across the snow in a monochrome wave, all black, color leached from the world. Only her face seemed to reflect any light, a pale gleam punctuated by the pinpoint terror of her eyes.

"Get in truck get in truck get in the fucking truck!" she shouted at him as if he'd been the source of her rage.

Teig shared her fear, felt the undercurrent of weirdness and menace in Akhust. He thought of the lost colony of Roanoke, thought of ghost ships found adrift with no crew, but this wasn't some legend. Unnerved he might be, but he had too much firsthand experience with hoaxes to not think about all the rational explanations first. They'd seen footprints, seen abandoned meals. No signs of struggle. The locals hadn't been abducted, they'd gotten up and abandoned their homes.

"Nari," he said, raising one hand to slow her down.

She slapped his hand away, grabbed his biceps, and forcibly turned him around. "Move!"

Teig stumbled, nearly fell in the snow, then picked up his pace. "Goddamn it," he snapped. "What are you—"

Running from, he would have said.

But even as he'd begun the question, he glanced back and spotted another figure coming after them, slinking through the shadows. Flowing, back there, and gaining on them.

"The *parnee,*" she said, searching for a translation. "The forest!"

Awhirl in confusion, Teig let her urgency carry him back to the truck. His stray thought about people putting on a show for the showman came back to him. Whatever he wanted to believe, this could all be a performance piece. Kaskil had been the one to recommend they stop at Olonkho's, where they'd seen Nari for the first time. Nari had been pulled over on the side of a road Kaskil had known they would travel—there wasn't another. Had she been broken down at all? It felt like a stretch, but the economy of this godforsaken corner of the world could use a boost, and if Teig managed to launch a hit reality series about them, it would certainly put money in everyone's pockets.

Would they go to these lengths? Were they desperate enough? Clever enough?

Nari had him by the arm. He glanced over his shoulder, stumbling. His bones hurt with the cold. When he inhaled, the air seared the insides of his lungs. The warmth inside the truck called to him. The engine revved like a summoning, but Teig resisted. He pulled his arm away from her grasp. From the corner of his eye he saw Nari reach the truck, saw Prentiss helping her into the back with Kaskil and his niece. The little girl had her face pressed against the window, peering out as if it were the porthole of a boat in rough seas—but with a total absence of expression. She stared at Teig and he stared back, but then her gaze shifted past him, at the dark figure striding across the snow toward them, walking between houses now, twenty feet from the street.

"Parnee," Teig whispered, trying the unfamiliar word on his lips. He needed to get in the truck, get out of here, but with all of the people missing he could not leave this mystery behind. Could it be real? The little girl would have to be in on it, and that would mean she had to be an excellent actor.

Was Prentiss filming?

Shit. Whatever the fuck this was, he needed it on camera.

The parnee stepped into the snow-covered street and for the first time Teig noticed the black streaks he'd left on the pure white behind him. Black . . . or red? Like Nari's cherry red hair, he had a feeling the true color of that stain had been made even darker.

That was no special effect.

"Who the fuck are you?" Teig roared at the parnee.

The man halted in the street and raised the dripping head of a slaughtered wolf in a fistful of fur. Blood spatter rained from his fist.

Inside the truck, the little girl screamed. And screamed.

Prentiss roared a warning.

Teig spun to his right, hands up for protection, but whatever blasted out of the dark alleys between houses, there was no protection against that.

They moved so swiftly that at first Prentiss saw only shadows. The man with the bloody wolf's head shook it angrily, holding it up like a lantern, black droplets scattering to the ground. He shouted something and gusts of wind blew along the road, frigid little maelstroms that picked up snow and ice and became quick shadows, silhouettes that darted low to the ground, racing toward Teig.

Prentiss launched himself away from the truck, leaving Kaskil, Nari, and the little girl to fend for themselves. From behind his camera, he'd seen things in his life that were so magnificent that he'd felt true awe, that flicker of confusion when you have to adjust to the idea that what you're looking at exists in the world you've always known. Prentiss saw that look in Teig's eyes as he barreled toward his friend. Confusion, fear, rejection of the impossible.

"Teig, get back!" Prentiss grabbed him by the hood of his parka.

Their eyes met. Sadness, doubt, denial.

In his peripheral vision, Prentiss saw the shadows slow to a predatory lope. They had something like fur, but the shadows rippled and for a flicker he saw not fur but the needles of an evergreen, prickly and bristling. Fucking Teig. Always had to be rescued from himself.

Prentiss hoisted him by his hood and his belt, half-turned, and hurled him back toward the truck. Teig let out a panicked cry and hit the ground on one foot, careened into the truck shoulder first. He bounced off, fell to one knee, but Kaskil was there to help him up.

The first shadow bit into Prentiss's left leg, teeth ripping through the thick layers protecting him from the cold.

Prentiss twisted, his own movement driving the teeth deeper, and he swung his right leg, smashing his boot into the creature's belly. On impact, it let out a whimper and a snarl and bit harder, fangs scraping bone. Prentiss howled in pain then stared at the thing and saw it as more than a shadow for the first time. What he'd thought were pine needles was actually dark fur, and tangible reality returned.

The wolf ripped at his left leg again, tugged so hard that Prentiss fell. He hit the road, blew the air from his lungs, groaned as he turned and began to pummel the wolf with a fist. But things flitted at the edges of his vision still and now he knew what they were. More wolves.

The man from the forest hadn't taken a step closer but he still held that bleeding wolf's head high. He threw back his head and loosed an ululating cry. When he snapped his mouth shut, the echoes swirled in the air as if it had become the wind. The wolves stopped their running. One by one they turned to stare at Prentiss, pacing, enormous skulls drooping low, ears back, watching him the way predators always watched prey. Planning the kill.

The echoes died. The wind gusted harder. The wolves crept silently toward him.

Behind him, the truck's engine revved.

"Goddamn it, Jack, let's go!" Teig screamed. "This is really happening!"

Prentiss turned and rumbled toward the truck. Through the open passenger door he saw Nari behind the wheel. Her eyes were bright with shock but her hands were locked and ready to drive. The girl Una sat in the middle of that front bench seat and the space beside her was empty, waiting for him, door hanging open. The rear passenger door was open, too, but neither Kaskil nor Teig had gotten in. They were half a dozen feet from the truck, shouting and waving at him to run. Prentiss wanted to laugh. He could lunge and he could careen but with his bulk, running wasn't as simple as that.

A massive wolf smashed into the side of his ravaged left leg. Its bulk struck right at the knee and Prentiss felt the bone crunch on impact. Something tore. Something cracked. He flopped onto the road and his head bounced on frozen snow. Seething, hissing in pain, Prentiss turned and held up an arm to fend off the wolves.

Kaskil and Teig were there. Each of them grabbed him under an arm and dragged him to his feet. His shattered knee blazed with pain but Prentiss moved. He voiced a torrent of the filthiest profanity he knew and tears sprang to his eyes, but Prentiss moved.

The wolves hit Kaskil next.

Two at once. Then a third. He fell, hit the road. Hard.

Blood fanned the snow and ice.

Prentiss listed to the left, started to go down, wondered how many wolves there were. If they were even wolves at all. Teig cried out, held Prentiss up though it made him grunt with effort. They were both falling when Teig spun Prentiss like some kind of swing dance. Prentiss smashed into the truck, his hip denting the metal right next to the open rear door.

"Get in!" Teig barked, grabbing him by the jacket, yanking and pushing and forcing him into the backseat.

Teig slammed the back door, climbed into the front, closed his own door an instant before two of the wolves slammed into the truck, enraged that they had been denied their prey.

"Help Kaskil!" Teig shouted at Nari. "Run them off! Use the horn, the headlights!"

Nari swore at him, dropped the truck into gear and hit the

accelerator. The truck powered forward, tires digging in as it swung around. The wolves were there, watching the truck eagerly, hungrily, as the headlights washed over them. Kaskil tried to rise, the wolves dragging at him with their jaws. A flap of skin and muscle hung from the left side of his face. Screaming, he smashed a fist into the eyes and muzzle of the one biting into his left arm. A wolf came from behind him, larger than the others and less defined, as if it hadn't entirely decided it wanted to be a wolf and not a shadow.

It caught Kaskil's right hand in its jaws, ripped its powerful head back, and took the hand with it. Kaskil staggered to his feet and wavered for several seconds, staring at the jets of blood pumping from the ragged stump, and then the wolves flowed over him in a wave, burying him beneath undulating fur and shadows. Herder, hunter, guide, criminal, convict, loving uncle, his life had not prepared him for this.

"Run them over!" Teig turned to Nari. "Save him from this!"

Instead, Nari spun the steering wheel, turning them away from Kaskil's final scream, from the wolf pack and the shadows, from the abandoned house where they'd found the little girl who now sat between Nari and Teig in the front, silent ever since her two screams, eyes forward, as if her uncle's violent death concerned her not at all.

Prentiss glanced out the window and saw the wolves stepping away from what remained of Kaskil. Their paws left bloody prints on the snowy road. One of the wolves cocked its head and watched the truck pass—watched Prentiss, eye to eye. A wildness slithered into Prentiss, then, as if he felt the brutality of the wolf. His gut churned with a new hunger and he flexed his fingers with an instinct that frightened him.

Prentiss shifted on the backseat as Nari sped up, tires tearing at the road, leaving the abandoned town behind. The blood on the leg of his torn trousers had begun to freeze. His flesh throbbed where the wolf had bitten him, as if the creature's teeth remained embedded there. His nostrils were full of the stink of his own blood. He'd need to stop the bleeding soon. But for now he was alive, and Kaskil lay torn and broken, back on the road. The guide's little niece remained silent as they stole her away.

Hissing with pain, Prentiss took one last look over his shoulder, searching for the wolves. The man from the forest had vanished already, gone as if he had never been there, but the wolves pursued the truck until they became shadows again, one by one, and the wind swirled them away as clouds of black mist that floated into the forest and were gone.

8

Nari tried to keep her eyes—and the truck—on the road, but she didn't like the way Teig sat forward, one hand on the dash, craning around so he could peer out the rear windshield.

"You see something?" she demanded. "Are they following?"

Teig gave a frustrated grunt. "It's too dark to see."

She glanced over her shoulder but a scrim of frost covered the rear windshield. Even if the glass had been clear, the night would have made it impossible to figure out if they were being pursued. The rumble of the engine filled her head, but she felt only vaguely aware of the tangible world around her.

"They were wolves?" Nari said, frustrated with these men for not speaking her language. Certainly the things in the dark had looked like wolves—*don't be stupid, they were wolves, of course they were wolves*—but she knew they had been something else, too.

"Kaskil . . ." Teig said, still looking back, barely hearing her. "I can't believe he's . . . did you see that?"

"Of course I—" Nari began, but he was talking to Prentiss, who lay bleeding and half-conscious in the backseat.

"I saw plenty," Prentiss rasped. "I just don't know what to call it."

Nari focused on the road and tried not to shout at them. "I told you. I saw the . . . the parnee . . ."

Teig cut his gaze toward her. "Which is what, exactly? The guy with the severed wolf's head? That's the parnee?"

Nari tapped the brake, careful going around a curve in the road, then sped up as fast as she dared. "The parnee. He is . . ." It was hard to explain how something could be two things at once. "A shaman. But also he is the spirit of the forest."

Teig frowned at her. "What does that even mean?"

In the backseat, Prentiss started taking quick breaths to fight the pain of his broken knee and ravaged leg. "Christ, mate, this hurts like a bitch. Look . . . someone needs to call the cops, get the authorities in here. Kaskil's dead and who knows what happened to the rest of them."

Nari shut them out. The two men were strangers to her but friends to one another. They were sharing their shock, diluting the panic by relying on their rapport, leaving her to fend for herself. Kind as they'd been, in this moment she could only depend on herself.

For a moment she wished they had never stopped to help her, but of course then she would already have frozen to death. Her heart raced and she kept her eyes on the road, trying to work the math in her head. Another three-quarters of an hour before they reached her broken-down SUV. How many miles beyond that to Olonkho's? The bar would be closed, but Timir and Sayaara would be upstairs in their apartment. There would be a telephone, hot tea, a door that bolted to keep the world outside. Did they have enough fuel to make it there? She glanced at the gas gauge and mentally checked that worry off her list. Plenty of gas.

They'd be okay.

I'll be okay, she thought.

The truck bounced through a rut. Her elbow struck the girl. Nari had nearly forgotten her, this poor, shattered thing, only nine years old. Una remained in shock, sitting between Nari and Teig. She stared straight ahead, jostled by the movement of the truck but otherwise immobile. Psychologists would have to determine the depths of her shock, the horror of the scars in her mind. Nari had no idea what she had seen back in the village to make her shut down so completely. She wondered if the girl had seen Kaskil die, had seen the wolves rip her uncle apart on the snow. Una had been in the truck by then, already nearly catatonic. Perhaps she had managed to avoid the sight, but she had to have heard the screaming and the noises the wolves made when they attacked Kaskil, when they tore into him, when they began to eat.

Then they vanished into the shadows, she thought, the image rushing up into her mind.

Impossible. Nari had grown up hearing the folklore of her country, but those were just stories. Even if the parnee had been there, he was just a man. Even if he'd killed a wolf, performed a ritual, shouted at them, he was just a man.

"Hey, little one," she said quietly in Yakut, careful to keep the truck steady as she glanced at Una. "You don't worry, okay? We'll be safe now. I'll look out for you."

The girl gave no sign she'd heard the words, and yet the second they were out of Nari's mouth she regretted them. She had no business making promises to this little girl. Of course she felt protective toward Una, would shield her from further trauma if possible, but she had her own life to live. If growing up with a mother whose narcissism and manipulation were like an emotional prison had taught her anything, it was not to surrender to empathetic obligation. Nari had been searching for freedom her whole life, and mostly failing to find it. Now she had been thrust into a terrifying scenario with total strangers, and she couldn't let herself start thinking she owed them something—at least, not enough to risk her own safety.

Being here tonight, in this place and time, had been purely

accidental, and the moment they connected with anyone in authority and she could get her own vehicle running again, she would be heading north. Heading home. But she had made the girl a promise.

Una kept her eyes locked straight ahead, her hands folded on her lap. The rise and fall of her chest proved she was breathing, otherwise she'd have looked like a particularly convincing mannequin. Something about her expression, maybe the way her brows drew together or the set of her mouth, made her appear as if she might be on the verge of tears, but those tears never fell.

Still, she was just nine years old. Her uncle had just been killed and the rest of her family had vanished. Now Nari had made a promise to her and, reluctantly or not, she'd stay with the girl until she felt confident they were both safe.

Ludmilla had only three and a half fingers on her right hand. Frostbite had taken the missing bits of flesh and bone and left permanent scars on her face and neck. People noticed the missing fingers but somehow never thought to ask about her toes. She'd lost three on her left foot and one—the pinky toe—on her right. At the insistence of her nephew Alfrid, she saw a doctor the first week of June, every year. Ludmilla lied to the doctor, who was the only person who ever saw her with her socks off. She insisted that she'd lost those toes at the same time as she'd lost the finger and a half. She didn't think of herself as an especially proud woman, but she would have felt ashamed to admit that the various bits and pieces had been lost over the course of four separate incidents.

The doctor, of course, advised her to stay indoors. To stay warm.

He didn't understand.

Alfrid also did not understand, but he had long since stopped trying to advise or control her. Ludmilla always told him yes, agreed with his advice, and then went out and did whatever she felt like doing regardless of his fears. Last winter, he had waited until February and finally confronted her, face red with frustration, hands fisted at his sides like a toddler throwing a tantrum.

"I lie to make it easier for you, Alfie," she had confessed. "I don't want to worry you."

"And I don't want you to die, Auntie."

Ludmilla had cupped his cheek just the way she'd done when he'd been a little boy, not a forty-three-year-old construction worker with sons of his own.

"I promise I'll be careful," she'd told him. "But I must do this. Your grandmother wouldn't allow it while she lived, so I had to wait until I was an old woman. Now I don't know how long I have left on earth and there is no time to waste."

Alfrid had taken her hands in his, gazing at her with the same pleading eyes he'd always used to get extra sweets from her as a little boy. "In midwinter? Surely there's no need—"

Ludmilla had grown angry then, and impatient. "They died in winter. Their spirits sleep in summer. I've told you all of this before. It does no good to offer blessings when they can't hear me."

He thought she was crazy, of course. Dear Alfrid. But short of dragging her off to his own house—already too small for his family—and locking her away, what could he do but accept her promises that she would be more careful?

Tonight, however, alone out on the highway, Ludmilla would admit only to herself and to the ghosts that she feared the cold. It hurt to be out here like this. Her joints ached and her bones hurt as if someone had just rung her whole body like a bell. Though she covered all but her eyes, the scars on her face and neck hurt as if the wounds were fresh, like someone had just sliced off a bit of cheek or half an ear, or scraped away the skin just below her jaw.

Still, she sang softly to herself as she went about her work. It was only pain, after all. And what was pain before the eyes of God? Pain was human. Something of the flesh. Her work concerned the spirit, and the life that came after death.

No more frostbite, Alfie had said, at the end of that argument last winter. *Is that so much to ask?*

Ludmilla had promised to try. She couldn't do more than that.

Her car puffed exhaust into the red glow of its taillights. Some people longed for the warm lights of home, but this view had become the one that gave her comfort. Ludmilla trudged along the road toward the car, but she still had another hundred yards to go. Her gloves were thick and she used hand warmers inside them every night. Her remaining fingers needed to remain nimble so that she could wave thin fir and juniper branches as she walked, and each time she stopped to pray.

They'd had a bad death, all of these ghosts. Ugly deaths, often violent, unutterably sad. They called this the Road of Bones and yes, the bones were still there, under the permafrost, but what Ludmilla had felt since she had first traveled this road as a babe had been pure sorrow. Their spirits were trapped here in the fog of that sorrow, never blessed, never given a proper funeral.

Since the night her own mother had died, Ludmilla had gone out for seven or eight hours every day the temperature became cold enough for her prayers to reach the dead. She prayed a half mile at a time, walking away from her car on the east side of the road and then back to its warm taillights on the west. A half mile at a time, ten stops each day, a full five miles before she lay her head on her pillow at night.

"In a blessed sleep, O Lord, grant eternal rest unto your departed servants and make their memory to be eternal," she chanted, teeth chattering from the cold, despite her scarf and balaclava. "Memory eternal. Memory eternal."

Ludmilla paused. Over the summer, she'd gotten much of her

strength back, but ever since the cold weather had returned, she'd had to pause more and more often in her work. Sometimes she couldn't get through the first verse of a song, or the first few lines of a chanted prayer, without stopping to catch her breath. She ignored it because she had to; she had chanted and spoken prayers along hundreds of miles of road by now, but there were still many hundreds of miles to go.

"Not tonight," she said to herself with a chuckle.

The taillights of her car glowed up ahead and Ludmilla began to trudge toward them. She wanted to sit in the car and catch her breath before driving home, but she would not do that. She might not complete hundreds of miles tonight, but she had a few miles more to go, and if she didn't finish them tonight, she would only need to add them to her tally for tomorrow.

Her lungs ached with each icy breath. Older now, she felt the cold more fully, more deeply. No matter how many layers she wore, no matter how heavy the coat or how thick her boots, the cold penetrated down to the marrow. The wind picked up, swirling ice crystals and snowflakes along the road toward her. The little whirlwind danced around her boots for a moment and then swept off into the sky.

Ludmilla smiled. Her mother had always scolded her for her flights of fancy. Her grandmother, though, had more than indulged her. In this part of the world, belief had undergone vast changes from one generation to the next. Her grandmother had been an udagan, a female shaman of the white tradition, and had taught Ludmilla all she could about the ichchi of the forest, the living spirits of rocks and trees and the creatures of the woods, the soul of the land itself. In her mother's generation, the Soviets had discouraged not only shamanism but all religion, so as a girl Ludmilla had learned from both of the women she venerated. The animistic shamanism felt true and right in her heart, as did the Christian lore she learned as a girl when visiting the homes of her two closest friends.

From what she'd read, a strong fifteen percent or more of people in Yakutia still practiced shamanism, and Ludmilla tended to like those people more than the others she met. She had found her worship in Orthodox Christianity, but the two faiths blurred together in this part of the world. Bears and saints shared reverence, and Christ himself blended with the Bright Creator of shamanistic belief. So though her grandmother would have preferred she stick to animism and the prayers of the shaman, Ludmilla knew her own faith would suffice. It powered her, warmed her, and frozen marrow wouldn't stop her any more than losing another finger might.

She paused again, about twenty feet behind her car. Opening her arms, palms up, she hung her head and began to chant in prayer for the dead beneath the road. In her mind she could see their bones there, could illustrate the contours of spines and clavicles. In the dark hollows where eyes once had been, she saw a spark of awareness as her prayers woke them, comforted them, assured them they could seek the eternal rest they had been denied.

Ludmilla smiled when she heard their whispers.

"That's right, my friends," she said. "Bless you all. Cast off the deeds of life that bind you here. The Lord awaits."

It might take them only moments to begin to ease from this plane to the next or it might take them months, but they would go. Kindness and prayer and true faith had been all they ever needed to find release.

Every day, every prayer, Ludmilla yearned to weep for the souls she set free, but her eyes stayed dry. Tears might freeze.

Smiling, she went to her car and climbed inside, pulling the door shut behind her. Bathed in the warmth from the struggling heater vents, she rested a few minutes. Her face stung, her old frostbite scars ached, but the pain in her bones eased.

At last, she checked the gas gauge, confirmed she still had plenty, and put the car in drive. A half mile, that was all. If it had been warmer, she might've done these prayers in mile increments, but ghosts were so much closer to the world in winter.

Ludmilla pulled over again, passenger-side tires up on the snow, but she basked a few minutes in the heat before she opened the door and climbed out.

"All right, my darlings," she said, turning to walk back the way she'd come. "Time to wake from your slumber. Time for the mercy you have been denied for so long. The Lord awaits you."

She began to sing, and pray, and walk, the cold digging into her bones as it always did.

The little girl leaned forward, reached out for the heater vent, and turned it aside so it blew directly at Teig. She hadn't moved quickly, but just the fact of her moving at all made him stare at her. Like a music box ballerina, she froze again just as suddenly as she had begun.

Teig stared at her. "Hey, kid. You okay? Can you hear me?"

In the driver's seat, Nari jerked the steering wheel a bit, following a turn in the road. She'd been distracted ever since they had passed her SUV, seemed almost as if she were trying to outrun not just the horror back in that little village but the people she'd been thrown together with. Teig understood. Somehow he would have felt safer alone than with the little girl who'd survived it all, and the constant reminder of Prentiss bleeding in the backseat. Nari glanced from the swath of road illuminated by the truck's headlights to the blank face of the little girl, lit up by the glow from the dash.

Teig looked at the woman. "You want to try getting through to her?"

Nari gave Una a nudge, hands still on the wheel. She spoke in her own language, which Teig found both guttural and lilting. If he ever got to make *Life and Death on the Road of Bones,* he wanted to learn some of that language.

What the fuck are you thinking? It's over. It's fucking over.

Kaskil had died in the street, dragged down by wolves, Prentiss lay bleeding and feverish with pain in the backseat, and an entire town's people had vanished except for this one little girl. The idea of making television seemed very far away, but he couldn't help himself. For the past hour he had been trying to figure out a way to salvage this trip, to find an angle that would allow him to do a show. There might be a single documentary in it. Maybe. But no matter how he tried to wrap his head around it, he knew his grand plans for the Kolyma Highway had been shattered.

He was going to lose everything. The company would fold.

But inside him, an old desperation had awoken. There'd been something unnatural about those wolves—either that, or he'd been hallucinating. And the guy with the severed wolf's head . . . he might just be insane, but he hadn't looked normal, had he? Teig had seen him mostly in darkness, but his body looked strange and he seemed abnormally tall. And hadn't there been something sticking out of his head, like he wore some kind of crown?

The cynic in him fought hard against the voice inside that told him he had finally encountered something unnatural. Some kind of dark magic, though just the word made the cynical part of his brain scream laughter. Teig had to fight the temptation to turn the truck around and go back.

Don't be stupid. Don't be heartless.

Kaskil was dead. That hadn't been an illusion. Any thoughts he had about all of this being some kind of performance had been obliterated from his mind. Now he felt sick with revulsion at his selfish thoughts. His best friend needed medical help fast. How much blood had Prentiss already lost? How much damage had the wolves done? And the girl had no family to take care of her now.

Teig glanced at her again, watching to see if she blinked, if her eyes focused on anything at all. The girl seemed utterly catatonic, except that a minute ago she had been irritated enough by the heat blasting out of the vent that she had turned it away. Teig knew Una wasn't likely to understand English, but she was ignoring Nari, too.

"It's okay, kid," he said, wanting to put a comforting arm around her but not wishing to frighten her. "I've got you."

Teig glanced out his window at the darkness. He watched his reflection for a minute or so, seeing but not really seeing. His mind's eye focused instead on that day so long ago, with the van and the puppy, the last time he'd seen his sister. He'd let her down that day and the monster who'd taken her had murdered her. Burned her. Done other things that his mother had prevented him from ever hearing about, but which he couldn't help assuming.

Not this time. Not this kid.

"The grandmother," Teig said.

Nari gripped the wheel, giving him a quick glance. "What?"

"The gas station where we met Kaskil is maybe two hours from here. The little girl's great-grandmother owns it. We can bring her there."

"Okay. That's good," Nari said.

In the backseat, Prentiss coughed to clear his throat. "I don't wanna be a bother, but I'm bleeding a fuck-ton and two hours sounds . . . long."

"We are maybe thirty minutes from Olonkho's," Nari said. "We stop the bleeding there. They will have . . ."

Teig saw her struggling for words but he got the gist. "Bandages. A first-aid kit."

Nari waved her hand and nodded. "This. Yes. And whiskey. I would very much like whiskey."

In the back, Prentiss coughed laughter. "Me too, darling. Me, too."

For the first time since they'd bolted out of Akhust, Teig felt some of the tension slip away. "We saw you there. Olonkho's, I mean."

Nari shot him a sidelong glance. "My friend Sayaara and her husband are the owners."

"Excellent reindeer burgers," Prentiss said. He made himself laugh, then groaned in pain and quietly cursed at himself.

"Do you know if police go in there? Are there police nearby?" Teig asked.

Nari snickered. "You think you are in America? That police are on every corner? We have few people. Traffic police, maybe, but not here."

Teig glanced at the little girl between them, but still she seemed to be lost in some interior world, where whatever went on around her mattered not at all.

"What about a phone?" Teig asked. "To call for help?"

"There will be a phone," Nari said. "We call someone."

In the backseat, Prentiss had started to breathe faster, fighting his pain, but had otherwise fallen silent. Teig began to feel guilty, wondering if they should have stopped sooner and tried to do more to help Prentiss, but they'd just seen Kaskil die in the street in the middle of that abandoned, creepy-as-fuck little town. They were high on fear and adrenaline that was only now beginning to taper off.

"You'll be okay, brother," Teig said, looking into the backseat.

Prentiss managed a single nod.

Teig smiled, but the thrum of the engine had been grinding into his brain, nurturing a headache that promised to only grow worse. Between him and Nari, Una began to hum quietly, a low, rhythmic noise not unlike the sound of the straining engine.

"Hey," Prentiss said in the background, his voice weak, almost lost under the drone of the truck. He cleared his voice and spoke up, louder. "Teig, mate . . . Jesus, Teig, look out the window."

Off to the left, up a snow-covered hill, barely visible in the darkness at the edge of the forest, wolves kept pace with the truck.

They darted through the trees, vanished and reappeared in the night and its deeper shadows, but there was no mistaking them.

It couldn't be the same wolves. Not a chance.

"Speed up," he said.

Nari paled, glancing out the window. She accelerated, the truck lunging forward, thundering over ruts in the road. Teig watched the wolves and a terrible suspicion spread through him, a fear that no speed would be enough. The wolves were tracking them. Hunting.

Nari skidded the truck around a curve in the road. The little girl swayed against Teig, but didn't crane her neck or say a word.

Out in the frozen woods, the wolves ran silent and cold.

In the apartment above Olonkho's, the woodstove crackled with heat, spreading the glow of firelight through the bedroom. Sayaara sat in a threadbare, cozy old chair near the window, wrapped in a blanket and caught up in an Olga Grushin novel that had proven quite a departure for the author. Sayaara loved her work, but this dark fantastical journey seemed almost a rebirth for Grushin.

Most of the time, she felt pure contentment in her life with Timir, loving him, running the bar. They were never so busy they couldn't have a laugh together or dance in the kitchen where the cook rolled his eyes at them, but the bar stayed busy enough that they were never bored. There was always work to do, were always people to converse with. But occasionally, in one of the books she loved, Sayaara would stumble upon an unexpected yearning to be somewhere else, someone else. Grushin often had that effect on her. It struck her as ironic, since if Timir had his way, they'd have moved to Moscow years ago. Timir longed for more chaos, more city life, but she only wanted the quiet, a good book, and her woodstove.

A discordant note rang out in their living room. The apartment wasn't much—two bedrooms, a bathroom, a little kitchen, and the living room with its sofa and comfortable, worn-out chairs. A flat-screen TV hung on the wall, but neither of them were much interested in what they could find on television. She had her books and Timir had his guitar. When the bar closed and everyone was gone, they'd clean up, climb the stairs to their apartment, shower—together, if they had the energy to make love—and then settle in for the reward of quiet time. They slept a bit late on winter mornings because the earliest deliveries didn't show up until at least half past nine, and customers did not show their faces at Olonkho's before noon.

Sayaara put a finger in her book, listening to Timir play guitar in the other room. He had a beautiful acoustic, a work of art, his one indulgence. The guitar had cost nearly a thousand dollars and she hadn't batted an eye. He never asked for anything, her lovely husband, and he deserved the world. She'd wanted him to have that guitar, to learn every beautiful song, every tune that made him happy—like "Million Scarlet Roses," which he was playing just now. Whatever made him happy.

Except moving to Moscow. That was off the table.

Olonkho's had become its own little community. Aside from the bar and the garage with its gas pump, there were a dozen gray, boxy homes and a squat building that functioned as a truck stop and minimarket. Thirty-one people lived in and around Olonkho's—with two more due in the spring when Nina Volkov's twins arrived—and Sayaara liked nearly all of them. Most people didn't stay long, driven a little crazy by the remoteness of the place, or the inconvenience involved in laying hands on items that would be simple to find in a city.

Sayaara sighed and dipped back into her book just as her husband changed songs in the next room. A slow, almost funereal version of Prince's "Purple Rain" that always made her somehow both sad and happy, like the memory of love lost. He was a good man. She only hoped he would stay.

Logs shifted in the woodstove, making a clatter. A few sparks drifted up and out of the black iron grille, wafting in the air. She watched them to make certain they wouldn't land somewhere and ignite. While she tracked the little floating sparks, a sound reached her ears. She frowned and cocked her head. The sound mingled with the crackling fire and the sound of Timir's guitar, but quickly resolved itself into the urgent blatting of a car horn, over and over.

"Love?" she called as she rose from the chair, setting aside her book. "Do you hear that?"

His music stopped. She heard the last chord linger. "Hear what?"

"Come in here!"

Sayaara went to the window. The panes were frosted at the edges, but each had a small space that remained transparent. She pressed her forehead to the glass and twisted to see down into the street. The window was so cold that her skin hurt to touch it.

"I hear a car horn. Frantic, like an emergency." She turned right and left, trying to get a good look at the garage and at the little homes that clustered behind Olonkho's.

Timir put a hand on her shoulder, trying to scoot her out of the way so he could peer out the window. "Someone must be hurt. We need to—"

Sayaara shushed him, holding up one hand. She backed away an inch or two from the glass, because she no longer needed to look down into the street. There were headlights on the highway, a truck barreling in their direction. The horn grew louder, somehow more urgent, and the truck began to slow for the turn. Its rear wheels skidded on the road.

In the red glow of its brake lights, she saw a small dark shape loping behind the truck.

"What in God's name?" Timir whispered, just over her shoulder.

She turned from the window, grabbed his hand. "Hurry!"

9

Teig knelt on the seat, one hand on the dash as they turned into the narrow access road for Olonkho's. They bounced over ruts. His head smashed into the roof of the truck and he steadied himself to keep from collapsing on top of Una. The little girl swayed as they skidded, leaning into him almost as if she wanted protection, but he knew it was only momentum that made her come nearer.

"No lights," Nari said. She smashed down on the horn again. Instead of a beep, it sounded like a klaxon. "There are no lights!"

Teig turned to glance through the windshield. "Top floor. One window with lights on!"

Even as he said it, lights flickered on inside the bar and his heart leapt. They needed shelter, needed walls and a solid door between them and whatever pursued them. He told himself they were just wolves, but they had kept up with the truck for more than twenty miles and only fallen back in the past ten minutes or so.

He turned to look over the top of the seat again, crouched down to see what he could through the rear window. Something still moved, way back along the road. Most of those loping shadows had stayed in the trees but a couple of them had come onto the highway. It had to be one of them he saw now, not loping but flowing along the road about eighty yards back, barely visible in the dark, but still giving chase. Still hunting.

They hit another rut. Prentiss groaned.

Teig turned fully in the seat, held on with one hand and reached down with the other to grip his friend's hand. Prentiss opened his eyes but they were bleary, as if he'd had too much whiskey instead of not enough blood.

"Asshole," Prentiss rasped.

"True enough," Teig agreed. If the man could joke—or maybe it wasn't a joke, but even if he could be angry—he was still with them. "Muster up whatever strength you've got, Jack. You're gonna need it in a few—"

Nari jammed on the brakes. Teig slammed backward into the dashboard and whacked his skull against the windshield. Prentiss let out a shout of pain before Teig realized he'd hung on to his friend's hand, yanked him up off the backseat. Prentiss's eyes had flared wide and now his head lolled to one side, barely conscious from the shock of it.

"Come on!" Nari barked. She popped the door and practically leapt out of the truck, turned back in to undo the little girl's seatbelt.

"I'm . . . I think I'm okay," Teig said, blinking. Still stunned. He touched the back of his head, felt a tacky dampness that could only be blood, then turned to see the little spiderweb pattern of cracks where his skull had struck the windshield.

"Teig!" Nari shouted.

She had Una's seatbelt undone, but was struggling to drag the catatonic nine-year-old across the seat. Teig shook himself, trying to focus, but he hefted Una and shoveled her out of the truck and into Nari's arms. As Nari slammed her door, Teig poured out of the truck and did the same on his side.

He heard voices behind him. Nari's voice, and maybe her waitress friend. Maybe the bartender, too. None of it mattered. Teig took one look toward the road and saw two wolves in the road. They were too big, their snouts too long, their bodies too low to the ground. Their legs should not have carried them so swiftly, and yet they were coming. Hungry. Their eyes glinted white in the dark, like pinprick holes in the fabric of the world.

Their paws made no sound, even as they turned from the highway and raced along the rutted access road toward the bar. But even now, at sixty yards away, fifty-five yards, fifty, he could hear them breathe. Could hear the huff and moan of their efforts, and something that seemed like laughter.

He yanked the rear door open. Prentiss grabbed hold of the frame around the door and dragged himself partway out of the backseat before Teig could put a hand out to help him. He'd been halfway unconscious a moment ago, but now he held on to Teig and twisted, planting his good leg on the permafrost.

When Prentiss hauled his ruined leg behind him, he unleashed a scream that clawed the air. Teeth bared in pain, he stood on one leg. In the glow of the truck's dome light Teig could see the blood painted on the backseat, pooled in the creases. Sliding his leg out, Prentiss had left a wide streak of red behind, but it didn't stop him from slamming the door shut.

"Move!" he roared.

Teig obeyed. He saw the wolves closing in. Saw a third come out of the forest just north of the bar. He slung Prentiss's arm around his neck, grateful the big man could still hop on one leg. The ruined knee had to be broken, and he'd bled so much from the wolves' mauling, but somehow he summoned the strength to move toward the bar without dragging both of them to the ground.

Shouts came from farther along the access road. The blaring horn had woken a few of the people who lived in this little settlement. A bright light winked on at the front of the nearest box-shaped house, but Teig had no interest in that light or those people.

The wolves were too close. Their huffing seemed just behind him, and suddenly he could hear their paws striking the road. They weren't shadows at all. Not apparitions. Whatever they were, they were real and solid and, *fuck, Jesus fuck,* they were right there. Right on him.

"Go," Prentiss growled, so quietly Teig wasn't sure he'd heard.

But that was a lie he told himself—he knew the voice and the tone, and he understood. Prentiss had given him permission to run, to leave him there on the street, twenty feet from the front door of the bar. But no fucking way would he drop Prentiss. He'd carry the big son of a bitch if it came to that.

Then it did.

Prentiss let out a small cry, sagged against Teig, and started to go down.

Teig glanced over his shoulder at the wolves.

The forest seemed full of them. They slunk out of the trees and loped toward the truck. Toward the bar. These new arrivals, the slackers, weren't going to get a chance though, because the first two, with those pinprick white eyes, those fuckers were going to eat well tonight.

Prentiss hung against Teig. Half-conscious, he mumbled an apology. Teig told himself he was going to get Prentiss the rest of the way, but the guy had to weigh more than 250 pounds and one of his legs didn't work.

Run, Prentiss had said. Part of Teig wished he had.

"Teig!" Nari screamed. "Don't let him—"

The muscles in his back and neck were straining as he tried to force Prentiss to stand up on his good leg and he stared at Nari, who stood in the open doorway of the bar, the little catatonic girl still in her arms.

The door. He wasn't going to get there.

Then the woman pushed out past Nari and the kid, came through the door with a hunting rifle, notched the stock against her shoulder, and shot the first of the wolves.

Teig swore. Struggling to hold Prentiss up, he turned to see the bullet's impact. The wolf jerked backward, blown off its feet, but it made no sound. Not a howl or a cry of pain. Teig stared at it while Sayaara shot the second of the lead wolves with the same result. Across the street, where the others had come out of the forest just beyond the garage, the rest of the pack halted, pacing back and forth, eyeing the bar and the people and the gun.

The bartender—Timir—shunted past his wife and rushed over to help Teig with Prentiss. Together, they muscled him toward the door. Just as they managed to lug him over the threshold, Teig heard Nari and her friend swearing and the rifle went off again, three times in quick succession.

As he and the bartender lay Prentiss on the bar's scuffed, beer-stained wooden floor, Teig looked out the door and saw the two wolves that had been shot loping back toward the woods to join the others. He expected the pack to flee into the forest, but once their leaders joined them, the wolves simply spread out into a scattered line, pacing and watching the bar. Patient and waiting.

Still holding Una, Nari nudged her friend back and closed the door, turning two locks and then sliding a deadbolt home. Both she and the other woman had gone pale, there in the dingy light of the bar. For the first time, Teig noticed that the little girl had fallen asleep in Nari's arms with a little smile on her face.

Safe, Teig thought. *She feels safe.*

He wished he felt the same.

Prentiss drifted for a time in a dream of the sea. In the dream, he lay in a rowboat without oars but couldn't bring himself to care. The wind and the tide would take him wherever he was meant to go. The sky seemed so far away, a soft, misty blue, the late afternoon sun casting shadows so long that the side of the boat stood high enough to keep him from its glare. No worries. No oars. Just fate and the tide.

He woke up in pain so profound that tears sprang to his eyes.

"Oh, Christ," he snarled, hissing breath between clenched teeth. "Fuck me. Oh, Jesus . . ."

They were the only words he could manage. The pain tightened every muscle in his body. He levered himself up on his elbow to take a look at the source of that pain, the flesh that had betrayed him, the bones that had been turned into weapons against him. There were others in the room but Prentiss was only vaguely aware of them, or of the hardwood floor that stank of stale beer and decades of spilled vodka.

The leg. The fucking leg.

"Oh, Jesus."

The left leg of his trousers had been torn or cut off mid-thigh. Bandages had been wrapped around his calf and knee. A metal athletic brace had been snapped into place over his knee, reinforced with struts that might have been broken ski poles, then wrapped in black electrical tape to keep the whole thing together. The knee throbbed angrily, but despite the pain he could barely focus on that injury because of the deeper pain—the pain he felt deep, clawed into him, traveling up his femur and down into the tibia and fibula.

Blood seeped through the bandages in half a dozen places.

Prentiss thought he remembered a dark-eyed woman plunging a needle into the meat of his leg. *Oh, what the fu—*

Teig crouched beside him, snapped his fingers a few inches in front of Prentiss's face. "Hey, brother. Focus over here."

With the arm he wasn't using to prop himself up, Prentiss slapped his arm away. "Fuck off."

Whatever small burst of adrenaline the pain had provided bled away, and he lay back on the floor, leg throbbing mercilessly. There were fans overhead, not rotating. Cobwebs skeined across the fan blades and dust coated the wooden ceiling beams. He ought to talk to the owners about their housekeeping, he thought, with a dark little laugh. For a second, he questioned where he was—why the hell did they need ceiling fans in Siberia? But of course it wasn't always cold as a warlock's bollocks up here.

Again, he snickered to himself.

"You're laughing now?" Teig asked. "That hit they gave you worked."

Prentiss felt the pain clawing at his leg again, but the words sunk in. "Hit of what? Someone gave me drugs?"

Teig sat on the floor, legs drawn up in front of him. With a jerk of his thumb, he pointed out the people gathered in the bar behind him. For the first time, most of the room came into focus. It felt to Prentiss as if he'd existed for a time just in the small bit of floor his body occupied, and maybe the dusty ceiling over his head. But now he lolled his head to the right to peer past Teig and he saw the rest of them. Nari's black cherry hair gleamed in the lights over the bar, where she sat on a stool beside another woman about the same age. Halfway between them and Teig was a structural support post. Prentiss blinked a moment and thought about his reindeer burger earlier that day. His stomach gave a little twist of protest at the thought, but he recognized the man.

"It's the bartender," he murmured.

"Timir," Teig reminded him, reaching out to touch Prentiss's forehead, maybe checking for fever. "And his wife back there is Sayaara. How much do you remember?"

Prentiss frowned, about to cuss him out again until he realized it was a damn good question. A few seconds ticked by when all his memory could summon up was an image of their guide lying dead and bloody in the street. Kaskil, that had been his name. Eyes wide open, but unseeing. Cold and dead. Kaskil, torn and bloody and . . .

"The wolves," he whispered.

Now he propped himself up on both elbows, leg still throbbing, pain making him angry now more than anything. He looked around for the door, saw it, and saw a few shuttered windows. "They were right behind us."

"They were," Nari said from the bar, toasting him with a shot of vodka, which she tossed back before immediately pouring herself and Sayaara another. "They are gone now. But maybe not gone. If you are not going to die soon, I would like to stay here until the sun is up."

Prentiss tried to shift. Pain shot through him. He grimaced and looked at Teig. "Am I? Dying soon, I mean."

Over at the bar, Nari translated for Sayaara and Timir and a ripple of grim laughter passed amongst them. Prentiss bared his teeth at them in something that wasn't a smile, but he guessed you had to have a dark sense of humor to live up here.

"Not dying," Teig replied. "But probably having your worst day. Tomorrow's not going to be much better. Timir was in the military. He jury-rigged your splint with a brace he used when he sprained his knee—but yours is broken, brother. The knee's only part of the problem. Sayaara stitched up the two deepest wounds because they were still bleeding. They had some painkillers—not sure if they're legal, but they worked. You don't remember?"

The pain brought clarity, but the memory was still hazy. They'd barged through the door, hearts pounding. The bartender—Timir—had slammed the door and locked it. They'd all fallen apart at that point, emotions flooding out of them. Nari had hugged Sayaara for a long time and Teig had been hugging himself, trembling as he peered out the window, searching for the wolves. There had been shouting outside, a few people wanting to know what was going on, but maybe they'd seen the wolves and gone back inside.

Prentiss had passed out on the floor.

He'd woken up while Timir had been cutting off the leg of his trousers. Teig had put three pills in his hand, made him swallow them with a shot of vodka, then lie there until they took effect. The pills had knocked him out, and though he'd felt it when the needle had gone into his leg, felt the thread tugging at skin and meat, even that had not kept him conscious.

"There's a hospital about three hours south," Teig said. "That's your next stop."

"How long've I been out?" Prentiss asked.

"A couple of hours."

"Drugs wore off already," he said, grimacing. "Or they weren't really meant to be painkillers."

Nari slipped from her barstool, knocked back another shot of vodka, and walked over to him. She studied him, forehead creased with worry. "They are painkillers. Desomorphine. It has a scary name, maybe you heard? Krokodil?"

A memory flickered at the back of his mind, but Prentiss couldn't grasp it.

Nari shrugged. "It is dangerous if you take too much. Maybe a bad idea to give to you. But no matter . . . you take all there was."

Prentiss felt nauseous. Nothing to kill his pain? "How long till sunrise?"

"It's only just gone midnight," Teig said. "I'm sorry, man. Nine hours to go."

"Fucksake." Prentiss glanced around at the others in the room. "Well, don't all just stand around like a bunch of useless twats. Get us a bottle of whiskey, or I'm gonna make your night just as long as mine."

With a relieved grin, Teig rose and turned to get the whiskey. Only in that moment, with Teig, Nari, Sayaara, and Timir all in one glance, did Prentiss realize the little girl was missing. He vaguely remembered Teig saying in the car that they were going to take Una to the gas station where they had picked up Kaskil, the place owned by the girl's great-grandmother. But that couldn't have happened, not with everyone still here.

"Where's Una?" he asked. His leg throbbed and he had to ask through his teeth. "We should all be together."

Nari hugged herself, gaze shifting as if she didn't dare look too closely at anything. "She is sleeping. Upstairs."

"The girl's exhausted," Teig said. "She passed out and I carried her up. Sayaara and Timir let us put her in their bed."

Prentiss nodded, but while Teig went over to the bar to get a bottle of whiskey from Timir, he found himself troubled. Despite his throbbing pain, which seemed to want to drive out thoughts of anything else, he couldn't push images of the little girl from his thoughts.

"Help me up?" he said to Nari, reaching for her hand.

"Whoa, whoa," Teig warned, hurrying over to help. "I'm not sure this is a good idea."

"I'm not spending the night on that floor, mate," Prentiss managed, though fresh pain clawed at him as he rose to stand on his one working leg. His thoughts went gray for a few seconds while both Teig and Nari steadied him, but he took a few deep breaths and that cleared his head, for now. "I'm too old and fat for that nonsense. If there's a chair for me to flop in, I'd be grateful."

He glanced around, examining the few restaurant tables before his gaze landed on the row of booths along the far wall. Slide out the table of one of those booths and shove the benches together, and that'd do for one night—if he drank enough whiskey.

"How about over there?" he asked, glancing at Sayaara and Timir. The husband frowned a bit, but Sayaara got up from her stool, nodding, and waved a hand toward the booths. She spoke Yakut or Russian to Nari, but whatever she said was permission.

Prentiss wanted to ask for a pillow, but the grim expression on Timir's face persuaded him to be happy with what he'd gotten.

They were helping him around the bar. He mostly hopped, trying to keep his weight off the broken knee.

"I got you, man," Teig said, and he really sounded like he meant it. "I'm so sorry. Sorry I dragged you up here. But I'm gonna make it right. I swear."

Prentiss wanted to ask how he planned to make it right for Kaskil, but that would have been cruel. None of this had been Teig's fault. Even through his pain and the fog the drugs had left lingering in his brain, he knew that. What happened in Akhust . . .

What did *happen in Akhust?*

Abandoned homes. Doors left open. Footprints in the snow. A ghost town, except for that one little girl.

"Teig," he whispered, as Nari and Sayaara started to drag the table out from between the booth's benches. "Why did they leave her?"

"What?"

Prentiss braced himself by grabbing hold of Teig's shoulders. They were eye to eye now, and the history of their friendship passed between them. Friendship, brotherhood, the best of times and the worst. "The girl. I can't . . . whatever happened there, I can't think about it, but why was she left behind?"

Teig nodded, expressionless. He swallowed hard. "I wish I knew. But we can help her, at least. We can't do anything for Kaskil, but—"

"You don't get a weird feeling from her?" Prentiss asked, so quietly that Nari and Sayaara did not seem to hear.

"She's catatonic, brother. What do you expect, after what she's seen?"

"We don't know what she's seen," Prentiss said, lowering his voice further, as if afraid the shadows might hear him. He felt stupid, letting the little shiver pass through him, but he couldn't help it. "But she's just . . . off."

Timir clapped his hands and barked something that sounded

almost cheerful. Prentiss turned to see him smiling, gesturing toward the door behind the bar, which had opened without the rest of them noticing. Una stood there, still no expression on her face, but her eyes had come alive. She glanced at each of them in turn, and when her gaze found Prentiss, she smiled thinly.

Nari hurried over to her, speaking rapidly, though Prentiss understood none of it. There was maternal concern there, and Nari reached out a hand.

The girl took her hand. She remained silent, but allowed herself to be led toward the bar, where she scrambled up onto a stool and sat awaiting whatever came next. Prentiss knew they would feed her, give her something to drink, and that was the right thing to do. Take care of her. Someone had to, after all. Until they brought her to her great-grandmother, the girl had no one else.

Teig shoved the two benches together, their legs scraping the floor, and then helped Prentiss to sit. He hoped he could fall asleep on the benches without sliding down into the crack between them overnight, but he figured with enough whiskey, none of it would matter. And if the girl was going to eat, maybe Timir would feed him, too. He needed iron to counter his blood loss. And he needed to stop thinking about why they were not driving to the hospital right now. Why they were hiding inside this bar until the sun came up, though he needed a doctor as soon as possible.

"Teig, listen," he rasped.

But before he could continue, there came a pounding at the door.

Teig whipped around to stare at the door. For hours, he'd been fraying at the edges, able to focus only on the moment at hand. Akhust had turned into a ghost town. With Kaskil dead and Prentiss out of commission, that left him and Nari—a total stranger—to look after

Una, on a night and in a place so far from anything he would have called safety. The bar had given him his first chance to breathe. Akhust had been empty, but the little truck stop community around Olonkho's at least seemed alive. Timir and Sayaara weren't police or doctors but they were competent, caring people, and they'd given Teig hope.

Now the pounding on the door, the voice shouting from the dark, brought anxiety crashing back down.

Wolves don't knock, Teig told himself.

Timir went to open the door.

"Hey, hang on!" Teig shouted. He slipped past Sayaara, grabbed Timir by the shoulder. The man's eyes flared with anger. Teig pointed at the door. "What are you doing? You saw the wolves!"

"Those aren't regular wolves," Prentiss chimed in, his voice reedy, tired, struggling.

Teig agreed. Neither of them had any experience with wolves and they weren't from this area, but they had seen the animals up close in Akhust and on the road. The way they'd paced the car, their relentless speed . . . Teig had never seen a wolf with his own eyes before tonight, but these animals dragged some ancestral terror up from the depths of his brain. They weren't *right.*

This is really it, he thought, dropping his gaze to the floor, as if the old wooden planks held some secret that would make sense of it all. All these years, Olivia's voice had echoed in his memory, her teasing about how she would come back to haunt him. He'd hoped for that, clutched at any possibility it might be true, so that one day he could tell her he was sorry. He had wanted proof that the afterlife existed, that ghosts were real, that the supernatural existed alongside the tangible world.

These wolves weren't ghosts, but whatever had happened in Akhust, it sure as hell wasn't anything natural.

Someone knocked again, hard enough to shake the heavy door in its frame. Timir turned back toward the door and Teig grabbed his arm. Timir slapped his hand away.

"Hey, hey!" Nari said, inserting herself between them. "What is wrong with you?"

Teig wondered if she'd lost her mind. "The wolves that killed Kaskil are out there!"

"No, they are not," Nari said, shaking her head. She exhaled, grabbed his wrist to stop him from gesticulating further, and made him meet her gaze. "These are friends. What is the word—"

"Neighbors," Sayaara said.

Both Teig and Nari turned to look at her, surprised she knew the English word, but then Nari nodded. "Yes, neighbors. Worried for Sayaara and Timir. They saw the wolves but say they are gone."

"That's what they're saying, right now?" Teig asked.

"A moment ago, yes," Nari replied. "The wolves are gone, but they are afraid."

Timir stood by the door, his hand on the deadbolt. He cocked his head and muttered something in Yakut to his wife before looking at Teig.

"I open now," Timir said. "Is okay."

Teig exhaled. They were right, of course. If the wolves were still out there, nobody would have gotten close enough to knock on the door. He gave Nari a sheepish glance and she released his wrist.

"It's been a long day," he said, hoping she understood his fear.

Timir threw back the deadbolt.

"Wait!" Prentiss rasped. "Listen!"

Teig and Nari turned to look at the door again, in time to see Timir reach for the door handle to turn the secondary lock. Sayaara put her hand over her husband's to stop him. The five of them went quiet, watching the door, listening.

The knocking had ceased. No more shouts came from outside.

The door seemed to breathe. Teig could not have put the looming question in his mind into words, but it opened like a chasm before him as he stared at the door.

"Timir?" Sayaara said, turning her husband's name into a question.

The bar owner turned to look at Teig, his frown an accusation, wordlessly blaming Teig for the fear that floated in the room with them like motes of dust. They were all breathing it in, breathing it out.

ThumpThumpThump

Three muffled knocks, heavy, on the lower part of the door. Nothing like the knocks that had come before. These did not sound as if they'd been made by fists, or even the kicking of boots.

"Erel?" Timir called through the door, following the name with several staccato bursts of Yakut. Teig didn't have to speak the language to guess the questions. *Are you still out there? What was that? Do you see the wolves?*

Teig turned to Nari. "Go upstairs. See if you can get a view out the window. Before we open the door, we need to—"

A voice came from outside the door, soft and weak. The only word Teig recognized was the bar owner's name. Timir went rigid for a second or two before he reached for the door latch again.

"Erel?" Sayaara called, voice cracking as she lifted a hand to cover her mouth, eyes wide.

Nari moved first. Teig followed.

"Timir, no!" Nari called. The words that followed weren't in English, but words didn't matter anymore.

They were all breathing in the fear that filled the bar, but they were reacting to it differently. Timir and Sayaara were afraid for their neighbor, but the rest of them had heard the same anguish in that fading voice outside the door and come to a different conclusion. They didn't know Erel, and they didn't want to risk their lives for him.

Nari tried to pull Timir away from the door. Sayaara shouted at her, their old friendship not made to withstand a night like this. Timir shrugged Nari off, turned the lock, twisted the latch. Erel's voice turned to whimpers on the other side of the door and through the crack between door and frame, Teig saw the scruff of the man's beard and a glimpse of one eye.

Erel cried out, but it sounded like surrender.

Teig shouldered Timir out of the way, crashed into the door, and slammed the deadbolt back into place a heartbeat before something struck the door from outside. Something that wasn't Erel. Something that snuffed out Erel's whimper.

Sayaara had begun to cry. She shouted at Teig, managed to summon up two words in English—"fuck you"—but Teig shushed her. Nari called for quiet as Teig backed away from the door. They stood and watched, stood and listened.

The night had gone silent.

In the yellow glow of the bar's lights, the blood that began to seep in beneath the door looked nearly black. It pooled slowly, spreading, following the line of a crack in the floor. Timir reached for Sayaara, and husband and wife embraced in shared grief, breathing in more of those motes of fear that infused them all now. Sayaara turned to Nari, asked her something that left Nari shaking her head, eyes full of regret.

"What's she saying?" Teig asked.

"What do you think?" Nari said, slumping down on a nearby barstool. "She wants to know what's outside."

Behind them, Prentiss cleared his throat. Teig startled. He'd nearly forgotten Prentiss was in the room.

"Wolves," the Englishman said. "But something else, too. And maybe they're outside now, but seems fairly clear they'd much rather be in here with us."

10

The stink of decades of spilled beer gave way to the copper tang of blood. Teig and Prentiss sat in rustic chairs around a squat table defaced by carved graffiti letters that looked nothing like the alphabet they knew. Prentiss had been uncomfortable on the benches he'd sprawled across earlier, but it didn't look as if he found his chair much better. Teig stared down into his vodka and sighed, his warm breath fogging the glass.

Nari had gone upstairs with her friends, and that was for the best. Bad luck had put her in the truck with them, but at least she had friends.

You have friends, Teig thought, looking over at Prentiss. *At least one.*

"You don't have to keep me company," Prentiss said.

"Am I keeping you awake?"

"You're meant to be keeping me awake. What if I pass out . . . slip into a coma or something?"

Teig tossed back the vodka. It burned on the way down and he turned the glass over, slammed it down onto the tabletop, covering up some of that artful graffiti. He pushed up from his chair and stalked to the door, stared down at the pool of blood, which had finally stopped expanding. It had begun to cool, the icy air outside the door causing crystals to form on top of the scarlet puddle.

He turned back to Prentiss. "We can't wait till morning."

Prentiss groaned, reached out to shift his ravaged leg. Splinted and braced and bandaged, it looked even more a wreckage than it truly was, but Teig knew the reality was bad enough. Prentiss kept drifting off to sleep, then waking with a hiss or moan from the pain gnawing at him. Maybe he hadn't lost enough blood to die of it, but he needed surgery, needed that knee set, and they were a hell of a long way from the nearest hospital.

"I'm fine where I am for tonight," Prentiss said. "It's not as if I can make a run for it, and we've got the little girl to think of."

The two men watched one another across the bar. They were alone again. Since this trip began, they had spent plenty of time together, driving in the car, on the plane, in hotel rooms. How many opportunities had Teig found to have the conversation that waited, unspoken, between them, and yet never broached the subject? Never taken it seriously, anyway. Now they were stuck. Prentiss sat with his ruined leg outstretched, propped on an extra chair. Teig could have left him there, could have run away from the things that needed saying. He'd tried to say those things before, but nothing ever came out exactly as he wanted it to.

"Teig," Prentiss said.

They stared at one another again.

"Yeah?"

"I'm afraid to say out loud the things that are going through my head."

Me too, Teig thought. But he wasn't really afraid of his thoughts, only to speak them aloud. To admit how badly he'd fucked up his life.

"Wait, what are you talking about?" Teig crossed back to his chair. "I've got a million things on my mind, and yeah, a lot of them scare me."

Prentiss shifted in the wooden seat, wincing in pain. "It's quiet in here now. Quiet enough that I can't keep these thoughts out of my head. If it was just the wolves, I'd find some way to brush it off. Tell myself some bullshit fairy tale, even though I know it's not natural behavior for wolves to attack people, especially in groups the way they did in Akhust."

Prentiss paused. His body seemed to deflate and his breathing turned deep and steady, like he was fighting the pain, or sleep, or the urge to puke, or all three.

"Jack . . ."

His eyes opened to narrow slits. "Yes, *Felix*?"

"Fair enough." Teig put up his hands in surrender. "You were saying about the wolves' behavior?"

Prentiss fixed him with a withering stare but his head swayed a bit, like a drunk about to lose a fight with his booze. "You know . . . you know what I'm saying, Teig. The people vanished from that town. The way those wolves came at us, half the time they only looked like wolves when I was staring at them straight on. Out the corner of my eye, I couldn't have even said they were there at all."

Teig felt ice creep up the back of his neck, though it was more than warm enough inside the bar. "It was dark."

"Fuck you, 'it was dark'!" Prentiss growled. He tried to sit up in his chair and then grabbed hold of his ruined leg with a stream of profanity that would have felled a forest of church ladies.

"Settle down, man," Teig said. He didn't like Prentiss's pallor, or his breathing, or the way for a moment he thought the man would just give up the ghost, right in that chair.

Prentiss wiped a hand across his forehead, where a sheen of sweat glistened. "You're pissing me off, mate."

"What do you want me to say? That this isn't normal?" Teig chuckled, and it made him feel sick. "They kept up with the truck, man. They tracked us here, they hid out, and they killed a guy at the front door when they thought maybe the door was about to open. Wolves aren't that fast and they aren't that clever, but there's a puddle of blood by the door that says otherwise. But we're still here, Prentiss. We are still sitting in this bar when we need to get you to the fucking hospital and get that little girl to safety, because we both know those things are still waiting for us outside."

Prentiss had begun to nod off. When he snapped up, trying to stay conscious, his eyes were glazed.

"Hey," Teig said, moving to kneel at his side. "Hey, hey, Prentiss. Man, if you need to sleep just go to sleep. I'm sorry, I shouldn't be—"

But he saw that sheen of sweat and the yellowing complexion and he put his hand on Prentiss's forehead, and then it all made sense. It wasn't sleep trying to drag Prentiss down. It was fever. And with his leg torn up like that, not to mention the bacteria in the bite of a wild animal, fever could only mean one thing—infection.

"Prentiss." Teig shook him, and Prentiss opened his eyes. "I'm getting you out of here. Tonight. Now."

"How you going to manage that trick?"

Teig smiled. "Remember when Discovery said they'd only greenlight my Shark Week idea if I could get Richard Dreyfuss to host it?"

Prentiss coughed a little when he laughed. His eyelids fluttered a bit, like he might drift off any moment, but it was clear he remembered. Teig had pitched a dating show to run during Shark Week wherein couples would float on rafts in a Texas quarry and watch their favorite shark movies projected on the quarry wall, talk about why they loved sharks, what frightened them, and see if they could make a love connection. It was ridiculous, but had enough absurd charm that Discovery was willing to give it a shot . . . if he could deliver Dreyfuss, who had devoted much of his life to The Dreyfuss Civics Initiative, getting civics learning back into schools. Any idiot knew the actor would never agree to host *First Bites*, but Teig promised Dreyfuss he could get at least two NFL team owners to make donations of a million dollars each to the Initiative, and he made it happen.

"You fucked up . . . a lot of shit . . ." Prentiss said. "But sometimes you're crazy enough to pull off a miracle."

Teig put a hand on his shoulder. "I'm just too dumb to believe it when people tell me something can't be done. I'm glad we stopped here because without Timir and Sayaara patching you up, I think you might've bled to death before I could get you to a hospital. But we can't just wait around. I'm going to have to get the truck. I'll drive it up to the door. Maybe they'll help you get in, or maybe I'll have to do that, but either way—"

"The wolves, Teig. You'll never—"

"We don't know that," Teig said. "No idea how many there are, or where they're at right now. I'll borrow a rifle from Timir. If I shoot one, it'll spook the rest of the pack long enough for me to make it to the truck."

"You ever fired a gun in your life?"

Teig cocked his head. "I've been making reality TV for years, my friend. I've done all kinds of shit that might surprise you."

"What about gas? If we run out, we're screwed."

"We should have enough to get to Kaskil's grandmother's place. We can fuel up there and get you to the hospital. It's only another hour past that, I think."

At the mention of Kaskil, Teig felt a pain in his chest. He knew the wolves hadn't been his doing, but couldn't help feeling that if not for him, Kaskil might still be alive.

"Teig," Prentiss said weakly.

"Close your eyes for a few minutes, if you can. I'm going to sort this out."

Prentiss sighed and his eyes closed, but he kept talking. "Remember your whole thing about the Texans?"

"You mean the Alamo?"

"Exactly. That's you, mate. End of the day, you're one of the Texans."

Teig squeezed Prentiss's shoulder, then sat back in his chair. "Always, brother."

He'd explained to Prentiss once that he often took stock of the people around him in terms of the battle at the Alamo. History said the men there knew they couldn't win, but they kept fighting as long as they could. Teig wanted friends who would have stood shoulder to shoulder with him on the wall of the Alamo, knowing it was hopeless but fighting on regardless. People like that were few and far between, but Prentiss had proven himself one of those "Texans" by coming on this trip, despite the times Teig's plans had gone awry.

No way would he leave Prentiss behind.

"I've made mistakes," he said quietly, listening to the way the wind moaned outside the bar. "Too many times I've let my ambition take casualties. People have lost a lot of money on me, but never once did I take a dime without intending to pay it back or to earn people's trust. Sometimes my enthusiasm just runs ahead of my good sense."

Prentiss opened his eyes. They were slightly yellowed and glazed with pain. "I know, mate. That's why I'm here."

The last sentence came out barely above a whisper and then Prentiss took a deep breath. He seemed, finally, to be asleep or he'd passed out from the pain. Either way, Teig meant to give him a little rest while he figured out how to get the two of them out of here. He had a lot of regrets in his life, many of them from the people he'd let down in business, but at the root it all went back to Olivia. His hopes for *Life and Death on the Road of Bones* were already crushed, but business and career didn't matter at all in the midst of this. They had entered another world, where the concerns of ordinary life seemed like a dream. Maybe he'd get back to that dream someday, but for now they had to make it through the nightmare.

Nari had never been upstairs at Olonkho's. Timir and Sayaara had made themselves a rustic, comfortable home there, with a small kitchen, a living room, two bedrooms, and a bath. They'd put Una in their own bedroom earlier, leaving the door open just a few inches to let in light from the narrow corridor. It ought to have felt safe and warm, but Nari kept glancing over her shoulder, watching the windows, suspicious of every dark corner.

"Don't go," Sayaara said, squeezing her hand.

They sat on the sprawling sofa, wrapped in knitted blankets, two old friends who now shared an awful new bond. Nari hugged herself, watching her reflection in the darkened screen of the old television. She looked down the corridor toward the couple's bedroom. A banging of cabinet doors echoed along the hall—Timir had gone to get his guns from a cabinet in the guest room. Nari knew she ought to feel safer—there were at least two hunting rifles and a shotgun they could use to defend themselves—but somehow the knowledge changed nothing.

She put aside her blanket and stood up. Sayaara's comforting hand fell away as Nari went to the window and looked down at the street. From this angle, she couldn't see the front door, but she knew the man who'd been banging to be let in must be dead. Nobody could lose that much blood and survive.

Nari shut her eyes and pressed her forehead against the window. The glass felt so cold it seared her skin, but at least she felt something. As a girl she had fallen from a tree and given her head a ferocious knock against a branch on the way down. The concussion had left her more confused and disoriented than she'd ever been since. The numbness inside her now felt like that, only it extended from her head to her heart.

"Nari," Sayaara said from the sofa. "You don't need to go with these men when they leave. You're safer here. Just stay with us. Whatever this trouble is, it doesn't belong to you."

There were dead people in the street. Sayaara couldn't see them from the sofa, but they both knew the bodies were out there. Timir had been the first to spot them, right before he went rummaging for his guns. The thuds against the front door and the shouts of their neighbor must still be echoing in their heads, just as they echoed in Nari's, but they seemed far away now. The corpses were more immediate. She couldn't see what might be left of the dead man at the front door but there were at least three bodies to the right of the window, north of the bar. The little settlement around Olonkho's might not amount to much, but even just a few dozen people were a community. They were friends, depending on one another.

Now some of them were dead.

Three? Or were there four bodies? Hard to tell, because Nari thought two of the dark lumps she saw out in the dark, up along the road toward the deep forest, might be two pieces of the same dead neighbor.

She had to be numb or she'd never make it to sunrise.

"Nari," Sayaara started again.

"I can't," Nari replied at last. "They don't speak Yakut and they're determined to take the little girl to her great-grandmother. At some point she's going to come out of the shock that has shut her down like this and she's going to need someone there to communicate with her. I have to help her until I know she's safe."

She turned to look at Sayaara, who had draped one of the blankets over herself so she looked like some kind of cloaked witch. "Her whole town vanished. All the people went off into the forest. Then she saw the wolves . . ."

Nari shook her head. Enough. She had played that mental recording back through her mind too many times already. She didn't want to see Kaskil die again.

"Just think about it, please," Sayaara said.

The urge to agree tugged at her. How much simpler it would be to cast off any obligation to Una the way she had cast aside her blanket a moment ago. Hadn't she spent hours driving toward home and daydreaming about what it would feel like to be free of obligation?

"Nari?"

She nodded. "I'll think about it. I promise."

Her gaze shifted toward the window again. Something skittered off in the dark between the parking garage and the next building, and though it looked like a shadow she knew it was one of the wolves. They hadn't gone far. They were out there, waiting.

She pressed her forehead to the glass again. Several shadows moved between the buildings. Yellow eyes gleamed in the dark. One of the wolves paused in the street and looked up, and she felt certain it knew she watched from that window. Neither of them looked away.

Wolves in shadows, or shadows in wolves?

The thought slithered through her mind, intrusive, as if it came from elsewhere. A shudder ran through her, a trill of nausea. Nari tried to focus on those shadows but something else moved along the street. She narrowed her eyes, craned her neck to try and make out the shape of the thing in the darkness down beyond the last of the buildings.

For a moment she was sure it was a tree, winter branches twitching in frigid gusts of night wind, but when she pressed the side of her head harder against the glass, neck aching, she felt sure they weren't branches but antlers. A reindeer, maybe, but if so then the biggest reindeer she'd ever seen.

"You look like a contortionist," Sayaara said. "What are you doing?"

"Do you hear that?" Nari whispered.

"I hear the wind."

It wasn't the wind. Nari felt it in her skull, as if it struck the glass from outside the window and traveled from glass to bone. Not a song, not really music, but somehow still melodic, like the galloping heartbeat and lilting inhale-exhale of some enormous beast that had swallowed them all whole. It lulled her, mesmerized her, and now she went down on her knees to press her cheek against the glass so she could hear it better. Feel it better.

"Nari," Sayaara whispered, with a quaver of fear. "What are you doing?"

"Sssh," Nari said, reaching for her friend's hand. "Listen."

The moment their fingers touched, Sayaara gave a shuddery exhale. "Oh. Oh, wow."

Nari smiled. She inhaled the music, breathed with it, absorbed its vibration in her bones, and when she looked along the street into the darkness again she saw not tree branches or reindeer antlers, but something like a man. She recognized this figure instantly, even at such distance, and even though it had *changed*. Once one had seen the parnee, it might be erased from recollection, so that it would be impossible to describe . . . but it could not be truly forgotten.

Upon seeing the parnee again, Nari smiled even wider and felt awash in joy. But that was the surface Nari. Down inside her was another Nari, the true heart, locked inside a little birdcage, helplessly flapping its wings, screaming without a sound.

She had told the American the parnee was a shaman, and this was true, but how could she explain the difference between the shamanist faith shared by so many people in her country and what the parnee was, what the stories said it had been in the past, how powerful and terrifying it could be when the times demanded it? A summer rain could be called a storm, but a winter blizzard that might bury a town or freeze a horse dead in its tracks . . . that was also a storm. The shamans, who were people, might speak with nature, but the parnee breathed nature, danced nature, screamed nature's grief. And like nature, the parnee could be merciless.

Nari had never seen it before tonight. Never really believed.

Now, face pressed to the glass, she sang the parnee's song and surrendered herself. Tears formed in her eyes. Tears of joy and relief. No more fear, no more running.

"It's calling to me," Sayaara said, squeezing her fingers.

"Yes," Nari agreed.

The music grew louder. She took her head away from the window, undid the latch, and struggled to slide it open. The window resisted until she smashed her fist against the frame, but even then it only slid up an inch. Enough for the cold to stab into the room, raking them with frigid claws. Nari flinched, knew she ought to back away from the cold, but even as it whispered around her bare throat and made her fingers hurt to the bone, she fought to open the window further.

Timir appeared in the doorway behind them, rifle in hand. He called his wife's name twice, three times. At first he sounded alarmed, but by the third time he said "Sayaara," the word floated across the room like a breathed prayer.

"Do you hear it?" Timir asked.

Nari closed both eyes, so pleased to know that her friends were here, that they could share this moment.

"He's calling us," Sayaara said, as she moved beside Nari. Together, the two of them struggled to jerk the window open. It squealed in its frame. One side gave way, twitching up a fraction of an inch, but as stuck as the window had been before, this only wedged it more firmly into place.

Sayaara began to whine.

"Open," Nari said. "Open."

She needed to be out in the street. The shadows were all moving down there now. The bodies were only dark lumps on the frozen road, but the night breathed, and with every breath it came more alive.

Timir wore heavy boots but she didn't hear a footstep. One moment he had entered the room and the next she felt his big hand grab the back of her sweater and drag her out of his way. He had the rifle in both hands, cocked it back, and used the butt of the gun to smash the window. The cold air swept in and stole Nari's breath, stinging her face, and the lure of that night song tugged at her more fiercely. But the sound of shattering glass pierced her brain, reached down inside her and opened the birdcage where Nari's true self lay captive.

Free now, for a moment. Whatever darkness that song had woven around her, she could resist it. But what of the others?

Timir smashed the rest of the glass out of the window. Alert, mind seared by sudden awareness, Nari saw him put a knee onto the windowsill, snapping the bottom of the stuck frame, and she knew the song still held him in its grasp. She shouted for him to stop, shouted at Sayaara to grab him, afraid even as she spoke that her friend might also still be trapped inside the song.

Sayaara grabbed her husband by the hair and turned to Nari with wild eyes. "Help me!"

Nari wrapped her arms around Timir's middle. Another noise filled her ears, a kind of nonsense burble, a constant repetition, and she realized the sounds were coming from her own lips. Just noise, blotting out the parnee's song.

She shoved Timir back, cocked her arm, and slapped him hard across the face. For a moment he gripped his rifle harder and she thought the next thing he shattered might be her skull, but his eyes cleared and he shook his head.

Timir clapped his hands over his ears.

"It doesn't help," Sayaara said. "It's not just in your ears. It's in your bones."

Nari gave them both a shove toward the door. Wordlessly, they all understood, shuffling into the corridor. Timir slammed the door behind them and they all paused to listen. Nari ceased her babbling and cocked her head.

"I still hear it," she said.

"Feel it," Sayaara corrected. "But not as strong, out here."

Timir glanced from one woman to the other. "What do we do now?"

In the silence that followed that question, Nari realized that she'd nearly forgotten all about Una. The little girl was meant to be sleeping in Sayaara and Timir's room, but with the smashing glass and their shouts, never mind the parnee's song, she could not have slept through it all. Yet not the slightest noise came from behind the closed bedroom door. A flicker of alarm went through her and she left her friends in troubled silence.

She went to the door, took a deep breath, and opened it as slowly and quietly as she could manage. The bedroom seemed to disdain illumination. Even the light from the hall barely penetrated, but she saw long, branching shadows. Her breath caught with the memory of the antlers in the dark at the end of the street, in the moment before the parnee appeared outside, but when she blinked those shadows were gone and the bedroom seemed to lighten a bit.

"Just go in," Sayaara said, nudging her from behind. "Is she asleep?"

Nari could not refuse. This was Sayaara and Timir's bedroom, and Sayaara herself had just chastened her for not entering. Of course it had to be safe. To Sayaara, it would be the safest place on the face of the planet.

Nari stepped into the room, but caught the toe of her boot. She stumbled, arms outstretched, but her shoulder struck something hard and the impact spun her sideways. Only when she lay on the floor, looking up, did she see the thin, bare branches overhead. Her eyes had begun to adjust.

"Is that . . . are they . . ." Sayaara tried several times to form a question, but failed.

Breathless, Nari grabbed hold of the trunk of the birch tree and hauled herself up. Eyes wide, she stared at this impossible thing. It had been lost in the shadows before but now the white bark appeared gray in the gloom. Taking a step back, Nari saw the thick roots growing from the hardwood floor, one of which she'd tripped over. There were half a dozen bare birch trees, branches spread along the ceiling, growing into the beams and pushing through the ceiling. Near the bed were three small spruce firs.

She laughed at herself, then clapped a hand over her mouth to keep the madness from escaping. Trees didn't grow in bedrooms.

"Nari," Sayaara said. "How can this be?"

The dull rhythm of the parnee's song still played in the back of her mind, but Nari shook it off along with her friend's question. She moved through the birches and around the nearest of the spruce firs. Somehow Una had slept through all of this. She'd be lying in the dark, asleep, still catatonic.

But the little girl was not in the bed.

Nari's heart clenched. She couldn't fight the impossible, couldn't unsee the wolves or the corpses in the street, but goddamnit she could protect one little girl who'd already lost everything.

"Ariuna!" she called. "Where are you?"

On her knees, she searched under the bed. There were roots there, and a baby spruce that would soon push its way up through the bed itself. Nari leapt up, turned to Sayaara. "Help me!"

But though the room was large, there were few places the child might be hiding. Not under the bed, not in the closet, not behind the bureau or buried beneath the blankets Sayaara had recently laundered.

Nari scrambled over the bed to the other spruce fir tree. The only space they hadn't looked was behind it. The scent of its needles filled the room now, as if an artist had created this place and forgotten that one last detail until this very moment.

She looked behind the tree.

Timir had built them a romantic window seat that looked out over the back of the building, nothing but starlit trees and hills in the distance. The little girl sat on the window seat with her knees drawn up to her chest and her fingers plugging her ears.

"Una." *Thank God.* Nari went to the girl, laid a hand on her shoulder, but Una ignored her, as ever. "Hey. Child, listen to . . ."

Only then did she notice the way the girl hummed. Una stared out the window at the snow and the wildwood and the hills, and she hummed the same primal rhythm that still resonated in Nari's skull.

Sayaara had crawled across the bed. "Do you hear it? She's—"

Nari whipped around to glare at her. "I hear it! Fuck! We have to go!"

She scooped the girl off the window seat, made her way around the impossible spruce, climbed over the bed with Una in her arms, and weaved through impossible birch trees, telling herself they weren't there at all. The parnee's song had done something to her head, some fucking mesmerism. The darkness had not yielded up shadows of antlers or branches. No.

Nari refused.

No.

Sayaara touched her arm as she carried the girl into the hall, where Timir was nowhere to be seen. "What do we do now?"

Nari stared. "Now? Now, we get the fuck out of here."

11

Teig took another shot of vodka. Sweat beaded on his forehead and trickled down the nape of his neck. He sat on the floor, flush against the door, and purposely banged the back of his skull against the wood. Minutes ago he'd been trying to figure out how they could take Una and leave this place and now he feared he might be too late.

"Stop!" he shouted at nothing and everything. Again he whacked the back of his skull against the door, trying to make the music stop. The chanting, or whatever the fuck it was.

Not music. Music is the wrong word. It's a goddamned fish hook.

That felt right. A fish hook in his brain. The grieving kid who'd lived inside him for more than twenty years had always longed for proof of the supernatural.

Careful what you wish for, idiot.

A groan reached him. A whimper. Teig glanced to his left and saw Prentiss crawling on the floor toward him, wounded leg leaving a smear of blood in his wake, blood to soak in with the decades of whiskey and vodka and beer.

"Prentiss, brother . . . no," Teig said. "Stop. You're gonna rip open those . . ." He couldn't think of the word. *Wounds,* a voice said inside his skull. His lips might have formed the word but he wasn't sure he spoke it aloud. The song had slithered in there and rewired some things.

Teig grabbed the vodka bottle. Drinking dulled his mind. It seemed to be dulling the song's ability to nest in his brain, but if he wanted to get out of there, how much could he drink and still drive the truck? Still keep them on the road?

If they managed to get out of here, crashing the truck would kill them anyway. Dead by dawn, if not before, frozen to death. Not for the first time, that image of Jack Nicholson at the end of *The Shining* came into his head. *Fuck, I don't want to be that. Sitting in the snow, icicles on my nose.*

So much easier to go outside. That had been his destination to begin with, hadn't it? Get to the garage, get into the truck, pull it up to the front door, load Prentiss and the girl and Nari if she wanted to go, and leave this icy little outpost in hell behind.

Teig groaned. Grabbed the vodka bottle as he hauled himself to his feet. Took a slug from the bottle, but his left hand was on the door latch. The wolves were out there in the dark. People were dead.

"Nunhh." He grunted a couple of times, sneered, and smashed the vodka bottle against the doorframe. Droplets glinted from the razor edge of the shattered bottle. He took a deep breath, pulled his left hand away from the door latch, and stared at the rough skin of his palm.

Stab that palm, twist the broken glass, and the pain would clear his head.

But it was so much easier to grab the door latch again, turn it, and open the door . . . so that was what he did.

The night air punched into the bar, so cold it stole his breath, but it shocked him upright. His spine straightened, his eyes widened. He stared out at the night. To his right, farther along the little access road in this grim, forlorn hamlet, an enormous wolf dragged a human body across the snow and into the darkness behind the garage. Beyond that, farther back, a figure moved along the road.

It stood like a man, but if so, the man was huge, hunched like an animal, and when he went still he seemed like just a trick of the light.

A hand gripped the hood of his parka and hauled him back into the bar. For half a second, Teig thought it must be Prentiss, but then that strong hand spun him around and he spotted Prentiss on the floor and remembered that it couldn't be. Prentiss had a fever. Prentiss had a shattered knee. Prentiss had been attacked by hungry wolves.

The guy who'd grabbed him was Timir. The big barman had a rifle in his left hand, so he slapped Teig hard across the face with his right.

Teig snarled. "What the fuck was that?"

Timir gazed at him, concerned and fearful. "You okay?"

"The song?" he asked, looking at Timir. "The chanting?"

He started to imitate the rhythm he'd heard in his head, but Timir gave a vigorous shake of his head and tried to cover his mouth.

"Teig!" Prentiss croaked.

He was still crawling toward the door. The frigid air still swept into the bar. Prentiss's face already looked red, stung by the wind. He looked pitiful. For a moment Prentiss managed to stop crawling, and he began to bash a fist against his own skull.

"Get it out!" he barked.

Which was when Teig realized the chanting hadn't stopped. Timir slapped him, and that had cleared his head, but now that he became aware of it again he felt the fish hook still there, tugging at him. Groaning, he slapped his own face, feeling stupid but knowing he'd do anything. On the floor was the broken vodka bottle. He'd dropped it when Timir had grabbed him, but if he had to, he would follow through on the pain he'd planned for himself.

Teig grabbed the barrel of Timir's rifle. "Give me this." Timir tried to pull it back, but Teig turned and gestured outside. "I'm going for the truck. I need a weapon."

"You know how to shoot?" Timir asked.

"My father made sure I could shoot the tail off a running rabbit. I do just fine."

Timir spoke decent English but he understood even more. He released the rifle, narrowed his gaze, and gave Teig a shove toward the door. "Run faster than a rabbit."

Out the door and into the street, he should have felt free. The night should have felt infinite and open but instead it swallowed him up. As the air swept around him, pressing through clothing and flesh so it felt as if the wind slashed him to the bone, Teig wanted to scream. The sound in his skull remained but the cold tamped it down, and as he ran across the road toward the parking garage, he barked a manic laugh. *Cold?* What sort of word was that? Even *freezing* seemed absurd, when the temperature had dropped below the freezing point fifty or sixty degrees ago. Language failed at this temperature. Did the locals have vocabulary for cold like this? Air so cold it scoured, punched, sought to steal your life?

Rifle in hand, he scanned shadows, expecting them to move. *Jesus Christ, don't let them move.* Out here in the dark, stomping across the road, he could barely make out the shapes of two or three bodies on the ground. Up the road a door opened, a head poked tentatively outside, and Teig knew he should scream at them to hide, but he'd never met the people who lived in these other homes and they weren't his responsibility. If he wanted to save Prentiss, and if he wanted to save Una, he couldn't think of anyone else.

When the van with the puppy had taken his little sister away, he'd been a child himself, incapable of helping. That horror had given him nightmares for years, his subconscious mind painting hideous pictures of his sister in the back of that van, the things that had been done to her. But Teig wasn't a child anymore. He could do this. He could save this little girl, and the man who had been the closest thing to a brother in his life.

The cold bled what little strength remained in him but he reached the garage, hauled open the heavy door, and stepped inside. Only after the door shut did he realize how much noise there had been out in the dark. The wind, the creaking of the trees, the loud pop of the settling snow and ice. Now it all ceased, including that seductive rhythm in his skull. It had vanished, cut off from the source.

Prior to coming to this part of the world, he would have considered the temperature inside the garage too cold to sustain life, and likely it was, long-term. But compared to out on the street, it felt like the tropics. All that mattered was the purpose for the garage's existence, which was to keep vehicles just warm enough that their engines would still start in the morning.

He darted across the garage. With the bar closed, there weren't many cars. Some of the other buildings must have had their own small garages, but the dozen or so vehicles belonged to residents. All except the truck that had brought Prentiss and Teig here, and had carried Kaskil to his death.

Don't start, he thought. *If you're gonna feel guilty, save it for when you're all safe.*

Teig hurried to the truck, opened the door, slid into the driver's seat, and set the rifle beside him. His thoughts had begun to fray and scatter. Why hadn't the wolves come for him? Where had they gone?

Hope flared in his chest but he tamped it down. Hope could be a mirage, the vision of an oasis in the desert, and he wouldn't surrender to it.

He turned the key and the engine roared to life, not even a cough.

Teig set the rifle more firmly on the seat beside him, ready for anything as he put the truck in gear and drove over to the garage's exit and back out into the mind-numbing cold.

It couldn't have been more than fifty yards from the garage exit to the bar's front door but he tapped the accelerator anyway. Halfway there, he laid a hand on the horn. Though loud, the blaring honk seemed so much a part of the ordinary world that for a moment his fear seemed outsized, even absurd.

The front door of Olonkho's opened. Timir and Sayaara were first out the door and Teig felt a flutter of resentment. Prentiss needed him. The girl, Una, needed him. They should've been the first priority. Timir should help him with Prentiss. What the hell was wrong with—

He hadn't finished the thought before he saw the wolves. They came from the shadows between buildings and around the side of the bar, low to the ground, and what wan starlight passed through the clouds barely seemed to touch them.

Sayaara screamed. Teig swore, grabbed the rifle, and jumped out, engine still running. He could see their ears, the shape of their snouts, the malevolent glow of their eyes, and the swift flicker of their legs moving beneath them. They ran silently, full of purpose.

Teig took aim and shot the first one in the neck. The wolf spun around, jerked by the force of the bullet, and skidded on the snowpack, but it did not cry out. Not even a whimper.

"Run!" he screamed.

Timir had another rifle, this one slung over his shoulder. He had one hand on his wife's back, but the moment he hauled open the door and shoved Sayaara into the backseat, he took up position beside Teig and barked something in Yakut. Teig hoped he understood, but even if Timir hadn't meant for him to go and help the others, that was what was going to happen.

Nari had stepped out of the bar with Una in her arms, carrying the girl as if she were a toddler. Catatonic as she was, that was for the best. Kids trapped inside their own heads weren't known for hurrying.

"Where's Prentiss?" Teig asked.

A groan from the front door. "I'm fucking coming."

Nari glanced between Teig and Prentiss. "I will come back," she said, which he assumed meant she wanted to help get the wounded Englishman to the truck.

"No. Get in, lock the doors," Teig said.

Something flashed across her eyes, a bit of anger and disdain at the idea of him trying to protect her over himself. *Don't play the hero,* those eyes seemed to say. He took it to heart, but it was too late to have a conversation about it.

Rifle shots kept booming, echoing off of buildings and the low-hanging sky. Timir shot two other wolves. Teig reached the door of the bar, braced the rifle butt against his shoulder, and shot another as it came around the corner.

"Help me up, goddamn it!" Prentiss grunted, but he seemed to be doing all right on his own. Using the doorframe for balance, he hoisted himself onto one leg.

Teig pushed up under Prentiss's arm and took his weight, half-dragging him toward the truck. The cold had settled in and he felt numb, even his thoughts beginning to slow. In the truck, Sayaara leaned over the front seat and smashed a hand down on the horn, maybe thinking it would drive the wolves away.

It didn't.

Timir shot another one. How many rounds did he have for that rifle? Teig had the other rifle over his left shoulder while he helped Prentiss, too tangled up to try to aid Timir now. If he wanted to shoot wolves, he'd have to drop his friend onto the road and he wasn't going to do that.

From the corner of his eye he saw something move and glanced that way, toward where he'd shot the wolf that had come around the corner of the bar. Two others were there now, advancing slowly, and he wondered how many they'd have to kill to get out of here alive.

Behind those two lay the body of the one he'd shot. Just before he looked away Teig saw a bit of black smoke rise and eddy from that dead wolf and move in the frozen wind. It turned to shadow and merged with the darkness until the wolf he'd killed vanished, as if it had never been there.

His gut twisted with the knowledge that nothing could be relied on now. Nothing could be considered solid or true.

"Hurry!" Nari shouted at them. She stood by the open driver's door of the truck and set Una down. Catatonic she might have been, but the little girl stood on her own two feet. "Move your ass!"

"My God," Prentiss huffed, almost a whimper as Teig stumbled toward the truck with him, "it's so fucking cold."

Prentiss hopped along, arm around Teig's neck, unable to put the slightest weight on his broken knee. When his boot caught on the ground, dragged a few inches, he cried out in pain and they had to stop. Head-to-head, leaning on one another, Teig and Prentiss took a breath.

"Felix," Prentiss rasped in his ear, voice cracking as if he might be in tears. "Do you hear it?"

Until that moment, Teig had blocked it out. Gunshots and shouts and maybe adrenaline had allowed him to keep from focusing on the rhythm that had slithered back into his head, the not-music that thumped and rolled in his skull. But the moment Prentiss drew his attention to it, Teig felt the fish hook set deep in his chest again. He stood up straight, forcing Prentiss to hold on, arm looped around his neck. Teig felt the lure, turned to peer into the darkness along the road. Several more people had come out, drawn by the horn and the gunshots and the screams. Or so he thought.

Sayaara did what anyone might do. She shouted to her neighbors and ran toward them. There were corpses on the road but these people were living and her instinct drove her to the familiar. Timir had shot the wolves that only a moment earlier would have kept his wife apart from their neighbors. Teig didn't know the language, so he could not be sure if Sayaara pleaded with her friends for help or cried out to warn them of the danger.

As if choreographed, the three dark figures in the street turned toward Sayaara. They began to shuffle toward her. Teig saw a hitch in her step, as if despite her desperation she sensed something wrong in them.

"Timir!" he barked, as he shuffled Prentiss toward the truck. "Stop her! Something's—"

But Timir had seen it, too. These neighbors had not come into the street earlier—those who now lay dead. They'd been lured outside by the urgent rhythm in the air, the song that dug into their bones. They didn't cry out to Sayaara in reply . . . but they did begin to run toward her, arms outstretched, and it was then that the woman realized something had happened to her neighbors. Something awful.

"In the truck!" Teig shouted. "Help me with him."

Prentiss snarled. "I don't need more help. Just dump me and move your ass!"

Nari looked up in fright and confusion, but she'd gotten the little girl into the front seat of the truck. Now she held open the door and helped Teig pile Prentiss into the back. Prentiss cried out in pain as he dragged his injured leg across the seat.

The people in the street moved swiftly. In the dark, these neighbors seemed to change, jagged fingers of shadow protruding from their skulls, as if these laborers and truck drivers and waitresses . . .

Ah, fuck no, Teig thought. *No way.*

It looked as if they'd sprouted antlers. Not at all possible. Not at all.

Timir ran after Sayaara, rifle in hand. He screamed her name. Too far away to help, Teig could only watch, his breath trapped in his throat, as Sayaara finally saw the things the night had done to her neighbors. Teig thought she would scream, but instead she came to a skidding halt and reversed direction. Sayaara stumbled once, running back toward Timir . . . toward the truck and the hope of escape.

"Teig." Nari grabbed his arm, drew his attention to the two wolves prowling around the corner of the bar.

"Get in the truck," he said, unslinging his rifle.

"But—"

The whipcrack echo of a single gunshot filled the air. Teig turned just in time to see Timir take a second shot. The three human figures raced after Sayaara as she ran toward her husband, only twenty feet from him. Now fifteen. Timir's shots had done nothing to slow them down, but he took aim again.

A growl sounded from the other side of the truck. The two wolves, stalking them. Prentiss started shouting at him, cursing at him to get in. Now Nari grabbed Teig's rifle in both her hands and used it to shove him toward the driver's seat. She hurled herself through the open driver's door, scooped Una off the seat, and plopped the silent girl onto her lap, then turned to shout at him.

Teig handed the rifle to her as he slid into the driver's seat. He reached out to slam the door. As he grabbed the handle, a wolf lunged from the darkness. The door slammed, and the wolf collided with the metal with a solid thump that felt nothing like shadows.

Even with the window closed, Teig heard Sayaara scream in pain.

In the backseat, Prentiss swore, his voice rasping with pain and fear. "What the fuck is happening?"

Down the narrow dead-end road between bar and garage, the first of the neighbors had caught up to Sayaara. He bent his head and rammed her from behind. In the scrum on the road it was difficult to make anything out, but Teig threw the truck into drive, cranked the wheel to the left, and turned toward the screaming. The headlights turned the whole scene into a garish diorama, as if the horror unfolding there were a bit of frozen fakery. Whatever the neighbors were now, the things jutting from their skulls *were* antlers. The woman behind Sayaara had impaled her, one long antler punched through her left shoulder as she drove her to the frozen ground.

Timir shot the woman through the forehead. She toppled over, dragging the impaled Sayaara with her. The other two neighbors paused, shying away from both rifle and headlights. The engine roared as Teig drove toward them, but Timir did not turn. He didn't dare.

Part of that good man had broken. He shouted his wife's name as he reached down and yanked Sayaara forward, not daring to do more to help her. Sayaara cried out again as she wrenched her body off the antlers that had punched through her back. Somehow she lurched to her feet and the other neighbors lunged.

Timir screamed at her to run. Screamed at Teig to save them. He pulled the trigger on an empty chamber and had just begun to turn the rifle around to use as a club when the two neighbors fell on him, thrashing him with their antlers.

Nari clambered over the backseat, barking at Prentiss to move aside. She threw open the back door as Teig brought the truck to a shuddering halt. Nari stepped out, caught the bleeding, crying Sayaara in her arms, then dragged her into the rear of the truck and hauled the door shut just as the wolves caught up to them from behind.

"Drive!" Prentiss rasped.

Teig caught a last glimpse of what the neighbors were doing to Timir. He ratcheted the truck into reverse, cranked the wheel, and backed up, trying to turn around. Something slammed into the passenger door, right next to the little girl. Out the window, he spotted another door opening, another neighbor emerging, this one larger than the others. Impossibly large. Then the wolf jumped up, punched its slavering snout against the window, growling. The little girl didn't even flinch.

He shifted into drive, hit the accelerator, cranked the wheel again and lost the passenger's side mirror when he clipped the corner of the garage, but the tires churned up the permafrost and they were rocketing back toward the highway.

Up ahead, the headlights illuminated the shape of another antlered man, different from the others. This one seemed barely a man at all, just shadow and the glint of yellow eyes, the ripple of a brown pelt.

Sayaara screamed, right behind him.

Nari pushed over the seat to point at the creature in the road. "The parnee. Don't stop. Don't stop!"

Teig tightened his grip on the steering wheel. If this was the parnee, he had changed, less human now than before. The truck hit him at forty miles per hour. The impact drove him under. The truck jumped as the passenger side tires bumped over him.

Then it was over. The path ahead was clear. The headlights found the highway, Teig tapped the brakes, then spun the steering wheel to the left. Just as he pulled them onto the Road of Bones, he glanced in the rearview mirror. In the red glow from his brake lights, the parnee stood up as if lifted by some unseen puppeteer. His shadow seemed impossibly long, larger than before, and with antlers that seemed to scrape the darkness. As he began to lope after them, the trees on either side of the road seemed to lean in toward him, drawn in his wake.

A quarter mile down the Kolyma Highway there was only the night behind them. Teig's heart still pounded in his chest, louder than he'd ever heard. Inhumanly loud. In the backseat, Nari whispered to Sayaara, promising she would be all right. Sayaara sobbed, repeating her dead husband's name over and over. He glanced at Prentiss, alarmed by his friend's silence, but the big Englishman only slumped in his seat, grimacing in pain, eyes glazed with shock.

Beside Teig, Una remained as they had found her, wordless and expressionless, entirely unfazed. Teig wanted to scream or cry or just to wake up from this nightmare, because this could not be the real world. Some people believed in ghosts, and he had always wanted to, but this wasn't anything as simple, as quiet, as a haunting. The things he'd seen—they had to be hallucinations. A psychotic break. He'd known people like that. He ought to ask the others what they'd seen but he bit his lip hard enough to taste blood, just to avoid asking any of those questions. He was so afraid of what they'd say, so fearful of the answers.

"Drive," he whispered to himself. "Just drive."

He took a deep, shuddery breath, sat up straight, and kept his eyes on the road, ignoring the pain and fear and grief in the truck with him. *Be more like the girl,* he thought, and it nearly made him laugh out loud. *That's right, Teig. Model yourself on a catatonic nine-year-old.* But he would do exactly that if he had to. Anything to make it to the end of this road.

He didn't know if Sayaara would survive her wounds, but he would get her and Prentiss to a hospital. Get Nari to safety. He would get this little girl to her great-grandmother. He would make it home alive, and find himself a different line of work.

The truck bumped through a pothole, rattled across ruts in the road, and for the first time he wasn't thinking about all of the bodies buried under the Road of Bones. He was thinking about the parnee, stark and patient in the glare of his headlights.

He glanced in his rearview mirror and saw only darkness, but still, he pressed his foot harder on the accelerator.

Teig had never wished so hard for sunrise.

12

Ludmilla understood zealotry, but never saw herself as a zealot. There were people of much more single-minded faith than herself. Her nephew Alfrid often complimented her on the strength of her faith, and though she could have argued with him, she typically resisted the urge. How could she explain to Alfie that her faith might be strong, but that did not mean she was without doubt? She had questions, of course. Doubts and curiosities. Her own grandmother had practiced an entirely different faith, lived and breathed a religion whose fundamental tenets were the sorts of beliefs Christianity had replaced in many parts of the world. Of course Ludmilla had questions.

In her purpose, however, she was entirely single-minded. Her little personal crusade, as she thought of it, was pure.

Yet even that was not without its moments of weakness.

Now, for instance. She stood in the dark, the cold gnawing down to the bone, and kept the gas can tilted so fuel would burble out and fill her tank. All of the walking she did, the moving and lifting, kept her fairly fit for a woman her age, but she could not pretend her little crusade had not begun to wear her down. There were four gas cans in her trunk. She was on the second one now, replenishing the fuel she had burned by leaving her car running as she moved up and down the highway, saying her prayers and singing funeral songs over the bones of people who'd been dead for decades.

The truth whispered in the back of her mind. A truth she rarely admitted to herself and would never have admitted to Alfrid, would never even speak aloud to the ghosts on the Kolyma Highway or in the quiet prayers in which she spoke to her late mother and grandmother. That truth made her feel dishonest, as if to acknowledge it aloud would be a betrayal of the purpose she had chosen for herself.

Tonight, she felt more exhausted than usual. Her neck had been hurting for the past hour and now it had spread to her jaw and down her back. Somehow she had pulled a muscle, and in Ludmilla's experience, that often led to a chain reaction, where a little muscle knot could radiate down to her hip and up into her teeth. Her left ear hurt.

She wasn't one to complain. Never had been. But her reluctance to give voice to the little pains that life brought did not make her immune from them. Growing old was not for the weak, Alfrid had once told her, and she had laughed.

Tonight she was not laughing. Tonight, her big secret was that she wanted to be home listening to Springsteen. In the summer of 1988, already in her late thirties, Ludmilla had gone to visit East Germany at the invitation of her brother and his wife. It would be the first of only three times she would leave Siberia, but it changed her forever. Still in the grip of Soviet rule, East Germany had teemed with people, and East Berlin had a life and a youth that overwhelmed her. On the evening of July 19, her brother took her to see the American rock star Bruce Springsteen perform live in front of the Berlin Wall. The authorities had allowed this concert to appease the growing murmur of rebellion amongst the East German youth, but instead of appeasing them it incited them to strive harder to break the stranglehold of Soviet authority.

Ludmilla didn't care about politics or government. Living along the Kolyma Highway, such things never really affected her way of life.

But that night, sweaty and dancing in front of the Berlin Wall to this wailing, raspy-voiced American, she fell in love with rock 'n' roll. She only knew half the lyrics to any given song, understood half of what she knew, and got most of the words wrong for the other half, but still, thanks to Bruce she spoke a little bit of English. Remembering that night tempted her to go home right now, make some tea, and listen to her old cassette of *Darkness on the Edge of Town*. But there were more prayers to be said tonight.

The spirits of the dead beneath her feet needed her to release them. She believed they had become aware of her, that whispers passed along the road from one set of bones to another, telling each other Ludmilla was coming and would set them free. She knew they needed her. So if sometimes she just wanted to rest and listen to Bruce, that would remain her secret—the thing she would never admit to Alfrid, and rarely even to herself.

The gas tank gurgled and she tipped the can down, pulled it away, and set it on the road. The wind snuck inside her hood, into the gap where her balaclava did not quite meet the collar of her sweater. It stung the exposed skin like rope burn from the hangman.

Too cold to dally, she drew a breath and hoisted the gas can up from the road, maneuvering it to the car's open trunk and depositing it into its place, second in the row of gas cans. A moment of lightheadedness struck her and she put a hand on the trunk, trying to catch her breath. With the cold and the wind, breathing did not come easily on the best nights, and tonight was no different.

Or perhaps it was. It took a few seconds for her to clear her head.

Ludmilla slammed the trunk, screwed the gas cap back on, and closed the flap, then went to sit in the driver's seat. A few minutes' rest with the heater cranked up high, that would be all she needed. No music, though. If she put on music, even Bruce, she would doubtless drift off to sleep, and she still had another mile and a half to do tonight.

She tried to catch her breath, wincing at the pain that ran up her arm to the back of her neck. *Get out,* she thought. *Moving around will help relax the muscles. Forget about home and Bruce.*

That got her moving. Now that she'd erased any chance of the car running out of gas, the only thing keeping her from completing the night's work was exhaustion and advancing age, and she wasn't going to let them get in the way.

Ludmilla climbed out of the car, took a breath, and slammed the door behind her. Exhaust smoke rose in plumes from the tailpipe, bathed in brake-light red. She forced a smile onto her lips and made friends with the frigid cold. The temperature bit into her but she knew she could survive it, that after losing fingers and toes over the years, she had mastered exactly what to wear and how much time she could be exposed before she got back into the car. She had hand warmers inside her gloves, foot warmers in her boots.

Inside her balaclava, very softly and in spite of the pain throbbing in her neck and back and arms—the bite of old age—she began to sing. "Tonight there's fallen angels and they're waiting for us . . ."

She frowned, angry with herself, both for forgetting the next bit of the song and for letting herself become so unfocused. The tune had stuck in her head. "Drive All Night," by Bruce, of course. Sometimes it snuck into her subconscious out there on the road, driving all night, but it was one thing for her to be distracted while driving and another to do so when she was meant to be praying.

A tremor of guilt went through her and Ludmilla looked down at the road beneath her boots. Still in range of that brake-light glow, she whispered an apology to those spirits around her, but a smile followed. They would forgive her. They knew her heart, knew how much she had dedicated herself to them.

She took a breath, cleared the song out of her thoughts, and then started walking again. Her boots crunched on the permafrost. Hands raised over her head, she began to sing, but this time her song became prayer, and her prayers became ritual. Now she could feel them again, so close she knew that if not for the mask that covered her face, she could have felt the breath of the dead upon her cheek.

"Hello, my friends," she said. "You know me. The whispers that reach you have spoken true."

Ludmilla looked down, certain that she could see the outline of their bones in the road, each ridge and rut and divot part of the silhouette of a skeleton. "Bless you all," she intoned. "Cast off the deeds of life that bind you here. The Lord awaits."

The wind gusted, the cold biting deeper, but her mind had gone elsewhere now. She kept walking, kept praying, her heart wide open. Ludmilla could hear their quiet voices and feel their longing, and their gratitude. Her feet grew numb in her boots, as they always did, and she ignored them, but she could not ignore the pain at the back of her neck and along her arms. She lifted her hands and began a new blessing. Her voice cracked and faltered and she had to lower her hands.

Her vision blurred, and so did her thoughts.

Ludmilla tried to reach up to massage the bridge of her nose. That sometimes helped, even through gloves and mittens and the balaclava on her face. But as she raised her arm, a fresh shock of pain punched her in the chest.

Thank you, a voice whispered in her ear. Many voices at once, all swirling on the icy wind. Ludmilla had heard the gratitude of the dead a hundred times, but this did not sound like simple thanks—it sounded like farewell.

No. She managed to turn. The glow of her taillights seemed quite close. It had felt as if she had walked much farther, but now it appeared that she had walked only the first hundred yards or so.

She drew a deep breath, mustered her determination, and started back toward the car. The spirits that lay beneath the Road of Bones had been suffering for decades, unable to move on to whatever world awaited them after death, and she had dedicated her life to them. But she had already freed thousands, and after decades, this next mile or so of bones could wait until tomorrow.

She needed rest, and tea, and possibly a doctor.

Shuffling back toward the car, she grew unsteady and nearly lost her footing. The glow of the taillights blurred. More whispers reached her, but after a few seconds she realized what she heard was her own voice, softly singing Springsteen.

"I swear, I'll drive all night," she sang, then smiled to herself because the rest of the line was about buying shoes, and she'd never understood that part. *Lost in translation,* she thought. *Americans are so strange.*

Pain clawed at her chest. Her shoulders pinioned protectively inward. Ludmilla stared at the blurred taillights still fifty yards ahead, saw the exhaust fumes swirling behind her car, and started forward again. One step. Two and three. But on the fourth step, her legs gave way and she crumpled to the road, clutching at her heart. Her vision blurred. She reached one trembling hand toward the warmth that awaited inside her car, the warmth that might save her life.

Beneath her, she heard whispers. She could feel the dead lying below her, and knew that for once, it was they who were praying for her.

She closed her eyes, and slipped away, still breathing. Heart clenched, but blood still pumping.

The killing cold wrapped its fingers around her, digging in. Frost settled onto her eyelids.

It wouldn't be long.

Nari would have given anything to go back to the morning and begin the day again, to wake up from this horror in her own bed, heart racing from a nightmare. But wishing could not erase this night, no matter how unreal it seemed.

"You're all right," she told Sayaara, in the language they shared. "You're going to be all right." Two very different things, she knew. The first was certainly a lie, but the second was an ambition.

They were jammed into the back of the truck—Nari and Sayaara and Prentiss. The big man made room as best he could. His skin had gone deathly pale, even a bit yellow, and a sheen of sweat glistened on his face, but he managed a tight smile behind his beard. They'd done all they could for him back at the bar. His bleeding had mostly stopped and he had that brace on his ruined knee. The doctors would have their say once they made it to the hospital.

While Nari struggled to get the coat off her, Sayaara wept and cursed God and the devil, and then passed out. There were three wounds in her back. Two were superficial, already clotting, but the third, where the antler had punched all the way through her shoulder, was worrisome. The bleeding had slowed on that shoulder wound, but not stopped. Nari wadded up a sweatshirt Teig had instructed her to grab from the back of the truck and pressed it against the back of that wound, then rested Sayaara against the seat.

Now for the front.

The truck rumbled along the road, silent but for the engine. Nari took hold of the edges of the hole in Sayaara's blood-soaked shirt and tore it open, exposing the exit wound in her shoulder. She forced herself not to think about how the wound had gotten there, drove out the image in her mind of those shadowy people, of the bloody antler and the way Sayaara had screamed.

And the other screams, as Timir died.

Nari's hands shook. She paused, fighting the emotion welling in her chest as she studied her unconscious friend. Laughing Sayaara, so in love with her husband, so happy with the life they'd made themselves in a place so many would have considered a frozen hell on earth. For them it had been paradise. Sayaara had liked to call it their love nest, though Timir would tease her for being such a romantic.

Nari knew peace could be found here, at the edge of true wilderness. But the trouble with living so far from other people was that when danger appeared, there was no one there to help.

"You're okay," Nari said, pushing her friend's hair away from her face.

She placed her hand gently on Sayaara's cheek, sad and frightened but unwilling to risk waking her friend back into a world where her husband lay dead in the street forty miles behind them. She had torn Teig's sweatshirt in half and now she folded the other half and pressed it against the bloody, ragged hole at the front of Sayaara's shoulder.

"Well?" Prentiss rasped.

Nari flinched. "Sorry," she said quietly, in English. "It's only that I am . . ."

Frustrated, she shrugged her shoulders. In the past few hours she had realized that her English was better than she would have believed. She had picked up much more over the years than she knew. But she did not have the English words to express the numbness and shock and dread inside her.

"I understand," Prentiss said, a gentle kindness in his eyes. "How's the bleeding?"

If Nari could have smiled, she'd have mustered one for him. She appreciated his effort to engage her, distract her. Prentiss had been grumbling and cantankerous at first, but now any pretense of normalcy had been stripped away. Together they had borne witness to horrors, had breathed in air filled with terror. They were survivors, and bound together by it. Nari had never been so grateful for a friend.

"Her back is . . . okay," Nari said. How did she say *clotting* in English? "The hole here"—she nodded toward the hand that held the cloth against Sayaara's shoulder. "It is smaller, but . . . ugly. But the bleeding is slow now."

Prentiss wetted his lips and gave a slow nod. "We'll be okay. Just need a hospital and a drink."

Nari flinched at this, and Prentiss must have seen her pain, for she saw the regret in his eyes.

"I'm sorry about Timir," the Englishman said, glancing at the unconscious Sayaara. "He seemed like a good man."

Her thoughts returned to nights she had spent as the unnecessary third, Timir and Sayaara welcoming her, laughing with her, letting her feel some of their warmth and love.

"He was very good," she said.

She shifted, muscles aching from being contorted in the backseat so long. Her leg bumped Prentiss and a little cry escaped his throat. She tried to apologize but he waved her away. His face had gone from pale to gray and she knew he needed room to rest.

Lifting the torn sweatshirt rag, she saw that Sayaara's shoulder wound had closed further. It remained bloody and wet, but no longer trickling.

"Watch her, please?" Nari said. "I am going in front. You need space."

"I'm all right," Prentiss lied, but his eyes were grateful.

Nari climbed into the front seat. Her boot struck the roof, smashing the dome light, but she managed to maneuver into the passenger seat next to the little girl. Una did not react at all as Nari nudged her more firmly into the middle of the bench seat, then took the time to belt both of them in. The growl of the engine and the rumble of tires on the road had become white noise.

Una sat with her head back, watching the barren road ahead as if entranced by every mile the headlights unveiled. Behind the wheel, Teig looked nearly as catatonic. His face had gone slack, his eyes dull, and at first she wondered if the drone of travel and the sameness of the view had lulled him nearly to sleep. Then she saw his lips purse slightly as he let out a breath and she understood that nearly an hour after they'd fled Olonkho's, he remained in shock.

"Teig?"

He kept his gaze forward. For a moment, Nari felt as if she'd become a ghost, invisible and inaudible to the living. Or given how vacant Teig's expression was, maybe he was the ghost, unaware that he'd left the world of the living behind.

"Hey. Teig." She didn't want to reach across Una to tug at his coat, so she gave him a wave instead.

Tightening his grip on the wheel, Teig gave a nod to let her know neither of them had become a ghost. He'd heard her, knew she existed.

"How are they, back there?" he asked.

"I am no doctor. But . . . not good."

Prentiss cleared his throat, nudged the back of the seat with his good knee. "Hey. Speak for yourself. I'm hanging on just fine."

Nari forced a smile. "You are not bleeding to death. If you say this is 'fine,' then you are fine."

Teig took his eyes off the road just long enough to glance at Nari. "Really. How are they?"

Instead of giving him the quick answer, she took a moment to consider. Prentiss might have been correct. He needed surgery on his leg and certainly would need to be treated for possible infection, but as long as they reached a hospital in good time, he would come out of this with nothing more than a limp and a lifetime of restless sleep. Sayaara had just become a widow and experienced hideous trauma, but if her wounds continued to clot, her condition was much the same as Prentiss's.

"We will be okay now." Nari looked at the little girl on the seat beside her. The glow of the dashboard made Una's eyes glisten. "Three quarters of an hour to the hospital."

Teig sank back into his seat, loosening his grip on the steering wheel. "So I can slow down a little? I'm afraid I'm going to drive us into a ditch, and then we'll all freeze to death."

A voice whispered in the gloom in the front seat of the truck. A single word.

"No."

Nari turned to look at Teig, and he at her, both with a confusion that made clear neither had spoken. Only when the little girl spoke again did Nari realize it had been Una's voice. She kept her expression impassive, eyes still straight ahead, focused on the icy road unfurling in front of their headlights. A single phrase now, but in Yakut.

"What'd she just say?" Teig asked, gaze shifting rapidly between Nari and the girl. "What was that?"

"You wanted to slow down," Nari replied. "She said 'drive faster.'"

Uneasy, Nari stared at the girl. Teig began to pepper her with questions in English, occasionally glancing at Nari for a translation, but Nari did not oblige him. In her mind she could picture the little girl sitting in an empty house, her parents and neighbors and friends nowhere to be found. An empty house in an empty village, until the wolves had come out into the street. Until the parnee had come out of the forest.

Una's sweet young face, so soft and sad, remained impassive. The way she gazed out through the windshield she looked almost unaware that she had spoken, as if the words had come from somewhere down inside her instead of from any conscious thought on her part. If Teig hadn't heard her speak, Nari would have thought she had imagined it, but no . . . the girl had not only spoken, she had urged them to speed up, aware of their circumstances. And she had understood Teig, who had been speaking English.

"Girl," she said in quiet Yakut, lowering her head, trying to will Una to meet her gaze. Then she asked the question that had been burning in her mind since they had driven out of Akhust hours before.

"What was that?" Teig said, eyes alert with fear. "What did you just say to her?"

Nari glanced into the backseat, where both Prentiss and Sayaara were now asleep or unconscious. "I asked her what we are running from."

Teig shot her a doubtful glance. "What makes you think she knows?"

"A minute ago, I thought we were safe," Nari said. "But Una does not think so. Which means she knows more than we know. It means she knows we should be afraid."

Teig replied with a smirk of disbelief. "I'm already afraid. Aren't you?"

Nari glanced out her window, peering into the dark at the forest across the snow. "I thought we were safe," she said again.

The soft sound of Prentiss snoring arose from the backseat. Nari turned back toward Teig, but he and the girl were staring out through the windshield again, faces slack. Teig's knuckles had turned white from the force he used to grip the wheel, but Una only sat calmly, emotionlessly, as if she had never spoken at all.

In the backseat, Sayaara grunted. Her breathing turned ragged. Nari peered over the seat at her, but she had slid down, mostly in shadow now, so it was difficult to make out the expression on her face.

"Hey, Nari," Teig said, his voice flat. Casual.

"Yes?"

Teig tilted his head to the left, drawing her attention to his window. "There's something out there. Pacing us. Right at the edge of the trees."

Of course there was. "Wolves?"

"I don't think so. I think it's something else. Something worse."

Ludmilla returned to the world slowly and in pain. The sharpness in her chest left no room for misinterpretation. It felt as if a knife had been driven between a pair of ribs at her sternum. If she'd had the strength to scream, she would have unleashed a wail of such sorrow and pain that the ghosts of the Kolyma Highway would have been haunted by it. But there was no knife, and no hand to twist it. Just her old woman's heart, overcome by age and exertion and the smoking she'd done for decades before her thoughtful nephew had finally persuaded her to give it up.

Heart attack.

The pain at the back of her neck and in her arms remained, but paled in comparison to the pain in her chest. She managed only small sips of breath, blinking her eyes, trying to clear her vision. Ludmilla whispered a prayer, the first time she'd ever prayed for herself out here on the highway instead of for the abandoned souls.

And what are you? she thought. *If you die out here, will you be any less forgotten?*

An absurd thought. Of course Alfrid would mourn her. He would see to her burial, with a priest and a funeral. Her spirit would rest in peace, loved and remembered, not like these poor souls. Yet a part of her could not escape the fear that she would be trapped here with them, and now that the thought had formed in her mind she could feel their yearning for her. Whispers of gratitude and sympathy reached her ears. She could almost feel them beneath the road again, as if they burrowed up toward her and wished to draw her down, keep her with them out of love.

"No." Her voice was a rasp. She blinked, still trying to stop the blurring. Half of her left eye had gone dark and she understood quite suddenly that this was not a lock of hair that had fallen across her face. Her balaclava had not shifted to block her vision. Heart attack had done it, or stroke, or both.

Ludmilla had assumed she would die in her bed. She had never thought it would hurt so much.

Lift your head. Get up.

Had those been her thoughts, or the whispers of the dead? She didn't care. They were necessary. Simply shifting her body, tensing her muscles to try to move, twisted the knife deeper into her chest and sent pain driving up her arms. But she moved, lifted her head. The balaclava had kept her face from freezing to the road. She sucked air through her teeth, would have screamed but the pain wouldn't allow it.

The car. Her car. The red glow of the taillights couldn't have been more than fifty yards away. Out here in the white silence, the world was so quiet that she could hear the engine purring. Still running, full of the gas she had topped off only minutes before.

Minutes?

How long had she been unconscious? She had no way to know, except that she was alive, which meant it couldn't have been very long at all. Had she been in motion, blood pumping, she could stay alert and alive much longer, but lying there in the road with the temperature down to sixty below zero or so . . . she couldn't have been unconscious for long and still be alive. And pain was all the evidence she needed that her life wasn't over yet.

Ludmilla gathered her legs beneath her, afraid to use her arms to lever herself up. The knife twisted harder as she rose from the road, and tears sprang to her eyes. She felt those tears freeze to her skin before they could travel the half inch to where the fabric of her balaclava clung tightly to her face.

Barely aware of her legs, she managed to shuffle toward her car, gaze locked on the taillights. The cold stroked her eyes and slithered beneath her hood, scraping the tiny strips of skin that were exposed, but it failed to inspire the old fear. Her lower half couldn't feel it at all, and the pain in her chest made the threat of freezing to death irrelevant.

The wind swirled in circles like a dog chasing its tail, and then swept up behind her as if she were a small child and the wind her doting father, a hand on the small of her back, hurrying her along even as he took some of the weight from her and made sure she kept her footing. In that moment if the wind had the strength, she knew it would have lifted her off her feet and deposited her in front of her car.

She also knew it wasn't the wind at all.

More tears fell and froze, but these were tears of gratitude. The ghosts loved her. The dead wanted her to live.

Barely conscious, she staggered along until she bumped into the back of the car. Fighting the knife that dug deeper, twisted harder, stole away her ability to catch her breath—or even to draw a breath—Ludmilla slid along the car until she reached the driver's door. Her vision went black and she felt the strength going out of her, thought she would die there.

Instead, she opened her eyes to find that somehow she had dragged the door open.

She spilled herself into the car. The pain of climbing into the driver's seat tore a real scream from inside her, the first time she'd had the wind to do it, but it only caused her more pain. The warmth blowing out of her car's heating vents would keep her from freezing to death, if only she could close the door. Crying, shaking, she managed, though it was the most difficult task she had ever attempted.

She collapsed on the seat. Her vision went gray, then began to swim with black. Ludmilla saw the knob of her radio and wanted so badly to turn it on. The cassette of *Western Stars* was in the player. It wasn't her favorite Springsteen, but she loved it just the same, and if she could turn the music on and hear his voice, at least she wouldn't feel so alone.

At least she wouldn't die alone.

Ludmilla couldn't lift her arm, not even enough to turn on the radio.

The keening sound that drifted from her lungs wasn't a song at all, just the sadness and the pain finding a voice. She would not freeze to death, no. Not yet. But if her heart didn't get her first, eventually the car would run out of gas, and what then?

Ludmilla felt herself slipping into unconsciousness but she managed to say another prayer, this one just in her head. Then she turned the little keening noise of pain and sadness coming from her lips into something resembling the melody of "Drive All Night." Weak and reedy, off-key, nobody else would have recognized the tune, but it wasn't for anyone else. Like the prayer, it was only for her.

Then, lulled by the rumble of the engine and awash in the heat from the vents, she allowed darkness to wash over her. Mercifully, it swept away the pain.

She did not dream.

13

Teig gripped the wheel so tightly the muscles in his neck and shoulders hurt. How far were they from the gas station run by Una's great-grandmother? *Fuck*. He'd lost track of both minutes and miles. Prentiss kept snoring in the backseat, despite the way the truck juddered over the ruts in the road. Sayaara huffed and groaned back there, too, and he thought she'd either fallen unconscious from her injuries or focused so keenly on her pain that she had no room for conversation.

That left Teig with Nari in the front seat, and the little girl between them. Una had spoken a few sentences in Yakut, startling the hell out of him and Nari, but now the girl had fallen silent again. With the growl of the engine and the rumble of the tires, he couldn't have said it was quiet in the truck, but goddamn, it seemed quieter than any moments he'd ever passed in his life.

"Are they still there?" Nari asked, breaking the silence.

Teig gripped the wheel so hard that his fingers hurt and he had to force himself to sit back and flex his hands and keep his eyes on the damn road. He glanced over the low snowbank to his left, across forty feet of mottled snow and into the woods that ran alongside the highway. Nari had asked if they were wolves, and he'd told her honestly he didn't know, though they'd taken great pains to seem like wolves.

"Okay, yes," he said, glancing to his left again. Shadows slid a few feet beyond the tree line, darting and bounding through the woods as though a forest offered no obstacle to them at all. "Yes, they're still there."

Nari settled deeper into her seat. Teig saw her staring down at the little girl as if both desperate for Una to speak again and terrified of what she might say. A hundred thoughts whirled in his brain, words he wanted to unleash even though he knew he ought to keep them chained in the dungeons of his head. He had impossible thoughts, but the things he'd seen since nightfall had already defied his definitions of possible and impossible, so it felt easy to slide further down that rabbit hole.

"Fuck it," he said, glancing left and right, then locking his gaze on the road ahead. The dirty white permafrost seemed the only reliable thing in the world right now. "Why are you looking at her like that? You think she knows something, you said. But like what?"

"More than us," Nari said again. "She talks when she wants to. So if she is not talking, she is . . . choosing to not talk."

"You think she saw what happened to the people in her town?"

Nari studied Una a few seconds longer, her gaze unsettled, and then blinked and turned away. Teig thought maybe Nari, too, didn't want to admit the impossible things in her brain.

"She saw something. I think she know something." Nari twisted in her seat and looked down at the little girl. "What do you know, girl?"

Teig felt his throat go dry. He stole a quick glance at them, striving to keep the truck on the road at speeds the Kolyma Highway had never been built for. Nari had one hand on the dashboard and glared at Una the way she might have at a vicious dog she'd hit with her car, afraid she had injured it, and afraid it might still bite.

Una's face was a smooth, expressionless mask, her body rocking with the bounce of the truck but no movement of her own. Her chest barely seemed to rise as she took a breath, as if she'd stopped breathing altogether. A lifeless thing. As if she had never opened her mouth to speak at all.

"Hey, Ariuna!" Nari said in English. "What you know?" She switched to Yakut, barked the question again, and then again. The third time, she grabbed Una by the arm and shook her.

Teig cringed, expecting Una to cry out, to whip around, to shout at Nari. Instead, the little girl stayed frozen, though Nari's grip on her biceps looked fierce and must have been painful.

"Let her go," Teig said.

He saw Nari's gaze flicker toward the windshield, saw her eyes widen in alarm. As she braced herself, he turned to face the road, already cursing himself for letting himself get so distracted. The truck had strayed left, with a turn in the road coming up. Teig twisted the wheel, heart hammering even harder. His fingers blazed with pain, too long and too tight on the wheel, but he held on tightly and drove the truck. He could feel the wheels beginning to slide out of his control and sensed another degree or two in the turn would send them spinning into the snowbank and maybe over it, down the slope to the right, into the trees. If they survived a crash and the cold, there were still the loping shadows to consider.

Teig held his breath, twitched the steering wheel slightly to the left. The passenger side tires plowed into the snowbank, tipped the truck to the left so that Una and Nari slid down into Teig, despite their seatbelts. In the backseat, Prentiss swore a blue streak and Sayaara let out a cry of anguish that sounded more like a wildcat in heat.

The truck thumped back down onto the road. Teig let up on the accelerator, but only a little. Heart in his throat, he used the palms of his hands to steer, letting the blood return to his fingers.

Nari sputtered in Yakut or Russian or something more comfortable than English, and he thought if he could translate these words it would have been a unique education. He'd been fascinated by her when he'd first seen her, that black cherry hair and her easy laugh, but he hadn't ever expected to get to know her. Certainly not like this.

Una remained silent and expressionless. Nari shifted back over to make more room on the front seat, but Una stayed where gravity had moved her, bumped up so close to Teig that he had to keep his right arm up a bit higher than was comfortable just to avoid elbowing her in the face. The girl unsettled him, but this close he could feel the warmth of her body and the protective feeling that had gotten its hooks into him hours ago dug in even deeper. The girl had started to creep him out, but in the back of his mind was the whisper of guilt, ever present, asking him to consider what Olivia would want him to do right now. His sister's ghost had never appeared, but she had managed to haunt him in other ways.

He glanced at Nari, knew the girl spooked her, too. But he told himself they couldn't blame Una if she had seen things she wasn't ready to talk about. If she knew what had come and taken her family and friends away and was too frightened to relive that horror, how could they hold that against her? Una was a survivor.

"We're gonna make it," he told her, a quiet voice meant just for her, though the others would all have heard. Teig glanced up at Nari. "Whatever she knows, it's not for us to worry about. We get her to safety. Shit, we get us to safety. Someone else can figure out what the hell is happening, and why."

He took a quick glance in the rearview mirror, afraid to take his eyes off the road again but wanting to check on Prentiss. In the dark, all he could make out was his friend's shadowed profile and a shoulder. Sayaara had slid so far down into the seat that he could see only the top of her head, the green glow of the dashboard creating a slight sheen in her hair.

"I thought you are smart," Nari said, her voice clipped. Cold.

Teig gripped the wheel again, focused on the road. Wishing he knew how many minutes were left, how many miles. "And now you think I'm stupid?"

Nari clucked her tongue. "You talk like wolves are behind us."

Teig had no reply. Nor did he bother to look into the woods to his left. He knew the loping shadows were still there, still pacing them, keeping up with a truck traveling seventy miles per hour or more. He didn't want to see them again, didn't want to think about them or tell Nari what she already knew—that wolves couldn't run that fast or this far, that they didn't slip in and out of shadows as if they were made of shadows themselves. Liquid darkness to fur and snapping jaws. That didn't happen.

So he didn't look to his left again.

Teig had his hands on the steering wheel and he had enough gas to get them to safety. Maybe he didn't know the others, but he owed that to Prentiss. He hadn't been able to save his little sister—he had been going to school and sleeping in the safety of his own bed while she suffered, while her kidnapper had destroyed her and then killed her and then burned her—but he could goddamn well save Una.

He told himself he didn't believe in fate or serendipity or any of that shit but a part of him couldn't escape the voice in his head whispering that maybe he'd been brought to Siberia for a reason. Maybe this little girl *was* that reason. Maybe after tonight, he'd be able to sleep. Maybe his life wouldn't always feel like such a disappointment.

The inside of the truck smelled like blood and sweat. The doors were frigid to the touch and the heater worked overtime, but the windows still had spiderwebs of frost spreading across the glass. But Teig could still see out the windshield and he could still drive.

"We'll be okay," he told Una.

And Nari.

And himself.

And—

In the backseat, Prentiss started screaming.

The burly Englishman had a scream like a lion's last roar, only it kept going. Weak as he must have been, Prentiss jerked up in the seat, smashed himself sideways into his own window. His skull bounced off the glass and a crack appeared, but Teig barely noticed the crack. He twisted in his seat, foot still on the accelerator, hands still on the wheel, trying to keep his eyes on the road and look in the rearview mirror and glance over into the backseat all at the same time, finding it impossible.

He tapped the brake. Slowed them down a little. Not thinking of the loping shadows at all. Teig whipped his head side to side, watching the road while trying to see just exactly what the holy fuck had happened in the backseat, because Prentiss kept screaming but now there were words in that dying lion's roar. Words that were mostly Teig's name.

"Get a light! Turn on the fucking light, Teig! Teig! Look at her, Teig! Oh, Jesus, stop the fucking truck stop and let me out and . . . Teig stop the fucking . . ."

Like that.

It all blew through Teig's skull at the same time, a dozen waves crashing at once. He glimpsed Nari's face, her lips opening wide and then wider, peeling back from her teeth in something about to turn into a scream of her own, like someone desperate to sneeze who can't quite make it happen.

Then Nari did.

She screamed like someone had just slit her open, and then her scream became a name.

Sayaara.

All along, little Una sat primly between Teig and Nari, safely belted in. No screaming, no turning, not a flinch. For an instant, just a glimmer in the midst of the unfolding chaos, Teig thought he saw her eyes shift to the left, not looking at him but past him, out the window at whatever loped in the darkness there. It made her more nervous than the screams.

Sayaara, Nari screamed again.

"Stop it! Jesus, stop fucking screaming!" Teig snapped.

He tapped the brakes again. Down from seventy to fifty-five. Now to forty miles per hour. In the dark of the backseat, Sayaara had curled up almost into a fetal position. Prentiss had lifted up his good leg as if he meant to kick her.

"Jack, what are you . . ." Teig started.

Then he saw Sayaara turn her head, and he saw the strange shadows back there. The shapes and angles that didn't belong.

Nari clicked on the dome light.

Teig saw the streaks of black blood on Sayaara's face and the bloody antlers growing out of her skull—growing even as he looked, lengthening. He heard the wet crackle of more skull giving way as the antlers thickened.

Now it was his turn to scream.

Later he'd tell himself he couldn't have helped but twist the steering wheel. What the hell was he supposed to do? He stomped on the brake, just the ancient caveman survival part of his brain reacting, but as his body recoiled from the sight of Sayaara changing in the backseat, his grip stayed firm on the wheel and the front tires turned to the right, sending the truck into a sideways skid. The screaming went silent, as if even Sayaara held her breath to see if they'd crash over the snowbank and tumble down the slope.

Maybe they would've, but the road was slippery enough that they kept skidding, the truck spun around and smashed backward through the snowbank on the other side of the road, where the slope went up instead of down. The truck carved off the top of the snowbank, hit that upward slope, then shuddered to a halt. The engine whined but didn't quit.

"Get her out!" Prentiss roared. In the backseat, he raised his good leg and smashed his boot into Sayaara's head. The antlers growing from her skull struck the window without breaking glass. She turned her malformed face toward Prentiss and spit on him, baring black teeth. Her eyes were wide and bloodshot, with hugely dilated black pupils inside a piss yellow iris.

Prentiss cried out curses to a God he'd never believed in. He reached back, unlatched his door, and fell backward out into the snowbank with a cry of pain that made him sound just as broken as his knee.

Nari scrabbled at her own door latch, muttering in Yakut. Teig thought it was terror mixed with pity for Sayaara. He heard the other woman's name many times, along with references to God. Out of the corner of his eye he could see that Nari had her arm around Una, holding the little girl against her, ready to drag her out of the truck no matter what it did to her to see her friend like this . . . whatever the fuck this was.

Teig slammed the truck into park. The engine's whine died down. His knee brushed the rifle barrel and relief washed through him. *No, no, you can't just . . . no.*

Sayaara spit again. The antlers scraped the roof above her head. Teig had been hated before, he'd been looked at with fury and disdain, but no one had ever looked at him the way she did in that moment. Was it Sayaara, hating him, blaming him for this, or was it the other thing, whatever had gotten into her when she'd been bitten in the street back at the bar? Either option made him feel like a child again, in the worst way. The wanting-to-cry way.

Her hand came over the backseat.

Just as Nari got her door open.

Sayaara's fingers tangled themselves into Una's hair, and yanked hard, trying to jerk the little girl over the seat into the back. Teig swore and sneered and grabbed hold of Sayaara's wrist with both hands, trying to break her grip. He saw her fingers in Una's hair, saw the way brown, leathery, bone-thin fingers were pushing out through the woman's flesh, splitting her human fingers. Thoughts went still in his head, leaving only action.

Nari pulled at Una, who'd remained near catatonic even now, as the thing in the backseat tried to claim her. When Una started to move, it was as if she had been moving all along. She grabbed hold of Nari with one hand and Teig with the other. Her foot shot out, caught under the dashboard, anchoring herself in a way that seemed like purpose not happy accident. The girl turned to look at Teig and her eyes had gone white as winter. As the thing in the backseat grunted and wrestled to drag her backward, antlers scraping the roof, Una's face crumpled into real fear for the first time.

"Felix, help me," the little girl said in perfect, unaccented English. "Don't let them take me." The voice seemed familiar, a ghost rising out of long-dead memory. Impossible, of course, but what was impossible now?

Teig let go of Sayaara's wrist. Una screeched, swore at him in what he thought must be Yakut. The winter in her eyes went whiter somehow. Teig grabbed the rifle. The piss-yellow eyes of the antlered thing in the backseat locked on the weapon, saw the threat, and reached out her free hand to grab it. Teig knocked away that hand and lunged, smashed the rifle butt into Sayaara's face. He struck the nub on the side of one antler, which slowed the blow, but the gun butt cracked her skull and Sayaara shrieked. Teig smashed the rifle butt down on the thing's wrist twice and finally she released Una's hair.

Nari hurled herself out the open passenger door with Una in her arms.

The hatred blazing in those yellow eyes drove Teig out behind her. He didn't wait to open his own door but scrambled across the truck's front seat and spilled himself into the snow. Into the cold. A gust of wind met him, sweeping under the open car door, scouring his bare face and stealing the breath from his lungs. He felt as if he hadn't been breathing at all in the truck, trying to live, desperate not to think about the thing in the backseat, but now he felt each desperate breath, and his heart pumped too hard, each beat a thump to his chest.

Rifle in one hand, he managed to rise. Behind him, Nari held a whimpering Una—or maybe the whimpers were Nari's. Teig raised the rifle and took aim at the truck. The dome light remained on, and Sayaara looked like some grotesque pantomime in the backseat. Blood slicked her face and hair. The antlers had grown so much that her head hung down, unable to rise because of the cramped backseat. Sayaara—the thing—whipped her head right and left in quick jerking motions, almost birdlike. The front passenger door hung open but she couldn't fit over the seat. Prentiss had gone out the rear driver's side door and Sayaara turned that way, as if unaware she could have opened her own door. As if she'd forgotten how, or the antlered thing growing inside her had never been inside a truck.

"Teig!" Prentiss screamed. "Jesus fucking Christ, Teeeeeeeg, don't just leave me here!"

"Coming! I'm coming!" Teig nodded to himself, as if he needed to confirm it. He'd been looking for a clean shot. The idea of shooting Sayaara, of killing her, set something off-kilter in his head. He knew this wasn't her, but they were so far into nightmare now that a part of him thought it all so unreal, so dreamlike, that it must be able to go back to normal. They must be able to wake up from this. Including Sayaara. And if he shot her . . .

He had no shot that wouldn't put a bullet through a window, and they needed the windows. They needed the glass to keep out the cold.

If they lived the next two minutes, they needed to avoid freezing.

He breathed in air so cold it'd make winter cry, but he marched around the front of the truck, through the headlight beams, and around to the driver's side. Prentiss lay on the road, dragging the wreckage of his ruined leg on the snow, smearing blood in his trail. Desperate, sad, confused by a life that had put him here tonight, Prentiss shot a pleading glance at Teig.

Sayaara crawled out of the backseat on all fours like she'd forgotten how to stand on two legs. The blood on her face and in her hair began to freeze the moment the wind hit her. A gust swept along the road so fierce it slammed the open doors closed. That rear door caught her left ankle, broke bone. The cry that came from her throat ululated and echoed across the permafrost and into the trees.

Prentiss swore at Teig. "For fuck's sake, Felix!"

Numb face, numb hands, numb heart, Teig lifted the rifle and took aim at Sayaara. As he did, the ground trembled beneath him. Not an earthquake, just a single boom, then another. And another. Confused, fresh fear putting the lie to his thoughts of numbness, he shifted over to put himself between Prentiss and Sayaara, kept the rifle aimed at the thing down on her hands and knees.

"What the fuck is that?" he barked. He shot a look at Nari and Una, who'd moved around to the front of the truck, then glanced at Prentiss. They looked as confused and as spooked as he felt.

The ground shook again and he heard the distant crash of tall pines toppling over. Teig turned toward the woods thirty feet from the snowbank that had swallowed the back of the truck. All the breath rushed out of his lungs. The moisture on his lips began to freeze as he stood there, gape-mouthed, unable to force his mind to define what his eyes were seeing. Something moved through the trees but this was no loping shadow. Trees fell, cracked, crashed . . . and then it stopped. Several hundred yards into the woods, something stood so tall that its silhouette blocked part of the night sky. Teig could see only the shape of it, as if it were invisible, yet where its shape loomed it looked as if snow fell. Like a blizzard in the shape of a giant stood looming in the distance, watching.

Una began to scream.

Sayaara turned toward her and lunged, Prentiss forgotten.

Teig took aim with the rifle and shot the thing that had been Sayaara right through the head, blowing out the left side of her skull and the antlers that had sprouted there. She collapsed in the snowbank, rolled onto the road, and lay there facing him. Still twitching. One side of her face had been destroyed, but a single eye remained and she glared at him, black pupil tiny as a pinpoint now, but that yellow iris blooming larger as blood began to spread through it, a film over the eye.

He felt the presence of the now silent, unmoving figure behind him, but he didn't turn. Maybe if he pretended not to notice, it wouldn't notice him.

"Prentiss, get in the fucking truck."

"I need . . . Christ it hurts."

Teig knew. He gestured to Nari, who understood immediately. She picked up Una and ran around to the passenger side, shoving the girl back into the front seat. Teig tossed his rifle into the back and helped Prentiss up onto his one good leg. It was harder than before. Prentiss had been stable, but now he'd lost more blood and more strength and with his size it took all Teig could muster to muscle him the ten feet to the truck, open the door, and dump him into the back. Prentiss groaned with pain that sounded like surrender, and Teig didn't like the sound of that at all.

As Teig tried to help him get settled, shifting him, Prentiss had his arms around Teig's shoulders like they were embracing. Prentiss grunted in his ear. "I'm gonna die out here, mate. I think we all might."

The chill that ran through Teig felt colder than anything Siberia could throw at them. He pulled back, held the open door, stared in at Prentiss. "Not a chance. You die out here and it's on me, brother. I won't live with that."

Prentiss closed his mouth, didn't express any further thoughts about what might happen next, but he didn't look as if he'd changed his mind.

"Fuck off," Teig said lovingly, and slammed the door.

When he slid into the driver's seat, Nari and Una were already back in place and buckled in. Una hadn't returned to her catatonia but she just kept her head hung, not looking at anyone. She shivered but he didn't think it was from the cold. A sheen of sweat had appeared on her face and that shivering seemed more like a fever.

"We are stuck," Nari said.

Teig nodded. He knew the rear wheels were in the snowbank. He wasn't stupid. But the truck had four-wheel drive and he'd rented it because everything he'd read told him it would be the perfect vehicle for moments like this.

The thought made him laugh. There were no moments like this.

He yanked his door shut, put the truck in drive, and eased his foot down on the accelerator as gently as he could manage. Too fast, and the tires would dig in. Instead, the weight of the truck rolled them out onto the road as if they hadn't hit the snow at all.

Teig exhaled.

The spinout had left them facing the wrong way, so he did a three-point turn slowly enough that Prentiss cursed him out from the backseat. Nari had her eyes closed, whispering something he thought must be prayers. Teig looked down at Una and the girl stared back with those white winter eyes that reminded him so much of the invisible shape looming over the trees off to the west.

Felix, he thought. The girl hadn't just spoken English, she had called him by a name he didn't think she'd ever heard.

As he sped up, he glanced out his window and saw the corpse of the thing that had once been Sayaara. Beyond her, beyond the snowbank, on the stretch between road and trees, a quartet of shadows had emerged. They cocked wolflike heads and watched as the truck pulled away, then they turned and dashed into the trees, where they loped along and kept pace.

Of the shape looming above the trees, there was no sign.

But in the rearview mirror, Teig saw one more figure. A shape he'd seen before, striding along the road in pursuit, as if he had all the time in the world. As if he knew with complete confidence that he would catch up to them in time. Tall and thin, with antlers of his own, the parnee walked on.

The truck sped up and Teig watched him getting smaller and smaller in the rearview mirror, until in no time the night had swallowed the parnee.

But Teig knew he was still out there. Still coming.

Hands shaking on the wheel, headlights searching the road ahead, he glanced down at Una again. Now that they were moving she had returned to her stillness, staring straight ahead, unmoved and unmoving.

She'd pleaded for his help. She'd said they were after her, or something like that. Teig had so many questions, but one burned brighter than the others—who the fuck were *they*?

It occurred to him, quite abruptly, that there was another question, equally important. Not just who was after this little girl, but why?

He wasn't sure he wanted the answer.

14

Nari wanted out of the truck. Despite the darkness and the murderous cold, and even in spite of whatever followed them, she wanted out of the truck. Anything to be away from the little girl.

"Stop," she said.

If anything, Teig sped up. He drove dangerously now, wide awake and focused on the road, but still more erratically than he'd been driving before. How many minutes had passed since they had left Sayaara dead on the side of the road? No more than a quarter of an hour, surely. How long before they reached this gas station Teig said was owned by Una's great-grandmother? It couldn't be far, not the way he'd described it. Half an hour? Less?

Nari turned to stare at Teig, trying to block out the presence of the little girl between them. "Stop the truck."

Teig flinched as if she'd shouted and looked at her as if she'd lost her mind, and maybe she had. "I don't think so. If you have to go to the bathroom, you'll have to hold on until we—"

"I want to get out." Nari heard the calm in her voice, the dull flatness, and wondered if Teig would understand she was in shock or if his own trauma would obscure that fact.

"You'll die," Teig said, as if that was the end of the conversation.

"If I stay in the truck, I will die, yes."

In the backseat, Prentiss coughed in his sleep. No snoring now, only labored breathing and the occasional unconscious whimper. She wondered why Sayaara had been . . . what, infected? Why Sayaara and not Prentiss? He had been bitten by those wolves, but Sayaara had been impaled on the antlers of the things back at Olonkho's. And what of those things? If Sayaara had changed, had they also been infected somehow? Had they started as ordinary people, just like she had? So many questions . . .

Nari pushed down her curiosity. She didn't want the answers—she just wanted to live.

Prentiss needed the hospital, but they would reach the gas station first. That was good. If they dropped the girl off before the parnee caught up with them, they might survive to reach the hospital.

Teig frowned at her. "You think you're safer out on the road than you will be when we get to the hospital?"

Nari exhaled sharply but did not bother to tell him she doubted they would reach the hospital alive. The little girl sitting between them kept very still, as if by making no movements she could make them forget the times she had spoken up. Nari turned to look at her, wondering if she imagined the slight upturn at the corner of Una's lips, as if the girl mocked her even now. Mocked them both.

"If you don't let me out, we put *her* out. Now, Teig. Stop the truck."

He shot her a confused sideways glance. "Put out Una?"

"How would you say? Dump her. Drop her. Put her out."

Teig glanced at the girl, and so did Nari, but Una reacted to the conversation not at all. As if she really were catatonic, or deaf and mute, but Nari knew Una was none of those things.

"We're trying to save her," Teig said. "Where the hell is this coming from?"

Nari looked down at Una again. Had the girl turned slightly toward her? Were her eyes . . . different from before? The truck hit a pothole and Nari nearly screamed simply from being startled. Teig kept driving as if they weren't having this conversation at all. Did he not smell the blood in the backseat or the strange animal stink that Sayaara had left behind?

Heart racing, Nari turned to look out the window. The night seemed darker than ever. Condensation had frozen on the inside of the glass. The cracked window in the rear driver's side door let in too much cold and even with the heat blowing full blast she could see her breath inside the truck. In the glow from the dashboard lights, she saw her own reflection and the ghostly images of Teig and Una. It felt safer, somehow, to study Una this way, and she had to remind herself this wasn't like the tiger pen at the zoo. There was no barrier between herself and this little girl.

"She spoke English," Nari said. Her voice caught and she cleared her throat.

"You speak English," Teig argued. "Can this wait until—"

"She spoke better than me, Teig. You heard it. She spoke it better than you. No accent. Nothing."

"Her uncle spoke excellent English," Teig replied, eyes locked on the road as he drove faster. Must be at least eighty miles per hour now, out there on the Kolyma Highway, with snow and permafrost beneath them. "Maybe she wants to be a tour guide, like him. It bothered me, too, at first, but it makes sense."

"You saw," Nari said, turning to look out the window again, watching Una in the reflection. "Sayaara . . . what happened to her. You saw the way she grabbed at the girl. You saw . . ."

Her head had begun to pound. Grief and fear and shock were churning inside her. Timir lay dead back in the road in front of his own bar. Now Sayaara, beautiful Sayaara, who had such a kind and welcoming heart and had treated her like a sister almost from the moment they met . . . Nari couldn't believe she was gone. It felt like a delusion, a waking nightmare. The change that had overcome her, the way her face had twisted, the antlers breaking through her . . .

Her skull. My God.

Breath hitching, Nari realized she had begun to cry. Angrily, she wiped the tears away. They would not help her, and it was too late to help her friends. She had suffered loss after loss, felt hollow inside, but she was still alive and she intended to stay that way.

"What are you trying to say?" Teig asked.

Cautiously, like he needed to hear it spoken aloud but feared the words to come.

"The parnee is not chasing us," Nari said, the words clipped, as clear as she could say it. "He is chasing her. And I think we should let him take her."

The growl of the engine grew louder as Teig accelerated. Nari glanced at the speedometer. Eighty-five miles per hour now. She felt a tingle in her chest as her heart quickened, and it wasn't at all pleasant.

"I'm going as fast as I can—" Teig began.

"Too fast," Nari said.

He shot her a quick, hard look, but only for a moment. At this speed, he had to keep his eyes on the road. The truck jumped and juddered, but it had been built for this and it was only a rental. Teig had to get it to the gas station and then to the hospital. After that, it didn't matter what happened to the truck, so maybe he didn't care. But they still had to get there.

"Teig, slow down," she said.

He didn't. "I'm not going to even try to say what's happened tonight. I only know that people are dead. I picked this girl up to save her life, just the same way Prentiss and I picked you up on the side of the road. Now I'm trying to save us all—"

"So am I!" Nari snapped.

Between them, the little girl actually flinched. Not catatonic at all.

Just pretending. Nari no longer cared—Una had already heard what she had to say.

"Stop the truck," Nari said. "Put her out, or let me out."

Teig's hands were fists gripping the steering wheel. "I'm not putting anyone out. You want her dead? I won't let you kill her."

Nari snarled words in Yakut. He thought she wanted to kill the girl? She was trying to save herself, and Teig and Prentiss, too. As for Una . . . Nari thought it might already be too late for her.

In the backseat, Prentiss began to cough. He cleared his throat, his breath becoming a wheeze. Nari thought he had lost too much blood.

"Teig, listen," Prentiss rasped. "There's something you gotta hear, mate, and I need you to really hear it. Take it in."

The road curved to the left. Teig eased down to seventy-five. The tires crunched on the snow and skidded a bit, but he kept the nose pointed south and accelerated the moment they were on a straightaway again.

"What's that?" Teig asked.

Prentiss grabbed the back of the seat and tried to leverage himself up. Nari realized he had never put on a seatbelt. Of course not, after the way he'd needed to be piled into the back of the truck. In her mind she could still hear him screaming as Sayaara changed, as she began to creep after him. Grief clawed at her insides, but Sayaara was dead. Nari had never met Prentiss before tonight, but he and Teig had been trying to save her life. She hoped he wasn't about to die trying.

"I know what's goin' on in your head, Felix," Prentiss rasped. "What Nari's saying sounds batshit crazy, but right now I'm not willing to doubt anything. Literally, *anything.* I'm not willing to put anyone out of the truck, not in this fucking cold and not with whatever's out there. But you're not thinking straight, Teig, so I'm gonna straighten you out."

"Oh, are you?" Teig said. "Jesus, Prentiss, can you just let me drive? I just want to get there, okay? It won't be much longer, I don't think. Can we just—"

"She's not Olivia, mate. What's happened to this girl, whatever happens to us or to her, this isn't your fault or your responsibility. She's not Olivia."

Nari saw Teig's face twist up, his jaw clench. Whatever words or emotions were caught in his throat, he didn't seem ready to share them.

"Who's Olivia?" she asked.

Teig said nothing. Prentiss sighed and lay back down with a groan. The engine rumbled and the truck shook and the cold coming through the cracked window bit deeper into Nari's bones.

They approached another curve in the road. Teig slowed again, but even less than the last time. The tires gripped the road, managing the turn, but Nari held her breath for a few seconds in doubt. As they made the turn, Una slid against Teig and the man let her stay there, as if she clung to him for protection and he was happy to give it.

Nari stared at Una. She hadn't been sure before, but now she saw the corner of the little girl's mouth twitch upward into what could only be the beginning of a smile.

Teig kept driving, faster than ever.

Too fast.

Growing old had taught Ludmilla many lessons. To young people, some would have passed for wisdom, but there were things she could have shared with her nephew and his coterie of friends that words could never properly communicate. Chief among those difficult lessons was the one about pain. Young people never understood their bodies, and how they were all connected. If you held a marionette, you could tug one string and it might move the leg but the arm and shoulder would also react. Likewise, pain. Muscles and tendons and nerves were far more in tune with one another than young people understood. They didn't know that hurting your ankle might lead to favoring the other, causing pain that soon moved to the hip, up to the sciatic nerve, into the spine and shoulders, the back of your neck, and your brain.

Ludmilla thought she'd earned a lot of wisdom where pain was concerned. Tonight she realized just how blissfully ignorant she'd been. Tonight, she was getting an education.

Pain had stripped consciousness away, and pain returned it. With a sharp gasp, she opened her eyes. At first it was just the back of her neck, pain like spikes at the base of her skull, but with the first eyeblink it stabbed into her left shoulder again. She tried to steady her breathing and felt the weight of the devil himself sitting on her chest.

She groaned, though if she were being honest, the groan came out as the kind of words that would have caused her to wash her nephew's mouth out with soap when he was a little boy. Words she hadn't even learned until she was nearly thirty years old. One of them was in English.

"Fuuuuuuuuuuuck."

It gave her a certain satisfaction, a weird relief. A little bit of rebellion against everything she believed in, everything she'd been taught. It felt like fighting back, and she needed to fight back right now. "Fuuuuuuuuuccckkkkk."

The tears had dried in her eyes. Her lashes were sticky with them. She thought more would come but no, there would be no more crying. The pain lingered, dug in hard, but fear spread atop it and suffocated it a little. Fear and sadness. It wasn't supposed to be like this.

The radio played quietly. Bruce. The Boss. The greatest thing to ever come out of New Jersey. Ludmilla had made people smile with such claims, because of course she'd never been to New Jersey and had only ever bothered to look at pictures of it the one time her nephew had done an internet search for photographs of Asbury Park, thanks to the title of Springsteen's first album. Still, she had no reservations. She didn't need to know anything more about New Jersey to know it had never produced anything better than this man and his music.

Bruce helped.

The heat blasting out of the vents in the car helped.

Ludmilla wasn't a fool, though. She exhaled and the pain clawed at her and she ground her teeth together so hard she couldn't even hear the music for a few seconds. She needed a doctor. More than that, she needed a hospital, and even then she thought it wouldn't matter very much. How long would it take to get to a hospital? To get into surgery? To save her life?

She choked out a laugh, or thought she did. It might've just been inside her head. She didn't have that kind of time. No time to finish blessing the dead beneath the road. The job would remain unfinished. Nobody would take up the mission once she was gone.

I'm sorry, she thought. *So sorry. Bless you all, every god and saint, every spirit of the earth and sky. I tried.*

Ludmilla knew she shouldn't have waited so long, shouldn't have let herself get so old. Her mother would have been disgusted, would have been dead set against it, called it blasphemy. But now she felt like a coward and a hypocrite for having waited all those years before beginning this mission, pursuing this purpose.

Her eyes fluttered and darkness flooded in again. Time passed and light returned. Light and Bruce and the warm air blowing from the vents. The rumble of the engine. How much time left before she ran out of gas? If her lips could have formed a smile, they would have. Hah. More fuel left in the car than life left in Ludmilla.

Consciousness ebbed and flowed but the pain remained.

One song ended. "Rosalita," she thought, though it all blurred for her now. In the quiet moment before the next song would begin, Ludmilla heard something miraculous. An engine, coming this way. The devil grew heavier on her chest, clutched her heart in his fist and squeezed, and she whimpered to herself as Springsteen played guitar.

A car. Maybe a truck. She wondered again how long it would take to get to a hospital.

She listened to the engine buzzing closer, and wondered if her heart would make it.

Teig saw the headlights too late.

His thoughts were churning so fast that he'd entered a kind of fog. Survival burned like a furnace in his chest, yet was somehow overridden by other instincts—save Prentiss, protect Una. Did Nari really think this girl was some kind of monster? Maybe her mind was a little broken—hell, no maybe about it—but who wouldn't be a little crazy after what she'd seen? What she'd lived through?

Living through it. That's the key.

Teig had gone a little crazy, too. He could feel it, tickling the back of his brain, down in the old caveman part where fear lived. Nari had to be feeling it, too, after what they'd just seen with Sayaara, after what they'd just done, after the antlers and those sounds. *God, those sounds.*

Teig had left a trail of disappointment and frustration in his wake for most of his life. He let people down as if that alone was his job, and now he was responsible for these lives. For this little girl and this unlucky woman, and for Prentiss, the brother he'd never had but who had chosen him as a friend. Had stuck by him when everyone else had decided to cut their losses and turn their backs.

Teig would not fail them.

And then he did.

His skull and teeth rattled in his head, the tires rumbling on the rough road. The cold had seeped in through the crack in the window. The glass had started to freeze. The truck juddered over the road and Teig could hear the little tics and pops as the cracks in the rear driver's side window continued to grow. The window wouldn't last very long now, he knew, but what could he do except keep driving? It couldn't be more than another twenty minutes to the gas station. With the heat blasting, they might freeze once that window broke, but not freeze to death. They'd make it to the old woman's gas station. Inside, she'd have something to cover the window, duct tape to seal it up. Something that would buy them time to get Prentiss to the hospital.

"What will you do?" Nari asked.

The words came at him slowly, his brain unable to ponder one more thing. Do about what? Prentiss? The total collapse of his purpose here? The people who'd died? What he would tell the police? The old woman at the gas station?

He shot her a hard look, realizing. "You mean about Una?"

Nari twisted her mouth up, glanced down at the girl between them, but didn't reply. As if she were afraid of Una. For the first time, Teig saw just how much space Nari had put between them. Yes, Una had moved closer to him on the bench seat, huddling close for warmth or protection, but Nari had also moved away, pressed herself as close to the door as she could.

Felix, he thought.

The little girl had called him Felix. And spoken in perfect, unaccented English. It had sounded familiar, the way she'd spoken to him, and it had reached down into his memories of long ago. But he knew that was his mind playing tricks on him. So the little girl knew English, so what? Her uncle Kaskil had been a tour guide, so that didn't seem very unlikely.

"I'm going to do the same thing for her that I'm doing for you and Prentiss," Teig said. "I'm going to save her."

The truck hit another pothole. The cracked window shattered. Tiny shards of safety glass blew around as the brutal cold blasted into the truck. Prentiss groaned, sent up a weak gasp of profanity. Nari swore, hugged herself for warmth. Una did not even flinch.

Teig swerved, but only a little. Startled, but he'd expected it. He kept his foot on the gas, the needle steady at eighty miles per hour.

Nari banged her hand on the dashboard in frustration. "Slow down!"

Did she not understand that this was all the more reason for them to hurry? That the cold only made it more urgent? Yes, this was her country, her territory, but it didn't take familiarity to not want to freeze to death, not want to let those loping shadows catch up with them.

The road curved to the right. Teig tapped the brake, dropped it down almost to seventy, trusting the tires to hug the road. Prentiss uttered a little prayer to a God he'd never believed in, and that scared Teig. He glanced in the rearview mirror for a second. Only a second.

Nari screamed his name.

Teig squinted, the oncoming headlights bright in his eyes. He knew he'd fucked up, but there was no time to be sorry. He stomped on the brake, the tires started to dig in, to slow down, but the truck hit a smooth patch and slid. Nari's voice filled his ears, pure sorrow and surrender. They were skidding toward the car head-on. He jerked the wheel to the right, trying to slide right by it, maybe rip each other's side mirrors off. Instead the truck spun out, the rear end whipped around, and suddenly the headlights were blazing straight at the driver's side door.

The impact felt like an explosion. Sounded like one, too. Shattering glass.

The airbag blew up in his face.

Then he was out.

Fifteen, maybe twenty seconds.

Teig opened his eyes to the grinding of the engine. The heater still tried valiantly to warm them, but the cold had been waiting for its chance and had made the most of every second that ticked by. His eyelids almost stuck together as he opened them with a groan. The crash had whipsawed his neck to the left and it felt as if he'd pulled every muscle. Bits of shattered safety glass filled his mouth and when he began to spit it out, he tasted blood on his lips and tongue. Carefully, he went to lift his hands to pick glass off his face only to find that he couldn't move his right arm.

Panic seized him. Teig twisted his head—pain shooting up his neck—and breathed a little sigh of relief when he saw Una plastered against his body, pinning his arm to his side.

Then he saw the blood on her face, the pale dent of impact. It took only a blink to put it together. The angle gave it away—her head had jerked to the left, just like his, only she'd smacked her skull against the steering wheel. If the collision hadn't blown out the driver's side window along with the windshield, Teig might have done the same.

"No," he whispered. Wincing with pain, he wiggled free of her, careful for her head and neck. "Come on, kid."

His words came out slurred. Whiplash concussion or just the cold? He didn't know.

With a shriek of metal, the passenger door rocked open. Teig looked up, angry with himself for forgetting Nari—and Prentiss. Maybe his head had struck the window after all. Nari had the door open and now glanced back at him as she slid her legs out. One hand on her right shoulder, the clavicle, where her seatbelt would have yanked taut, she bulled her way out and onto the road.

"Wait," Teig tried to say. It came out like a moan, so he tried it again and this time managed to form the word properly. He blinked, a flicker of anger igniting in him.

But who was he angry with?

Nari still massaged her right shoulder but she bent to look back into the truck and he saw the flare of her own anger. She'd told him to slow down multiple times and now those warnings came back to him. His anger seeped out like helium squeaking out of a balloon.

"Take her," he said, working himself around with great difficulty to undo Una's seatbelt.

Nari gave him a dubious look. She wanted nothing to do with the little girl. Teig knew that, saw it in her eyes.

"She hit her head," he said. "Help me get her out!"

For a second he thought she would ignore him, but if she left them behind, where could she go? In a less desolate place they could call the police and a tow truck. An ambulance would come, maybe more than one. But out here they were on their own, at least for now, and Teig wanted to take stock of their injuries and the damage to the truck.

Twenty fucking miles. He thought that was all they'd had to travel to reach the gas station. Might as well have been twenty thousand if they didn't have a vehicle to carry them.

He tried to set his thoughts in order. Get out. Check the truck. Check the car they'd hit and its passengers. Check his own passengers, and his own damn self.

Nervous, wincing in pain, Nari reached into the truck. Teig slid Una gently across the seat. Her hair veiled her face, but not completely—the dent in her head had become a bump, rapidly swelling. Bits of glass peppered her forehead and cheeks. Blood streaked her face, but she was breathing.

Nari lifted her out of the truck as if the little girl might explode.

Teig unbuckled himself at last. Head throbbing, he managed to look over into the backseat. Only then did he remember that Prentiss hadn't been belted in. When the window back there had blown in, he'd lain down on the seat, head on the passenger side, legs on the driver's side, which meant when the truck had collided with the car Prentiss had been thrown against that door feet first. One knee had bent properly but the ravaged left leg had been in a brace, which had crumpled. A metal strut in the brace had broken free and embedded itself into the meat of Prentiss's thigh. The broken knee canted at a hideous angle.

The only blessing was that the pain had knocked him out. Prentiss's chest rose and fell with shuddering hitches, suffering even while unconscious. Icy blood drooled from the fresh wound in his thigh, sluicing down the leg of his torn trousers to puddle on the floor of the backseat.

Teig might have wept for him then, but his friend was still alive.

"Fuck," he snarled. Then shouted. "Fuck!"

Nari called out to him. It wasn't the first time. He realized now that he'd heard her voice but not registered it. He wanted to rail at her for the way she'd distracted him, the way she'd ridden him about Una. None of it was her fault, but he wanted to scream at someone. Anyone would do.

Skull pounding, neck aching, he scrambled across the front seat and climbed out the passenger side. He had to pick up the rifle and scoot it ahead of him unless he wanted to climb over it, and once he had the rifle in his hands, he remembered they were being followed and that he might have occasion to use it. After that, he held on to the rifle like a life preserver.

"You wanted to get out and walk," he snapped at Nari. "Now you've got your fucking wish!"

Nari wasn't even looking at him.

Broken headlights cast diffuse illumination into the darkness, turning it all into a twilight dream. The truck's front right quarter had twisted and punctured the tire, which sat flat and useless. The engine still growled but the truck wasn't going anywhere without changing that tire, and maybe not even then. Teig took a sharp breath that seared his lungs. His eyes felt dry as the desert and when he blinked it was as if his retinas were covered with a fine grit. The wind lashed at them and he felt his body tense, ready for an attack he couldn't see, couldn't fight. Every time he had gotten out of the truck before this he had been wearing a balaclava but he had left it in the truck and his face and neck were bare. The air turned intimate, the cold slithering inside his clothes, caressing and embracing him, stabbing icy fingers down to the bone.

Even as the danger they were in really struck him, he looked at Nari in surprise. She carried Una in her arms as if all her concerns about the girl had been forgotten. Nari's focus had turned elsewhere.

The old woman stood in the road, just beside her open car door. Over the engine and the wind, Teig suddenly could hear the *ding ding ding* that reminded the driver that the door was open. He frowned, certain he also heard familiar strains of music, struggling to identify it. A saxophone. The rough growl of a voice. This old lady stood clutching both hands to her chest, halfway between prayer and pain, Bruce Springsteen drifting out of her car speakers. It would've been dreamlike if not for the night's terrors, and his pain.

The old woman took a step forward, then began to waver. Her brow furrowed but her lips bore a near beatific smile. Confused, Teig moved to help her.

"I'm so sorry," he said, before remembering that she likely couldn't understand a word he might say.

Her eyes were unfocused, as if she didn't see him at all. Definitely a head injury.

The woman stumbled and Teig caught her with one arm, rifle held out to one side in the other hand. He held her like a dancer who'd just dipped his partner. Her eyes were tight with pain, the skin around them crinkled and beaded with sweat. Her muffled voice rose from behind her balaclava, but of course Teig didn't understand a word.

"Nari, what's she saying? What's wrong with her?"

"Ghosts," Nari replied, as she knelt in the road, cradling Una in her arms. "Something about ghosts in the road. No . . . under the road. She wants to bless the ghosts. They wait for her, she says."

Teig held the old woman and managed to prop her up long enough to get her over to her car. He leaned her against it, and though she sagged a bit, she managed to stay upright. Her eyes were closed, but slowly they fluttered open again and she looked at him.

"Are you in pain? Can you hear me?" Teig asked.

But it didn't matter what language she might use to reply. He knew the answers. In the first few moments he'd thought her pain had come from the collision, but now he wondered if she had even been in the car when he'd smashed into it. She trembled and her breath hitched, and he was sure this was a heart attack or a stroke. For a second he felt like Dorothy in Oz, picking up stragglers on the Yellow Brick Road, only instead of the Emerald City, everyone he piled in the back of his truck needed a goddamn hospital.

Flat tire, he remembered. The truck wasn't taking anybody anywhere.

The woman pushed herself up, managing to stand. She clutched at her left arm, eyes bleary, and Teig wondered if she realized where she was. The wind whistled past the open car door, whipping around each of them, and though both vehicles were still running, their engines growling, the dread that had been gnawing at the edges of his mind since he and Prentiss first set out on the Kolyma Highway began to creep deeper into his heart. Twenty miles from the gas station or two hundred, the nothingness still yawned in front of him like the quietest, most beautiful of traps. The cold bit down hard, digging its teeth into them. He had tried summoning words into his head that might describe this kind of cold, but he felt as if he needed an entirely new vocabulary to achieve it. Teig wondered if Yakut had other words for the kind of icy reaper that stalked them now. A murderous air, a cold never meant for human beings to survive.

Something else crept into Teig just then. He'd felt terror and desperation, felt deadly cold and the nearness of death, felt grief and horror and felt the world tilt under his feet as every definition he'd ever had of ordinary and possible was simply erased. This new creeping something felt so different because he'd lost it and forgotten it existed.

Hope. It clicked like a switch in his chest. Urgency seemed to wake him up, but instead of desperation this felt like momentum.

"Nari, put Una in the backseat of the old lady's car," Teig said.

Careful not to jostle her much, he leaned over a bit and tossed the rifle onto the front seat. Taking the woman by the arm, he moved her carefully away from the vehicle, keeping her upright while he surveyed the damage. The front end had been partially stove in by the collision but no steam rose from the engine and the tires weren't blown out. Most importantly, the engine hadn't stopped running.

Nari might have argued with him, asked for explanation, but Teig had already realized she was smarter than he was. She'd understood immediately. The old woman's windshield had been shattered by the impact but the car could be driven. They could wait out there on the road, but it was late at night and the chance of someone happening to drive past and rescue them offered terrible odds. Traveling twenty miles with a blown-out windshield when it was at least fifty below zero . . . that wouldn't offer safety or comfort. There would be frostbite or worse. But he thought that with the heater blowing, they would at least get to Una's great-grandmother alive.

"What's her name?" he asked. "Can you ask her?"

"Ludmilla," the old woman croaked. "Is my name."

So she spoke a little English after all. He frowned, trying to remember where he'd heard the name recently.

"All right, Ludmilla. I've got you." He kept the pale old woman on her feet while Nari opened the back door and set Una down so the girl could climb in.

The space inside the car would be cramped. Una, Nari, and the old woman would have to fit in the backseat so Teig could get Prentiss in the front. He would need Nari's help to move Prentiss and even then it wouldn't be easy, but it had to be done or his friend would either freeze to death or bleed to death, and Teig wasn't about to let either of those things happen.

"It's okay," he said to Ludmilla, as the old woman exhaled a long breath, almost like surrender. "Hey. We're going to get you to a hospital."

Her eyes narrowed at that. Her English might be limited, but she knew that word and it upset her. Ludmilla shook her head. Fighting back pain, she tried to extricate herself from Teig as if she didn't want his help.

"Hey, stop it," Nari said in English, before rushing into a torrent of worried Yakut. Even as she guided Una from the UAZ into the backseat—the girl sliding into the car as if she were half-asleep—Nari barked commands at the old woman.

Ludmilla shook her head back and forth, lifted a wagging finger in admonition, and kept up a stream of Yakut that evidently rejected Nari's points.

"What the hell is—" Teig began.

Ludmilla dropped to her knees on the road. Teig cried out and reached for her, but she shook off his hand and started to caress the ruts in the permafrost, gazing lovingly at the ground.

"The ghosts," Nari explained, but Teig understood. The old woman thought there were bodies buried under the road. Given the story of the Road of Bones, Teig was sure she must be right, hundreds of thousands of times over.

"Tell her if she doesn't come with us right now, she's going to be one of them," Teig said.

But Nari only gave him a sad glance. "She knows. I think it's what she wants."

Teig felt his momentum ebbing just a little as he stared down at the woman on her hands and knees in the road. Ludmilla might be dying, right there in front of him. Maybe Nari was right and she wanted it that way, but how could she expect him—hell, anyone—to stand there and watch her die or, worse yet, take her car and leave her behind in the road.

"No," he said. "Help me with her."

He went down on one knee, speaking quietly to Ludmilla in English, hoping she could understand and that she'd cooperate. If she would just pass out, he would load her into the car. Instead she shook her head, brushed his hand away, and began to pray. At least he thought they were prayers, given the rhythm of the words and the reverential tone. He tried again.

"Teig," Nari rasped.

He heard her urgency and bristled. Teig knew they were in a hurry.

"Teig . . . look."

His heartbeat quickened at her tone. The ice crunched under his boots as he turned, Ludmilla forgotten. Teig stiffened, staring at the truck he'd left running, slewed sideways across the road with Prentiss sprawled unconscious across the backseat.

Just behind the truck, over the snowbank, a pair of reindeer looked back at him. Their eyes were black and glistening. Patient, and knowing.

In the backseat of Ludmilla's car, Una unleashed her little-girl scream and began to pound the seat in front of her as if that might make the car move. She wanted them to get in the car and drive away as far as the engine would allow, and Teig would have done it . . . but not without Prentiss.

He started to call out his friend's name, thinking if he were conscious, maybe they could make it. Then he paused as a thought struck him. In this part of the world, reindeer were common. He gave a small laugh, watching the big, lumbering animals. These were no loping shadows. These weren't wolves.

The first of the reindeer rose up to stand on its hind legs and stared at Teig as if daring him to move or speak. The other lumbered down the snowbank and also rose. Their bodies changed as they stood, becoming towering, manlike things, but their antlers remained. Antlers, and those black, glistening eyes.

The one nearest the truck ripped open the back door, reached inside, and dragged Prentiss onto the road. Pain shot him awake and Prentiss began to scream. The deer staring at Teig seemed almost to laugh as the other stomped its hooves and climbed the snowbank, dragging Prentiss by his good leg.

The reindeer dashed two-legged across the snow, running toward the trees with Prentiss skidding and screaming along behind them.

Teig heard it clear as a bell—Prentiss screamed his name.

In the back of Ludmilla's car, Una fell silent.

15

Ludmilla saw it all unfold through eyes blurred with pain. These people were strangers, but she knew their names from their shouting. The wind howled down the highway, whipped past the cars. The engines purred and the ghosts whispered in her ears. The man—Teig—screamed for his big, bearded friend, who'd been dragged off across the snow. Teig ran to the snowbank, then shot a frantic glance back at her.

Loss. Shock. Surrender. She saw them in his shifting expression as he realized that all choices had been taken away from him. What could he do now, this bereft American, ill-prepared to have his eyes opened like this?

She saw the moment he made up his mind.

Teig ran back toward her. Ludmilla remained on her hands and knees on the road. The woman, Nari, took her by the shoulder and helped her rise to sit on her haunches like a dog. Nari spoke but her words blended together into a slurred babble, and Ludmilla wondered if part of her own brain had begun to die. Her heart must have stopped beating by now. She imagined it hardening, blackening, a stone fist clutching the dying muscle and squeezing. Ludmilla's mother always said she had a hideous imagination.

"Get her up," Teig barked at Nari. "Put her in the car, now!"

Ludmilla understood. American music had taught her enough English to get most of it, but more than that, she understood the fear on his face, the way he glanced at the little girl in the backseat of the car—the little girl who wasn't what she appeared to be. She saw the way his eyes squinted, on the verge of sobbing or screaming in desperation, the way he stood, the urgency in the set of his shoulders.

Nari tried to pull at her arms, speaking Yakut to her, cajoling her into rising—into getting back into the car. Her own car, whose driver's door hung open still. Her Springsteen mix had come round to "Somewhere North of Nashville," off the melancholy masterpiece *Western Stars*. Ludmilla thought it was as beautiful a funeral song as she could ask for.

"No," she said, pushing Nari's hand away.

Pain made her grit her teeth. It might have looked like a smile.

"You . . . go . . ." she said, managing a bit of English.

Nari crouched by her, held Ludmilla by the shoulders, searching her eyes with a look of horror. "We're not leaving you here alone to die," she said in Yakut.

Ludmilla would have smiled but pain made it impossible. She nodded slowly, and replied in their shared tongue. "I won't be dying alone. I am in beautiful company."

She inhaled, relishing the warmth of the air. Illusion, she knew. The cold would have killed her if her heart hadn't gotten to her first. But pain had changed Ludmilla. Her face felt flushed with heat. The prayers she'd spoken for years and those she'd said tonight seemed to rise up around her now.

"Goddamn it!" Teig shouted, rushing at her, only halfway looking at her as he kept watch on the snowbank where the monsters had dragged Prentiss away. "Get her in the car!"

He tried to grab her other shoulder. Ludmilla prepared to push him away. Just before his fingers would have touched her, she saw a gentleness sweep over him, as if he realized only then what the moment had brought.

His eyes softened as he looked down on her. "I'll carry you. I'll be careful."

Nari rose to her feet. "No. Let's go."

Teig shot her a horrified glance, so easy to read. Did she really want to abandon this dying old woman? his expression asked. The sadness on Nari's face was her only reply. Of course she didn't want to leave Ludmilla behind, but there was no saving her. Nari's expression said it all, and Ludmilla agreed.

"Go," the old woman said to Teig, in English. "I'm okay."

Nari and Teig shared a look that was an entire conversation in three heartbeats, a moment in which they had to decide if they were willing to pick her up and force her into the car.

Nari spoke in Yakut again. "We'll be right back," she said.

But Ludmilla could see she wasn't certain they would make it back. Despite the fist crushing her heart, Ludmilla forced herself to smile for a moment just to give Nari the absolution she would need later. If she lived.

"Go. Let's go!" Teig snapped, rushing for the car.

Ludmilla watched him go, watched the regret in Nari's eyes as she followed. In the backseat of the car, the little girl who was not what she seemed realized the decision had come and started to get out of the car as if she meant to flee on foot. Nari scooped her up, shoved her into the backseat, and climbed in after her. The little girl began to shriek as if she were being abducted. One thing seemed clear, she didn't want to go where Teig intended to take her.

Teig slammed the driver's door, muffling Springsteen. But that was all right. Ludmilla would have his voice in her head and her heart. He was with her now, whispering in her ear just like the ghosts of the men and women who lay dead beneath the road. They watched her. She felt their eyes on her and their love for her, and that comfort wrapped itself around her in a beautiful embrace. She sagged a bit but remained on her knees, waiting to join them.

The engine of her car roared. The tires skidded as Teig pulled around his useless truck, revved it up, and drove right through the snowbank. The car wouldn't make it far on the snow and the permafrost, but that was all right. Ludmilla had watched the hornedones drag the huge man across the ground. She knew they hadn't gone far.

They were waiting.

Prentiss felt as if he were flying. A shushing noise filled his ears and his head bobbed. His shoulder jerked hard, pain ran up his spine, but mostly he felt cold and swift, like the angels had taken him before his time. The silky smoothness of his coat hissed along the snow. His head bumped again and he knew this wasn't flying. This was dying.

Darkness took him . . .

He inhaled sharply, lurching back to consciousness as his body rolled down a small slope and came to rest against the base of a tree. The wreckage of his left leg smacked the trunk before he came to rest, limbs splayed, but he felt nothing. Pain radiated up from his hip, into his spine, but from the leg, only numbness. If it had been amputated he might at least have phantom limb pain, but no—the leg remained attached to his body, it had simply stopped sending any kind of signals to his brain. Maybe that was a mercy, but it made him want to scream.

Snow had packed the inside of his jacket and up into his shirt, a product of being dragged across the ground.

Head muzzy from blood loss or concussion, Prentiss managed to hoist himself up on an elbow enough to look around. Something growled behind him and a musky animal stink enveloped him, so strong he winced and held his breath. He remembered the wolves that had attacked, the ways his flesh had torn, but when he turned toward the sound and saw the shape looming in the darkness nearby, it was no wolf.

He remembered the silhouette of moments before, the thing that had torn away the door of the truck and grabbed his leg. Though it crouched, bent and crooked as if unsure what sort of beast it wished to be, its antlers made it seven or eight feet tall. Its eyes might have been yellow or gold but when it blinked they seemed black, not like night or ebony or oil, but like someone had punched holes in the fabric of the world and inside its eyes were hints of what it might look like on the other side.

The beast grabbed him by the beard. Prentiss groaned as it dragged him up off the snow. He tried to balance on one leg as it bent its head to sniff at him, face to elongated face. It huffed out a breath. Prentiss smelled the animal stink of its exhalation, but its breath should have been hot and moist. Instead, he felt only cold. Colder even than the brutal night wind. Frost formed on his face . . . and then the beast let him go. Prentiss's ruined leg gave way and he flopped to the ground. When his face struck the snow, the frozen skin cracked.

He lay there as another set of hooves stepped over him as if he weren't there at all. Too weak to cry out his fear or protest his pain, he began to weep. His father had been a gentle man, but his mother had grown up in a household that taught her to despise emotion as weakness, especially in a boy. Even as a toddler, she'd shamed him if he cried.

Tonight, she'd never have forgiven him, but he wept just the same. His body had nothing left to give.

The second Nari shut the car door, she realized what a mistake she'd made. Teig had rescued her from the side of the highway when her SUV broke down. He was the one who got her out of the abandoned town where all this had begun. She doubted she'd have survived the attack at the bar without him. So when he shouted at her to get into the only drivable vehicle out there on the frozen goddamned highway, Nari had climbed in. Worse, she'd pushed Una into the car and climbed in after her. This little girl with the devil in her eyes.

Now she wanted out.

"Teig, stop!" she shouted. "Please!"

But he had gone beyond hearing her. Beyond thinking of anything but Prentiss. Nari held on to the headrest of the seat in front of her while he spun the steering wheel, the car skidding in a half turn before he gunned the engine. The car leapt toward the snowbank and all the breath went out of her. What had she been thinking?

She screamed his name again. Just his name, in a new and primal timbre, as the nightmare began to crystallize into truth. In the dark, full of fear, fighting for life, the human mind could slip into pure instinct. Survival mode blotted out rational thought, made it almost impossible to think about anything but shelter and safety, the ability to take your next breath.

The front end of the car thrust upward as they hit the snowbank. Winter air blasted through the broken windshield and Nari ducked down for protection from the vicious cold. The car slammed down on the other side of the bank, crunching a few inches of hard-packed snow. The winter tires tore through it, found purchase on the permafrost below, and momentum did the rest. The car wouldn't get far, but it didn't need to. She squinted against the frozen wind and saw the dark shapes thirty yards ahead, lanky, bent, looming things that stood at the tree line and watched them come. One of them reached down and dragged the portly form of Prentiss to his feet.

"Fuckers!" Teig roared, laying on the car horn like some kind of war whoop. "Fuckerrrrrrs!"

Nari looked at the door handle beside her. She could pop the door open and throw herself out. She might break something, but maybe not. Maybe she could make it back to the truck, drag Ludmilla into it, for shelter at least. If the things got what they wanted from Teig and Prentiss, maybe they wouldn't kill her. Maybe they'd leave her alone long enough to change the tire. Maybe she wouldn't freeze to death. Maybe, maybe, maybe.

She glanced back the way they'd come.

The parnee stood at the spot in the snowbank where the car had just burst through, watching them go.

Beside her, Una shook off the blow to her head and began to shriek again.

The little girl, shrieking, should have woken all sorts of feelings inside Nari, the desire to protect a child. But she looked over just in time to see Una scrabbling at her own door handle, trying the same escape Nari had considered only seconds before. The car slewed, fishtailed, began to slow, and Teig hammered the accelerator again, cursing the tires, hoping to get a little more traction, the nose of the car aimed right for the antlered men standing in front of the trees.

Nari grabbed Una by her hair just as the girl got her door open. The door swung wide. Nari yanked her back. Una screamed, legs kicking out in front of her, boots punching the door wide open until the car bounced into a rut and the door swung closed.

The scream made Teig break focus for the first time. He faltered a little, started to glance over his shoulder.

"Fucking drive!" Nari screamed at him.

Una clawed at Nari's hands, tried to rip free, but Nari held on to fistfuls of her hair.

"What are you doing?" Teig barked.

Una twisted around, still fighting to free her hair, and glared at Nari with eyes that could never belong to a little girl. The hate in those eyes, the intelligence and malignance, were so much older.

Suddenly Nari didn't want to get out of the car anymore. Not yet. Not until this was over. All her life, she had just yearned to be free, to sever herself from the weight of obligation, but if she did not see this through, she would never be free of it.

Ignoring Una's screams, she twisted her hands more tightly into the girl's hair and glanced up, meeting Teig's gaze in the mirror.

"They want her," she said. "We give her."

The snow deepened. The tires sank. The car caught one last bit of traction and leapt forward with enough force to lodge the front end in a little gulley just shy of the tree line. Barring a lot of work with shovels, the car would be there until late spring.

Teig forced the car door open. The snow stopped it from swinging all the way, but he forced his way out. He glanced back inside, looked at Nari and Una. The way Nari had her fingers wrapped in the girl's hair, like they were kidnappers instead of rescuers, made his stomach turn. He thought of a van and a puppy. No, he didn't like this at all.

"You hold on to her," he said, "but for her safety, not ours. We're all going home after this."

Nari went pale. Her upper lip curled. "You are fucking crazy."

"Just do it." Teig reached back into the front seat and grabbed the rifle.

He'd avoided looking at the creatures . . . *the antler men*. Or the trees, or the shadows, or even Prentiss. Now he held his breath, swallowed hard, and looked up. There were four of them that he could see, these enormous reindeer who'd unbent themselves, who'd stood up out of beasthood and become something else. But he saw eyes back in the woods and knew there were others. Low to the ground, in amongst the trees and the reindeer, several of those loping shadows slithered in the brush, afraid to come out or held in abeyance should they be needed.

Teig let his gaze drift from beast to beast, breathing in shallow, ice-burnt gasps. The ground shook beneath his feet. Snow shifted and cracked, trees swayed. He looked up and to his left—to the north—and saw the tops of trees shunted aside, some of them cracking off. The air went still, the wind died, and all was silent except for the rustle of those trees and the shaking of the world.

What have I done?

In the space between eyeblinks his mind traced his path backward. How had he come to this place? This moment, from which there could be no retreat? All he had wanted was a new beginning, a way to rebuild his life and reputation, to make his old friends understand he had never meant any harm, that he wanted—no, deserved—their forgiveness. All he had wanted was to prove his dreams were not beyond his reach, and to reward those who'd kept their faith in him. Make it worth their while.

But only Prentiss had stuck by him.

And now . . .

One of the unbent creatures held Prentiss by the back of his jacket and lifted him as effortlessly as if he were a rag doll. Prentiss had blood on his swollen face and snow caked into his beard. His left leg had been twisted around at the knee so his foot pointed the wrong direction. Little icicles of blood had formed on the leg of his trousers and on his boot. But he twitched, and he blinked, bleary-eyed but alive.

Still alive.

Teig had brought him here, this man who'd been a brother to him.

The ground shook again. The antler man lifted Prentiss a bit higher and shook him, a warrior brandishing a prize for the enemy to see. Prentiss's head lolled back, his mouth hung open, and he screamed out the despair of the truly lost.

Back in the woods, the loping shadows began to howl along with him, but Teig knew it was not harmony, but mockery. He felt Prentiss's despair, felt the hopelessness of this moment. They'd come to a dead end in the cold and the dark. The winter dug into him now that he had stopped moving, now that his adrenaline slid from fury and terror into funereal dread. His eyelashes stuck together when he blinked. The moisture of his breath turned to icy crystals on his lip and chin. Despite his gloves, his fingers grew numb. Only the pain in the little bones in his hands remained, and he knew that would fade, too.

He lifted the rifle and laid the barrel atop the door, in case the lack of feeling in his fingers interfered with his aim.

"Give me back my friend, you fuckers," Teig said.

For punctuation, he shot one of the antler men through the left eye, blowing out the back of its skull.

16

Ludmilla rested on her knees, there in the road with her head hung and her eyes closed. Sunk down like that, her body warm as midsummer though the wind whisked around her, she felt her pain bleed away and a sweet contentment settle in. She listened to the rumble of the useless truck's engine but it blended with the whisper of the air along the road and across the snowbanks, and with the quiet prayers that reached her—prayers not from her own lips, but from the lips of those long dead. They sang to her, prayed for her, just as she had done for them.

Snow crunched, breaking the quiet symphony of engine and ghosts, and she looked up to see a musk deer approaching. The moment their eyes met, the musk deer froze as if caught in the midst of something taboo. Ludmilla tried to smile at it, unsure if her face complied with the urge, but the musk deer's ears twitched and it took two more steps toward her. Its head cocked and it regarded her with the curiosity of animals, the fascination that could only be born from innocence.

Then a bear stepped up behind it.

There were others as well. Ludmilla felt a real and beatific smile stretch her mouth as the animals climbed over the snowbanks and began to investigate her. A trio of wolverines flashed their teeth as they trotted south along the road. One attacked another and they gamboled together for several seconds until the third cuffed them and they renewed their interest in Ludmilla. Beyond them, long shadows strode along the road. They were upright at first, but soon they dropped to all fours and as they grew nearer they resolved themselves into wolves, though Ludmilla had no confidence that they had begun the night that way.

A massive figure came up over a snowbank and leapt atop the idling truck that the strangers had left behind. A Siberian tiger.

My God, it's beautiful. She exhaled, though each breath now was more precious to her than the last. There were only five hundred or so Siberian tigers left in the world, and this one had come to see her. The tiger growled softly and then fell silent, or the rumble in its chest merged with the rumble under the truck's hood. Other animals arrived, including several more brown bears, one of whom had half a dozen brown chipmunks nestled in the fur on his back, their little heads peeking up for a look at Ludmilla and the truck.

From across the snowy ground there came the crack of a rifle. The shot echoed and most of the animals turned to look eastward, toward the sound. Two wolves stood on their hind legs to get a better look, their backs too straight for them to be ordinary animals, but Ludmilla had known from the start that these weren't simple beasts. Her grandmother had been a shaman and though she had never been in the presence of so many forest spirits, Ludmilla could see the wisdom of age in their eyes and taste the ancient flavor of their breath.

Snow crunched. Hooves clacked on the road. She looked northward again, where a pair of the largest reindeer she'd ever seen were approaching, side by side, bumping shoulders and antlers like nuzzling lovers, and perhaps they were at that.

Behind them walked the parnee.

The forest spirits turned their attention back to Ludmilla. With every step the parnee took, they seemed to tense, their eyes to narrow, and she knew they meant to drag her off into the forest and make short work of her there. She didn't mind, really. To be part of the forest would be far from the most undesirable ending.

Then whispers rose from below her. A song and a chorus of prayers that anyone else would have thought just the whistle of the wind. The wolverines seemed to hear it first. They sat on their hind legs, ears twitching. They cocked their heads and then seemed almost to nod in unison, a decision reached. Even as the chipmunks on the back of the brown bear did the same, and then that bear and his brothers followed suit, the wolverines turned and clambered over the eastern snowbank. The tiger didn't spare her a glance before it leapt away.

All of the animals departed, following in the trail left behind by the strangers in her stolen car. In the end, only the musk deer remained, the first one who'd caught her eye, and then it, too, left the road and vanished into the dark.

Ludmilla breathed quietly.

A boot scuffed the road.

She looked up into the face of the parnee. The last of the animals had gone, the mated reindeer pair included, and only this creature remained, the shaman of the forest spirits, not a man or an animal, not a ghost or a demon, but a spirit. Yes, he was that.

The parnee exhaled. She felt the warmth envelop her, caught the scent of the forest in spring, when the leaves of autumn were still moldering even as new leaves and flowers came into bloom. She wrapped her arms around herself, found that she could not feel her fingers at all. Her eyelids stuck together and she had to reach up a hand to rub the ice crystals off them. When she managed to look again, the parnee had gone. She could not see him, but off to her right, she heard boots crunching in snow and knew he had gone after the rest of them . . . gone to pursue the strangers . . . gone to claim that little girl with her cruel black eyes.

The truck's engine whined a moment and then quit. It ticked several times as the frozen air seized it, and then it went silent. Not so much as a hiss.

Now the only sounds around Ludmilla were the popping of the snow as it froze harder and cracked. That, and the ragged breaths that hissed in and out of her lungs. Her heart had gone quiet.

She slumped sideways, sprawling on the road.

For a moment, she thought she could see the spirits of the highway's dead surrounding her in the dark. "Oh, my friends," she rasped. For they were her friends. The spirits of the north had come down upon her, the rage of nature, which no man could turn aside, and they had left her alone.

Their prayers had done it—the songs of those buried in the unholy ground below the Road of Bones. For years, she had done her best to bless them, to free them, to protect and guide them, and now they had been the ones to protect her.

Ludmilla turned her head. The fabric of her balaclava and the skin beside her eyes had frozen to the road, and when she turned, both pulled away. But she was able to look down through the ice and the hardened permafrost, and she could see their bones beneath her. Bones, and skulls whose vacant orbits seemed to return her grateful gaze.

"Thank you," she said.

And Ludmilla left us. Joined them. Another body on the Road of Bones.

Teig didn't shout at the antler men to release Prentiss. He'd just shot one of them through the eye and seen it drop dead in the snow, so he thought they had gotten the message. The rifle crack echoed through the trees but otherwise all had gone quiet. Three more of those unbent reindeer stood near the trees, the gleaming eyes of loping shadows coming nearer through the woods behind them. One of the antler men still held Prentiss aloft.

"Felix," Prentiss croaked. "Don't . . ."

The words were so quiet that anywhere else they would never have reached his ears, but the wind seemed to aid them, a gust that carried past Prentiss and brought his voice to Teig along with the strangely human stink of the unbent reindeer.

Nari shouted at Teig, repeating his name several times with the urgency only terror allowed. Teig didn't dare take his eyes off Prentiss, but then the rear door of the old woman's car popped open and Nari dragged the little girl out of the backseat.

Una began to shriek and to claw at Nari's face.

The antler men banged their hooves on the ground, restless and alert. The one holding Prentiss shook him like a rattle. A warning.

"Stop it!" Teig shouted at Nari without turning toward her. "What are you doing?"

"Do it, Teig!" Nari cried. "Make the trade!"

Una's shrieking grew louder. She kept clawing at Nari, tried to break free, wild eyes scanning for an escape route.

Teig snapped a hard look in Nari's direction. "Stop it! I can't . . . she's a little girl!"

"We don't have any idea what she is!" Nari shouted.

The words echoed, somehow louder than the gunshot had been.

Teig turned to stare at Nari and Una, saw the terror in their eyes. Saw that these two weren't nearly as afraid of the unbent creatures who began to move nearer, or of the wolf-things that slunk from the trees and began to circle. No . . . Nari and Una were far more fearful of each other. Teig stared at Una's eyes, at the timeless intelligence there, the hatred, and he knew Nari must be right. But whatever those eyes said, Una was still just a little girl, and Teig wouldn't just hand her over to the monsters who'd come for her. They didn't drive a van or tempt her with a puppy, but they were monsters just the same.

He felt as if he were going mad. He wanted to scream.

"Teig!" Prentiss croaked.

The antler man holding him roared something at Teig in words that were not English but did not require translation. Prentiss shook. Piss ran down his leg, first dripping, then freezing solid. Teig wanted to cry for him. Instead he lifted the rifle, stepped out from behind the open car door, and started walking toward the antler men. Two of the wolves slid on their bellies, creeping closer to the car and to Teig, but he narrowed his eyes and focused on his aim. His gloved hands did not shake. If he pulled the trigger, he knew he would blow the brains of that antler man out the back of his skull. Prentiss would drop to the ground. His ruined leg, broken and twisted backward and frozen with icicles of his blood and piss, would crumble under him.

And what then?

Teig did weep, after all. *What then?*

The antler man holding Prentiss shouted. The others moved in toward Teig. Teig exhaled, took aim. A grunt came from Prentiss and their eyes met. Teig faltered, meeting the gaze of his only remaining friend, the only one who'd stood by him.

"Ruthie," Prentiss croaked. "Tell Ruthie . . ."

Then the antler man grabbed Prentiss's head and twisted, breaking his neck.

The monster dropped the broken body into the snow.

Teig couldn't find the breath to scream.

He leveled the rifle, took aim, and shot the one who'd killed Prentiss. The bullet punched through its shoulder, thrown off by the shaking of his hands. *Jesus, no. Prentiss . . . brother, I'm so sorry. I . . .*

The wounded antler man stepped over Prentiss's broken, bloody remains and extended a hand, pointing at the snowbound car. Pointed at Nari and Una, but Teig knew immediately that Nari held no interest for these demons, whatever the hell they were.

The ground trembled again and more trees cracked. Above the forest, the air had gone still. A shape loomed there, invisible but noticeable for the way the wind diverted around it and for the tops of the trees that seemed to grow from midair, as if the forest had risen up to watch the standoff unfolding at its edge.

The wolves closed in. One of them leapt onto the hood of the car and Prentiss swung the rifle barrel over to aim at its yellow eyes. Its claws did not scratch the hood. The metal did not dimple under its weight. The thing that stared at him now, daring him to fire, was a wolf only in shape and name, but not in spirit. Teig saw that now, as grief strangled his voice and choked off the breath from his lungs. The antler men began to close the distance, joining the wolves, and Teig wanted only to collapse to his knees the way the old woman had done back on the road, to surrender himself to whatever came next.

Then the little girl unleashed another scream, the most furious and forlorn yet, and he straightened up. Breath rushed back into his lungs and he squeezed the trigger. The bullet struck the wolf in the neck, twisted it around, slung it right off the hood and into the snow. He knew from the last encounter that soon it would be a slinking shadow again and then a wolf, if a wolf was indeed what it desired to become. But for a moment or two, he'd made it suffer, and for that he was glad.

Una screamed and Teig turned to see Nari with a fistful of the girl's hair, dragging her away from the open rear door of the car, muscling her through the snow. He saw the look in Nari's eyes, the way she used her fistful of the girl's hair to twist Una's head, to show the little girl's face to the antler men like the butcher presenting his customers with a choice cut of beef. The similarity made a little geyser of vomit churn up inside Teig's throat. He turned aside, threw up what little remained in his stomach, and then turned furiously upon Nari.

"Not a fucking chance!" he roared. "Put her back in the car! Put her back and—"

"And *what*?" Nari demanded, eyes wild, as Una thrashed and clawed and tried to escape her. "How many bullets you have? What can you do? Our choices are give her up or die and I do not want to die. Not for this thing! It isn't Una, Teig!"

Nari twisted the little girl's hair again and thrust her face toward Teig. Una screamed her throat raw, spittle flying, beyond words.

"They're here for *her*. Something's inside her. They don't care about us, but whatever is inside this girl, they won't let us take it farther south. They'll kill anyone who tries to protect it from them."

The girl fell motionless in Nari's grasp as if the words had stilled her, as if she had gone catatonic yet again. Teig stepped toward her—toward both of them—and as he did, the little girl brought her feet up behind her and kicked at Nari, tried to push free of her grasp and to lunge for Teig's rifle.

Nari yanked her back by the hair. Una spit and clawed at her. She turned and spit at Teig with the devil's hatred in her eyes.

Grasping his rifle as if it held some talismanic power, Teig looked around at the wolves and the three antler men who had encircled the car and its former passengers. They'd come close, but had stopped advancing when Nari had brandished Una as an offering.

Teig glanced at Prentiss, who lay dead in the snow, in the dark. He thought about all the things he should have said, about the halfhearted apologies he'd mustered up instead of taking full responsibility for all the times he'd fucked up. Teig thought about how much he owed to Prentiss, and he wondered what Prentiss would do, right now, if Teig had been the one lying dead in snow stained with his own blood and Prentiss had been the one left alive with a rifle in his hands.

Whatever evil thing hid behind Una's eyes, the body belonged to a child, and he was supposed to just hand her over without a fight? He didn't have to wonder what Olivia would have thought about that. He already knew.

"Nari, translate this."

She stared at him. The girl screamed again and Nari shook her by the hair. Teig spun on her, back turned to the monsters from the forest. "Don't do that! Don't hurt her!"

Nari looked at Teig as if seeing him for the first time. "They're here for *her*."

"Just translate what I'm saying, please." Teig took a deep breath and turned to face the antler men. The wolves had retreated slightly, watching warily. Wondering, perhaps.

The nearest of the antler men, the one he had shot through the shoulder, tilted its heavy head in curiosity, its crown of antlers weighty enough to made its skull sway a bit, almost hypnotic. Teig studied its face and began to speak.

"I don't want to die," he said.

Nari repeated the words in Yakut—or he assumed it was Yakut—and he hoped the creatures would understand.

"I can't let you take this girl," he went on.

Nari stared at him, expression a mixture of fear and fury. Teig stared back, unyielding, until she relented and continued the translation.

"I can't let you take the girl," he said again, "and I don't want to die. But I want to find another way if I can. If my friend here is right, it's not the girl you want at all, but something inside of her. Can you . . ."

Teig thought about his next words. He glanced over the treetops, at the place where the wind did not pass, at the way the air wavered to reveal something enormous watching, listening. Somehow he knew his words weren't meant for these antler men, but for the presence that bent trees and shook the ground, that breathed winter and bent the wind.

"Can you take the thing inside her without killing the girl?" he asked.

Nari repeated the question.

In her grasp, Una had gone still as she understood what Teig was attempting. The thing inside the little girl's skin began to whine like a dog that has only now realized that all of its barking will do no good.

One by one, the antler men bowed their heads. The wolves, those loping shadows, slipped back into the trees. Teig glanced around in confusion, until he saw the trio of wolverines slipping across the snow toward them, followed by a musk deer and three lumbering bears, and two massive reindeer who had not yet learned the trick of standing on their back legs, like these antler men.

The reindeer parted. Behind them stood the figure Teig had known would come. Of course he would. The parnee had followed them mile by mile, dogged and patient. In the dark, he looked made of the night itself. What passed for clothing hung from him like moss. His bare skin seemed like weathered tree bark in some places and dried leather in others, but most of his face was covered with a caul of soft antler velvet. As he breathed in and out, the velvet over his mouth puffed like spider-webbing in a breeze. In the time since they had first seen him, he had changed significantly, grown larger and more bestial, as if the farther south he went, the more he took the wilderness with him. The antlers that grew out of his skull, and the little nubs on his forehead and at his temples, weren't like those of the unbent reindeer—the parnee's antlers were yellowed and cracked like ancient ivory. They were new, but looked as if they'd been growing for so long that they resembled knots of coral more than the rack on a stag's head. Yet he held up that intricate weave of antlers as if it weighed nothing at all.

Teig could barely breathe. The time for running or screaming had passed. The time to live or die had arrived. He let the rifle drop into the snow at his feet.

"Take me instead."

Behind him, Nari whispered what sounded like a prayer, and then his name. "What are you doing?"

Teig didn't take his eyes off the parnee. It tilted its head. The velvet caul over its face billowed with its breath. A nub of new antler growth tore through the velvet on the left side of its skull. Teig had not expected the words to come out of his mouth but now that they had, they felt like the right ones.

He'd always wanted to believe in ghosts, yearned for evidence. All those times he had met people who claimed to be haunted, and it was only ever Olivia's murder that haunted him. If Teig survived this, he knew that Prentiss's death would haunt him, too. The one thing his sister and his friend had in common—maybe the only thing—was that both of them had trusted him to have their backs, to be there when they needed him. Maybe their deaths weren't his fault, but they gnawed at him, burrowed into his mind.

Prentiss.

Jesus Christ, Jack, I'm so sorry. Eight thousand dollars. Your life was worth so much more.

He wouldn't look at Prentiss's corpse again. Teig promised himself that.

"Nari," he said, without taking his gaze from the parnee—he didn't dare break eye contact, afraid that connection might be the one thing preventing these forest spirits from killing them all. "Translate my words. I need you to—"

"Teig, what are you doing?"

"Just fucking translate," he said, biting off each word without raising his voice.

This time Nari didn't argue. The parnee cocked its head in the other direction. The velvet veil across its face tore a bit more and a black eye gleamed in the opening. The other animals studied him with the same curiosity, but the antler men stomped their hooves and snorted warm breath into the frozen air, growing impatient.

"Something's inside the girl," Teig said, presenting his gloved hands palm-forward, as if in surrender. He hesitated, but when Nari began to translate the words into Yakut, he forged onward. "Whatever you did to the people in Akhust, that was connected to you trying to capture or stop it—the thing inside her. Am I right?"

Nari still held Una by a fistful of hair, her other hand gripping the girl's biceps. Una had gone deathly still, watching and listening, the malevolence behind her eyes so apparent now that Teig hated himself for missing it earlier.

When Nari had finished translating, they both watched the parnee's face, the inhale and exhale that billowed the velvet over his features. Seconds passed and Teig began to lose the last spark of hope, until the parnee gave a single, slow nod.

"Okay," Teig said. "Okay, I get it. And I understand you don't give a damn about my life or Nari's or anyone else who might get between you and . . . whatever you're hunting. But I can't let you have her."

As Nari translated that, the antler men stomped and snorted and the snow crunched as they began to edge forward. Behind the antler velvet that covered its face, the parnee seemed almost amused.

Teig raised both hands. "Please, listen. Whatever's in her . . . it wasn't always, right? From what I can figure out, before yesterday she was just a girl. Something got inside her. Possessed or infected her, something like that. Maybe you can't rip it out of her. Maybe it has to have a home, or a body for a host or whatever, but I want to know if you can move it. Can you take it from her and put it into me?"

As Nari translated, her voice quavered, and he wondered if that tremor came from fear or sorrow. Either way, she kept translating and the parnee watched Teig closely, eyes narrowing in suspicion and doubt, and then maybe judgment as well.

Seconds ticked by. The animals had seemed restless, but one by one they turned to look at the parnee and went still. Even the antler men seemed to pause, their menace to lessen. One lowered himself to all fours again and in the space between heartbeats went from a woodland god to an ordinary reindeer.

The parnee drew in a long breath, chest filling, and seemed to stand a little taller as he studied the three passengers and their stolen, useless car. Teig felt the heat of his own heartbeat. He had lost feeling in his hands and his nose, though both were covered. If he survived the next minute or two, he would still have to make it to shelter, and heat. *One miracle at a time,* he thought, staring at the parnee and his menagerie, astonished with every moment he found himself still alive.

The cold dug deeper. Teig clenched his jaw. Adrenaline had been surging through him, keeping him from feeling the worst of it, but now his bones ached and his muscles began to constrict.

"Teig," Nari whispered, her voice barely audible over the wind. "Do you know what you're doing?"

Before tonight he would have muttered some flippant reply, but the old Teig had been broken down and cast aside. Tonight's Teig had no easy answers. He just knew that he couldn't do nothing anymore, that he couldn't save himself and let others suffer for it. All his life he had lived by the same philosophy that underpinned the advice flight attendants gave after the plane took off. In the event of an emergency, you had to put on your own oxygen mask first because if you didn't save yourself, you wouldn't survive to save anyone else. For years, Teig had done whatever he had to do in order to stay afloat. He had abandoned project after project in the search for the ones that would succeed, that would put money in the bank and let him hire the friends who'd been loyal to him, often as a payback for the times he had abandoned or disappointed them.

He'd convinced himself that as long as he had one friend who saw his true intentions, who believed in him and knew he was a good guy, everything would be okay. Prentiss had been that friend, and now Prentiss was dead.

Despite his promise to himself, Teig let his gaze tick over to his corpse, twisted in the snow. His blood looked black in the dark. Instead of the terror Teig might have expected to see on Prentiss's face, in death his expression showed only sorrow.

"Fuck it," Teig whispered to himself.

He snapped his head up to stare at the parnee, raised his right hand and pointed a trembling, frozen finger. "Fuck *you*. Don't just stand there and wait for us to freeze to death, you son of a bitch." Teig slapped both gloved hands against his own chest. "Take me! I'm right here!"

The antler men snorted and stomped. One of the bears lumbered a bit closer, shivering in irritation as a few Arctic fucking chipmunks or whatever they were chased each other in a circle through the thick fur on the bear's back.

The parnee took a step toward Teig. A puff of breath blew a bit more of the velvet web away from its face. Those wet black eyes stared at him, unblinking, too large for the parnee's face. A flash of anger had made Teig brave, but eye to eye with the parnee, the vigor of courage failed him.

"Please," Teig whispered. "I just want to save someone. This girl . . . she didn't ask for this. Is there any way—"

The parnee reached out, grabbed Teig's coat in both hands, and snapped his head forward. Their skulls rammed together. Nubs of ungrown antler split the skin on Teig's forehead and he fell into the snow. Darkness encroached at the edges of his vision and his eyesight blurred.

The parnee let out a shout in a guttural language that wasn't Yakut, wasn't like anything Teig had ever heard. The antler men stormed toward the stalled car. Nari screamed as one of them grabbed her, fisting her hair into a ball and yanking her around just as she'd done to Una. But Nari's screams were nothing compared to the shriek of the little girl. The moment one of the antler men laid hands on her, her eyes rolled up to whites and she let out a scream as if she were being flayed alive.

Teig tried to rise. Down on one knee, he glanced up at the treetops, to the place where the wind and sky were obscured by the invisible monolith with parts of the forest growing out of its unseen flesh. Did the parnee serve this creature or did it serve him? Teig wasn't sure, but he gazed up in silent appeal at that empty bit of night sky nevertheless.

"Please," he said.

The little girl kept screaming, kept fighting.

An antler man stepped over, spit on Teig and kicked him in the head. Hoof connected to skull, and all went black.

Teig had saved no one—not even himself.

17

His first thought—muddled as it may be—is that his head is cracked. Pain radiates from the cheek and temple on the left side of his skull. Something carries him, swaying him back and forth. He wants to open his eyes but whether from swelling or freezing, the lids will not obey. He hears the crunch of snow and a grunt, something hefts him a bit higher, as though his weight has become burdensome, but it is only his mind that tells him this. Disoriented, consciousness little more than a flickering candle flame, he feels himself moving and the pressure of the wind buffeting his face, but the cold is taking its toll.

The black embraces him again, safe and comforting. It welcomes him warmly, and in the delicious moment as he transitions from awareness to soft nothing, he is relieved, craving the black as an insomniac clutches at the threads of promised sleep.

Sleep.

Soft nothing.

A bump, that isn't a bump.

Teig awakens in a seizure. His jaws grind together with such force he can feel the crack in his skull splinter further. He'd scream but he hasn't the strength. His body thrashes, bucks against the grasp of the thing carrying him, and he falls. He strikes the snow, pain stabbing through his torso and neck, but not his hands or feet, not his arms—those, he can't feel at all. Of course he can't.

Stricken with fear, brain fogged, facts present themselves, dredged up from research he's done for this trip. In times of panic or grief, he's always relied on facts. It's why the series he's produced for television are always these weird bits of reality. The adult human's core body temperature can drop as low as eighty degrees, possibly seventy-seven, and still hold on to some tether of life. Hands exposed to weather like this quickly go numb as the blood retreats toward the core, the body doing all it can to preserve life at the expense of extremities. Even with gloves and boots, out here with a windchill approaching seventy below zero, his body has already decided to sacrifice his hands and feet if necessary.

And it will be.

Teig thrashes on the snow. He strikes the back of his skull and hears the crack of bone, and refuses to think about anything but the pain, and the cold. This maximum shiver, this seizure, this is good. It means his core temp had dropped to ninety-four, maybe a little lower, but that's a long way down to seventy-seven.

His body still shakes, but it's slowing to a tremble.

Hands hoist him off the snow. He wants to open his eyes. There are others here. The woman. The little girl. Prentiss.

No. Prentiss is dead.

Fresh grief spills through him, but at least that pain is warm.

The thing tucks him under its arm like a sack of groceries and he settles into swaying back and forth, and the soft nothing of the black envelops him again. The ocean takes him. Ebbs and flows. He rolls on the waves. The pain in his face, his skull, has retreated into his brain, down deep, and faded to a dull ache. But even as he floats in nothing, he can feel the line where his skull cracked. Like a seam in the bone, and the cold has fingers that dig at the edges of the seam, trying to get its claws in to pry it open, to cradle his brain in frozen fingers. And maybe that won't be so bad. If those fingers can dig into the crack in his skull, the cold slips into his brain, and the pain goes away. Like it has in his hands and feet. Like it has in his arms, and the nose he is sure he used to have. He can't feel his nose anymore, or his face, really.

It's okay.

He's okay.

And then he's very much not.

When he's dropped a second time, Teig hits pavement. His arm gets in the way of his head, which is a blessing. His skull bounces off the thick padding of his sleeve and the meat of his right arm, which feels nothing. He rubs his gloved left hand over his eyes and it feels like a club, but it draws moisture, scrapes ice, and he manages to open his eyes again.

The breath goes out of him. He yearns to have that warmth back, the little bit of heat he has left. Ice crystals form in the mist of his lost exhalation.

Hooves clack on the road. Teig sees the antler man above him, straddling him. The one who's been carrying him, he thinks. His eyes flutter, the soft black nothing about to embrace him again, but the antler man sees it coming, reaches down and cuffs him in the side of his cracked skull, and Teig manages to scream.

It's the sound of his own pain that brings clarity.

The antler man grabs him by the coat and lifts him to his feet as if he weighs nothing at all. Teig's legs go out from under him but the unbent beast hoists him again, plants him again, shakes him until he forces himself to stand on feet he can't feel. Careful not to collapse, Teig glances down at his boots to make some kind of connection in his brain, to prove to himself that his feet are still there.

He hears quiet sobbing.

Someone is crying.

Teig nearly laughs. His brain is as numb as his hands and feet but he knows they are beyond tears, now. Crying will get them nowhere.

Down deep in the core of him, where his conscious mind and the blood from his extremities have both retreated, he knows that maybe crying is all they have, now. Isn't grief the normal response to hopelessness? He thinks maybe that's so.

But then he sees the parnee.

Carrying an unconscious Una in his arms.

And Teig thinks maybe there's hope after all.

He looks around and, to his surprise, recognizes their surroundings. They've made it back to Akhust, Una's home. Even the houses are familiar. Not far away, he can see the home where the guide, Kaskil, had put him and Prentiss up for all of an hour or so before the world turned upside down. The other direction, he can see the garage, and the place in the road where Kaskil died, and where Prentiss's blood had first been spilled.

Animals are walking through the little town. Up the street, two brown bears saunter northward, between buildings, headed for the forest at the edge of this little sliver of civilization. Loping shadows dart into the trees ahead of the bears. Reindeer and mule deer and other four-legged beasts continue the march, and Teig understands this is a migration. All of these animals, or the wilderness spirits inside them, share a destination, and he wonders what it could be.

Two antler men approach him from behind.

Teig turns and sees the source of the sobs he's heard—Nari, of course. That's her name. The woman with the black cherry hair. He remembers now the way he'd sat up and noticed her in the bar, how strikingly attractive she was. Now she's his companion, connected to him in a way he'd never have wished. They ran for their lives together, shared in unimaginable terror . . .

Now we'll die together.

Teig squints. His vision blurs but he can see she's still crying. That's easy enough to understand. What he finds confusing is the way she's walking. Nari is between two antler men, each of them holding one of her hands, like protective parents taking their toddler for a stroll. Head hung, she trudges between them, not a trace of rebellion in evidence. The left sleeve of her parka is torn and in the jaundiced glow of what little starlight comes through the low-slung nighttime clouds, Teig thinks he sees a splash of blood and the gleam of visible bone, as if she's been wounded. Or bitten, and the bite's gone deep.

"Nari?" he rasps.

She looks up. Something in her eyes makes even the core of him go cold. They're wide and black and gleaming.

Then the parnee barks something in that language that is not Yakut. The antler man who'd been carrying Teig gives him a shove. Teig flails and nearly sprawls on his face but the icy nubs inside his boots manage to keep their footing, and then he's walking.

They're all walking, headed the same way as the animals. North of Akhust, into the forest, out beyond the outskirts of the human world and into the white silence. The wild land, where human voices make no sound. The parnee carries Una. The antler men hold hands with Nari. The other one follows behind Teig like a prison guard.

They leave the empty town behind.

Nari did not feel as if she were dying. Her hands and face were cold, her feet ached, but they had been walking for hours before reaching Akhust and by now she ought to have been deeply into hypothermia. Death should have been whispering in her ear. The wound in her arm hurt and she felt the blood freeze up and then crackle and flow freshly when she moved the arm.

Her body hadn't gone numb, but her heart . . . that was another story. Her mind, too.

She had learned a great deal from the parnee in the past couple of hours, walking hand in hand with these impossible beasts. From time to time, Teig had grunted awake and then passed out again, usually dragged up from unconsciousness by the sound of Una screaming.

Not Una, she had to remind herself every time.

The thing inside the little girl had screamed and fought the parnee, then returned again and again to that catatonic state in which it either lay plotting, or resting. Gaining strength for another attempt.

The march turned the night and the minutes into a blur, so that Nari convinced herself it might be a glimpse of hell, a nightmare, a slippage of reality's mask from which she might return, like the hero of some fairy story. But then they had walked into Akhust, still empty, still echoing with the screams of hours past and the roar of the truck's engine when they'd made their escape and left Kaskil's bloody corpse behind.

She'd looked up and seen the shape of the towering, transparent presence that had led them all this way. It would not enter the town, but walked around the perimeter, trees swaying out of its path as though of their own accord, or as if the wind had reached in and parted them. Akhust had no life in it now, but in the houses she knew she would find ovens and cabinets and refrigerators, bedrooms and televisions and other reminders of the frantic, erratic thing called civilization.

Nari knew, also, that this was their last glimpse of it.

That was what had started her crying.

By the time they encountered the first of the frozen dead, her tears had run dry. They had marched only a couple hundred yards into the forest. The ground underfoot had deep snowpack, and her boots only crunched through the top two or three inches. There were other footprints, however, both human and animal. Many of the hoofprints were unnaturally large. Many of the human prints were barefoot. The first of those sightings, the thought of men and women and children in Akhust walking barefoot into the north woods, filled her with weary dread.

The trees were frosted with snow and ice. The fir trees looked nearly silver. Pine and larch seemed to offer a bit of color, needles spiking from beneath the frost. Nari still walked with one of the reindeer on either side, each of them holding one of her hands, stringing into a single file line like schoolchildren when they needed to thread between trees. Ahead of her, another of the beasts nudged at the stumbling Teig, and ahead of them, the parnee carried Una clutched close to his chest, as if she were a bomb that might destroy them all if he took one wrong step. All around them, the animals moved quietly through the forest. Chipmunks had taken to the branches while others scurried along underfoot. Nari thought she'd counted at least six wolverines now, but they were sneaky little things, slinking and darting. She'd heard wolverines before, knew the low, throaty growl like something between a bear and a hyena, but these were silent as penitents kneeling in church. Farther away, bears and reindeer snapped branches and crunched ice as they walked, but their voices were also silent.

Reverent.

Only Nari cried out when they came upon the dead man. His corpse leaned against a kigilyakh, one of the stone pillars that had formed over one hundred million years earlier in the mountains of Yakutia. The kigilyakh did not belong here, in this forest, any more than the frozen man belonged.

The frozen man.

He wore a robe and nothing else. The parnee had summoned the people of Akhust the day before, hoping to stop the thing inside Una from escaping into the wider world. The forest had kept the thing captive for many thousands of years and intended to keep it captive for thousands more.

The people of Akhust had left their homes. Left their coffee and their woodstoves, left their doors open as they answered the parnee's summoning. But they had not brought the girl, Una, with them, or she had escaped the grasp of the others in Akhust. The parnee and the rest of the forest spirits had no care for individual lives, and so when the people of Akhust found themselves deep in the woods, they also found themselves confused and abandoned, and freezing fast.

Nari knew this. Intuited it as if remembering it herself, and the intuition made her sick.

She tore her hands away from her escorts, knelt, and threw up in the snow. Vomit steamed and melted ice, and then began to freeze almost instantly. When Nari turned to rise, she saw the two antler men standing by the frozen man and the granite pillar. The man's face had been frozen with the sorrow of his ebbing life. His skin had turned blue and white, or the frost that coated him had added those hues. The two antler men tilted their heads side to side in curiosity, as if they recognized this man.

The parnee barked at them in its old language and they turned, reluctantly, to follow the strange procession ahead of them. They turned to reach for Nari's hands but she ignored them and quickened her pace. Head down, skull aching, the frigid air embracing her as if in welcome, she followed the parnee of her own volition, even though they walked through what now seemed a forest of the frozen dead. Children clung to their mothers. Fathers buried their faces in pain or in shame that they could do nothing to save their families. Some had vacant looks, as if the spell that had mesmerized them had blanked their minds, and Nari knew those were the fortunate ones. The ones who had woken from that spell, had known they were dying, had felt the cold sink to their bones and stop their hearts—those were the dead whose faces would haunt her. Pale blue and white, rimed with frost, beautiful and grotesque in the way of grieving cemetery angels.

And there were so many of them. Dozens, at least.

They trudged along for long minutes. Soon, Nari had lost any sense of time. The ice-sculpted corpses grew less numerous and she spotted one only here and there, but these seemed older somehow. Even their clothes seemed from an earlier era. A little voice at the back of her mind told her this was impossible. They would thaw in summer and collapse. No way could they remain frozen like this, remain standing or kneeling or bent over a stone pillar as if grieving for a wife or a child or a father lost to the north woods. And yet her eyes did not lie.

Up ahead, Teig dropped to the ground as if someone had switched him off. Nari called his name and ran to him, took his shoulder, and turned him over. None of the antler men tried to stop her. The parnee—at the head of their pack—did not slow his pace or even turn.

"Teig, wake up. Please . . . it's me," she said. Her voice sounded different, even to her own ears. Even echoing inside her aching head. It sounded rough and guttural.

She shook him again and this time Teig groaned and his head bobbed a bit as he opened his eyes, staring up at her.

"Nari? Aren't you . . . you don't even look cold. You don't look tired."

Her spine stiffened. How could she explain to him? How should she tell him that she no longer felt cold, that instead of exhausted she felt strong, that the bite wound on her arm that had ripped muscle away and exposed bone had now started to heal? Couldn't he see it in her eyes? Didn't he understand?

"Get up, Teig," she said. Some of the anger and resentment crept into her voice. She knew he could hear it, see it on her face. "You wanted this. You should be awake."

Teig frowned, visibly stung and confused. "I don't . . . why are you . . ."

"You should have handed her over."

The pain in his eyes might have drawn some sympathy from her, but Nari had none left to give. She'd reserved it all for herself.

"What difference does it make, now?" Teig said. "They're going to kill us all."

"No . . . they are not," Nari replied. She grabbed Teig by the shoulders and lifted him off the frozen ground as if he were a child, and set him on his feet. "You are going to get what you asked for. They're going to spare the girl, thanks to you. But I think you'll wish that you'd run, that you'd left her behind."

Nari felt sick. She turned away from him, started walking, her boots crunching in the snow. Boots that no longer fit her, not the way they should.

"I certainly wish it," she said. "But the time for wishes has passed."

Teig called her name. Asked her what she meant. Nari ignored him until he got to the question she could not ignore.

"How do you know all this?" Teig asked, his voice a plaintive rasp.

Nari coughed a laugh, her voice beginning to fail her. What could she say? What difference would it make?

Behind her, the antler men grabbed hold of Teig. He had managed to walk on his own much longer and farther than any of them could have expected, but now he needed their help. That was all right. Instinct told Nari they didn't have much longer to go. The knoll lay ahead, not much farther.

She looked up through a break in the trees and saw the beautiful shimmer in the sky, the shape of Bugady Musun. Nari's grandfather had been Evenki, not Yakut, and he had talked about her often. She could picture him still, a withered, leathery old man swathed in fur, smoking his pipe and reminiscing about his boyhood, those rheumy, ice-blue eyes gazing into some inner place, as if he could see the past replaying before him. He'd been nine or ten years old, he said, hunting with his grandfather in the north woods, miles from the nearest dwelling. They had seen reindeer that walked on two feet, but more than that . . . they had come into a clearing where several of them had gathered, some on four hooves and others on two, all of them with their necks craned upward. For a moment, the air had shimmered and grandfather had seen a reindeer woman, antlers scraping the sky, her hide the same hue as his own grandfather's weathered face.

The deer woman had looked down upon them. Nari's grandfather would later say there were trees growing amongst the antlers on her head, that a bird's nest had fallen from the branches when Bugady Musun bent her head to look down at them. Even when she had been a little girl, young enough to believe this story, she had been sure he embellished the part about the bird's nest.

Then Bugady Musun had vanished, at least to the eyes of the two hunters, young and old.

Not gone, her grandfather had been sure to stress. Just vanished.

The goddess was the patron of animals, the guardian of all the wild things of the north woods. In her honor, Nari's grandfather and *his* grandfather had put away their rifles and killed nothing that day, not even a bird. They went hungry that night, but Bugady Musun had honored them by allowing herself to be seen, and they would not disrespect her in return.

The next day, the hunting was the most bountiful Nari's grandfather could ever recall, and both he and his own grandfather believed it had been a blessing from Bugady Musun. She understood honor, and hunger, and obligation.

Nari watched the shimmering air up through the trees, saw a few trees that seemed to float way above the ground, and knew the goddess was with her. It did not stop the pain in her skull where the nubs of antler coronets had begun to form, or the sharp piercing as the brow tine burst through her skin. It did not stop her heart from racing with fear now, as the velvet began to form. Her eyes began to well with fresh tears, but she looked skyward again. The tree cover had thickened, so she could not see far above them, but the ground trembled slightly and she could hear the trees pressed aside as the goddess passed, and at least she wasn't alone.

Teig didn't have that blessing. Poor bastard.

No. Teig was dreadfully, entirely alone.

18

With each icy corpse they passed, Teig wondered how he remained alive. He had lost all feeling in his limbs and his arms hung lifeless at his sides, but his feet continued to shuffle. His balaclava covered most of his face but he knew it didn't matter. Frostbite would be killing exposed flesh, and the fabric of the balaclava could not have protected him all this time. Maybe it was the presence of the parnee. Maybe it had done something to keep him alive and moving. Or maybe it was just the sight of the dead people of Akhust, flash-frozen in the north woods, corpses as ice sculpture. If he let his legs stop moving forward, he knew his fate.

As long as he kept walking, he was still alive.

He wished it could have been different but as Nari had said, the time for wishes had passed. Only minutes since she had spoken those words, and now Teig looked up to see more granite pillars. These were different, though. The kigilyakh were natural rock formations but here they had grown in a circle, nine of them at equal intervals at the edges of a natural clearing. The sight jarred him. This was not Stonehenge, where the stones had been placed by ancient human hands. This clearing had formed this way. In this single, small space, the chaotic wilderness had created a small patch of order.

In the center of the clearing was a rough hillock, a knoll that rose up in the midst of those granite pillars. The wind had scoured most of the snow from the knoll, revealing hard permafrost and bald jutting rocks.

At the base of the knoll were a variety of animals, not the beasts who had been escorting them but others who seemed to have been awaiting their arrival. There were wolves and long-tailed gorals, what might have been an Amur leopard, and half a dozen scurrying things that looked like a cross between a fox and a very confused raccoon.

Raccoon dogs, Teig thought. He'd never seen one before, but they chased one another with playful exuberance.

He thought he might have smiled, but his face was too numb to feel it. He fell to his knees, then caught himself with his hands before he sprawled across the clearing. It did not escape his notice that now he was down on all fours, like the rest of the beasts here.

There were reindeer around the clearing as well. Waiting, like the other animals. He studied those reindeer for any sign that they might unbend themselves and rise on their hind legs like the antler men that now entered the clearing behind Teig, but these seemed only ordinary, four-legged beasts except for the way they watched him, the suspicion in their eyes. The distrust, as if they did not believe he would keep his word.

Teig saw the icy mist of his own breath. It seemed less and less, as though even the oxygen in his lungs had begun to freeze.

The parnee grunted. He stamped his boots as if they were hooves, and he carried the unmoving Una through the circle of stones, into the clearing, and began to climb the ten-foot knoll. As he did, the animals dispersed, trotting or scurrying away from that small hillock, out of the clearing, beyond the edge of that stone circle. A fresh breeze kicked up. It must have been cold enough to kill, but he felt only the pressure of it, the way it tried to tip him over. If he had been on two feet instead of four, he might have fallen. That breeze carried a sound like the baying of wolves, but somehow soft as a whisper, and when

Teig glanced up he saw that the loping shadows that had been pacing them all along had finally joined the rest of the parnee's menagerie. One by one, the shadows resolved into wolves, and other than the glint of pride and intellect in their eyes, Teig would not have known the difference between these and ordinary beasts.

The parnee stood at the top of the knoll. Cradling Una with one arm, he turned and beckoned to Teig with his free hand.

Snow crunched beside Teig. Hands grasped his left arm, helping him to stand. "Go to him. This is what you asked for."

The voice was a rasp. A grunt. Teeth clacked as if the mouth that spoke was unused to forming words. Teig glanced to his left and wished he hadn't. Even with the velvet that partially veiled her face and with the antler points that had begun to grow from her forehead, he could see much of Nari still remaining in her face.

He wanted to take her and run, but it was too late for her. Too late for either of them.

But Una . . .

Maybe not too late for her.

Teig shuffled across the snow to the base of the knoll and began to climb. He'd taken only two strides upward when Una began to scream and thrash and the parnee had to use both hands to restrain her.

It's not her, Teig thought. *It's the thing hiding inside her, the thing that tried to escape.*

Bitter bile rushed up the back of his throat, then, because the thing thrashing and clawing at the parnee and screaming the little girl's throat raw was also the thing he had agreed to take into himself. To free her, he would house this ancient thing.

Teig faltered.

The animals all froze, terrified of what would happen next.

Teig shifted his left leg backward, his boot searching for a foothold. He would die here, he knew. Even if the parnee didn't kill him, if the antler men did not tear him apart or feed him to the wolves, he would freeze to death. But he looked up to the top of the knoll and saw the spitting, snarling little girl and did not want the thing that had infected her soul to infect his own. If he had to die, he shouldn't have to die like that.

The parnee barked at him in that ancient, guttural tongue that seemed part human language and part animal. Teig shook his head. He didn't understand the words, but he could imagine what they meant. They had struck a bargain, he and the parnee, and if Teig did not keep up his end of it, this little girl would die. She had lost her family, her parents, her friends, her whole village. No one would come and save her now—nobody left alive knew she existed, or cared, except for Teig. Without him, she would die. What happened to his sister had never really been his fault, though he had choked himself with guilt all these years. He couldn't save Olivia, but this girl . . . this girl he could save.

How could he run from this?

The cold sank its claws deeper. His chest ached. His thoughts slowed and he blinked. Would he freeze right here, like this, a few steps up the knoll, an ice sculpture of death by indecision? When he moved again, his arms and legs felt like air, just ghosts of limbs. His eyes felt rough, ice crystals on his retinas, but his vision told him that he was moving. A step up the knoll, bent forward so he did not topple backward.

When she saw him begin to climb again, the thing inside Una stared at him, shrieking, shoving against the parnee as if to escape Teig. She knew what was coming. It knew.

A darkness exhaled from her open mouth. It misted before her face like a mask, and it made him want to scream. To shriek louder than this parasite inside a little girl. He looked at that darkness and saw its eyes, saw a madness and malignance unlike anything he had ever known. He'd known people who were awful, who relished cruelty, but he had never known real malevolence. Those eyes were puncture wounds in the world, and what bled from those wounds was a poison unfiltered by humanity, ravenous for the fear and pain it could inflict. That was malevolence. All his life, he had never understood the root of the word evil, but he understood it now.

His boot skidded on the knoll and he smashed his left knee against a jutting rock, but couldn't feel a thing except the impact. Teig threw out his hands and caught himself. The knoll was not steep enough that he needed to climb like this, but he didn't have the strength or the balance to go on otherwise. He climbed on his hands and knees. Would have crawled if it came to that.

Grateful that he didn't have to look into those eyes again. Not just yet.

The poison in her, the malevolence roiling inside that little girl . . . to invite it into himself would be like asking for cancer. Worse. But he closed his eyes while he climbed and he summoned memories of his sister, moments in which he had lifted her and swung her around, played on the slide with her, made a little maelstrom in the swimming pool. Moments in which he had made her nearly burst with joy. Moments when she knew he loved her.

Teig kept climbing.

He had owed emotional debts to friends and family his entire life, debts he had always intended to repay but never gotten around to covering. And, after all, he and the parnee had made a deal. Teig had made a promise, and this was a promise he was not going to break.

At the top of the knoll, somehow, he managed to stand.

The darkness inside Una glared at him with a hatred so pure it nearly felt like love.

The parnee nodded, threw his head back, and howled to the night sky. Around the base of the knoll, at the edges of that stone circle, the wolves-that-were-not-wolves bayed at the gray-shrouded moon and the antler men bent down and were only reindeer again.

The ground shook.

The trees beyond the stone circle swayed. Just to the north, some of those trees parted, and silhouetted against the sky he saw the shimmering air that told him that same towering observer had returned, or had been there with them all along. He saw trees in the air where they did not belong.

Teig swayed, nearly collapsed. His eyes closed and his thoughts went dark a moment until he shook himself back to consciousness. He wouldn't die just yet. He wouldn't fail, now.

When he glanced up again, for just a moment he saw the true face of that figure that towered above them all. Like a gift, she revealed herself to him, this reindeer woman fifty feet high, antlers stretching so high it seemed the clouds wove amongst them.

Then she was gone.

The parnee cried out in prayer, lifted a struggling Una over his head as if offering her to the one who watched over them all. Chanting in that ancient tongue, the language of the forest, he put Una on the ground.

As he did, the parnee seemed to fade. No longer flesh and bone, it seemed only spirit, a phantom in the shape of the shaman who had been there a moment ago. The parnee's hands pressed into Una, pressed through her, and the scream that escaped the little girl's lips now sounded as if, at last, it came from the girl herself. Somehow, that made it worse.

The parnee ripped the squalling, squirming darkness out of Una. It thrashed against him, wrapped serpentlike around the parnee's translucent arms, spitting and baring teeth black as oil. The parnee turned toward Teig and held out the shrieking darkness and that malevolence turned its eyes on him.

Teig saw it coming toward him, and he could not help but scream. All his determination bled out of him. How could he have made himself do this? God, no. No, no. Nothing was worth this. Yet here he was.

Then something moved in his peripheral vision and he looked down, past the parnee and the darkness, and he saw Una—the real Una—curled on the rocky, frozen knoll in a fetal ball. Beside her, for just a moment, Teig thought he saw another girl, sitting quietly and with one comforting hand stroking Una's head, whispering kind promises. Spectral lips mouthed five words. *Everything will be all right.*

Were those words for Una or for Teig himself?

He couldn't know.

Teig reached for the darkness.

Nari watched as the parnee grabbed hold of Teig. The thing inside Teig thrashed and began to spit and the reindeer stood upright again. The antler men rushed up the knoll and began to beat and kick Teig until he lay bloody and unmoving on the top of that little hillock.

The ground trembled with the footfalls of Bugady Musun as she turned and started north, to forest so deep and winter so cold that no human foot could ever find the trail that led there.

The antler men followed, dragging Felix Teigland with them, but Teig wasn't there anymore. Or if he was, he was just a cage now, a prison for something that should never have escaped to begin with. Something that would never be allowed out of the woods again.

In less than a minute, the clearing had emptied. The parnee had followed the antler men and the animals had followed the parnee, and now the only living creatures remaining in the circle of stone pillars were Nari and the little girl.

Nari climbed the knoll. As she reached the top, Una began to wake.

The girl sat up, rubbing at her eyes, shivering with cold, perhaps truly aware for the first time since the darkness had slithered into her body and tried to use her to escape its captors.

Una heard the huff of Nari's breath and the scritch of her ill-fitting boots on the permafrost. The girl turned to look, just as Nari reached out to her. Una shrank back, face a rictus of terror at the sight of her, and Nari could not blame her.

The little girl was still screaming when Nari snatched her off the knoll, turned, and fled into the forest, those screams trailing behind them even as the wind gusted and stole them away, and then—at last—the forest went quiet.

The trees whispered amongst themselves.

The darkness had gone.

19

Tuskulaana smoked too many cigarettes. Smoking had burned out her sense of smell, at least where the stink of her cigarettes was concerned. When she still had a husband, she cared about such things, but it had been a long time since he had left her alone with her little gas station and the tiny market that went along with it. The place needed work, but she was an old woman and not especially worried about a coat of fresh paint or nicer shelves. Tuskulaana knew she wasn't alone in this disinterest. The customers who came into the little market wanted gas, or snacks, or new windshield wipers, and they didn't expect much from a way station in one of the loneliest places in the world. If the floors were grimy, who the fuck cared? Not her customers, not her dog, Sacha, and not her. The only one who ever gave her a difficult time about it was her grandson. Kaskil wanted something better for her, wanted her to have something she could be proud of. Tuskulaana had told him a hundred times that she was proud of him, and that was enough. She loved the boy, even though he wasn't a boy anymore.

Her little house, though . . . that was something else. Every two years she repainted the walls in all four rooms, each a different, bright, cheerful color. She kept the place neat and clean, grew herbs in little pots on shelves in her kitchen, and when it wasn't so cold that it would kill her, she took her cigarettes outside. Even the dog tidied up after herself.

A small path led from the back of the market to her little house. One of her customers looked after the market's small parking lot and kept the path to her house shoveled in the winter. A mechanic who worked on the trucks that cared for the road, he was a broad-shouldered man with kind eyes and thick, wiry eyebrows. He laughed easily and his voice was throaty with damage from his own decades of smoking. Often they would smoke together. In nice weather, they would stand in front of the market and have a smoke and share gossip. Sacha liked him, and he would rub the scruff behind her ears for an hour without complaint. But her mechanic friend was only forty-seven and Tuskulaana had turned seventy-nine on her last birthday, so although sometimes she thought she saw a special sort of glint in his eye when he made her laugh, she never made anything out of it. Just the fancy of an old woman who liked her own company and not having to give a shit what anyone thought of her, or of how she spent her time.

Still, it would have been nice to have a man in her bed.

Not that she needed a man around, or the trouble they always brought with them. No, it was just that she couldn't sleep. Tuskulaana had fought insomnia for thirty years or more, and had been losing that fight since the start. She would fall asleep all right, sleep for a few hours, and then wake up in the quiet darkness unable to drift off again. At three or four in the morning she would surrender and leave her bed, careful not to wake Sacha, who snored throatily in her plush, fluffy dog bed.

She would drink tea and smoke cigarettes until it was time for breakfast, and sometimes tea and cigarettes were the only breakfast she had. Then she would open the market and the gas station, and wait to see if anyone would come.

Sometimes she went days without seeing another person. Once, when the truck that delivered supplies to the market had broken down, she had gone nine days without speaking to another human being. She often told herself—and the folks who might ask her about it—that she relished these long periods, that she and Sacha never got lonely, not when they were surrounded by nature and the ghosts out on the road.

Times like now, however, at five o'clock in the morning with the sun still hours away and Tuskulaana working on the last cigarette in the house, she had to confess the truth to herself.

But maybe not just yet.

Not until she'd smoked that last cigarette and had to go over to the market to get another carton.

No, not yet.

Tuskulaana sipped her tea. She liked a little sugar in it. Sometimes a lot of sugar. Old age had its prerogatives. She thought about the Victor Pelevin novel she had been reading, but could not bring herself to fetch it.

The little house was quiet save for the way the wind made the windows shake in their frames, and the creak of the timbers shifting and popping in the cold.

Her teacup was to her lips when the thumping began. Somehow Tuskulaana did not spill her tea. She sipped at it, relished the sweetness—she'd oversugared again—and then set it down and turned to look at the door. The thumping became a pounding. The knocking sounded like someone bashing a rock against the door. In her dog bed, Sacha lifted her sleepy head and offered a tired, befuddled growl.

Tuskulaana ought to have been terrified. The urgency of that pounding, there in the hours before sunrise, should have frightened her out of her wits. Instead, she felt only a dreadful, creeping sadness. Only tragedies arrived with such urgency in the small hours before dawn.

Sacha rose, barked twice, and then trotted to the door. She stared with suspicion, head cocked, listening to the pounding, then dropped her snout to sniff at the well-insulated threshold. Again she barked, but it sounded different now, and the dog began to back away from the door.

As Tuskulaana rose from her chair, a thump hit the door with such force that it cracked, and that was enough for her. She shouted at whoever had disturbed her insomnia, interrupted her lonely teatime, and frightened her dog. Tuskulaana stormed toward the door—insomuch as a woman of her age and shape could storm anywhere.

Hiding now behind Tuskulaana's chair, the dog began to whine.

Her visitor must have heard her shouting, because the pounding ceased.

Tuskulaana cursed that urgency for making her go to the door without a coat or a blanket, for it was insufferably cold outside. Hideously cold. Nevertheless, she unlocked the door and drew it open to discover a girl waiting just beyond the threshold. Half-frozen, ice crusting her hair and lashes, the girl shivered and gazed at her with eyes both imploring and terrified.

This girl had been pounding at her door? This girl with small hands, with tears frozen on her cheeks, with one foot booted and the other in only a thick wool sock?

No.

Tuskulaana saw hoofprints not far from the door, leading up and then away again. She leaned out, peered into the darkness, and saw the deer woman darting into the trees next to the little house, heading north.

"Come in, you poor thing," she said. "Come in and get warm. I have tea and sugar."

She brought the girl inside and closed the door, as Sacha eyed them warily from behind the chair. The little girl said nothing but drank tea greedily and held out the cup for more, eyes pleading not for food but for comfort. Anything that would make her feel less lost.

In that moment, Tuskulaana saw the resemblance.

This little girl wasn't lost and she was no stranger. It had been nearly a year since Tuskulaana had seen her great-granddaughter, but now, in the light, with her hair pushed away from her face, she saw the truth.

"Ariuna?" she said.

Named, recognized at last, the girl began to cry.

Realizing what her presence there must mean, Tuskulaana also wept.

But at least neither of them would cry alone.

At first, Nari thought she'd become a monster. She had seen it happen once already, to a woman she considered one of her best friends, and she thought now that the antler men might have once been people from Akhust and other places—people who had been anointed by the goddess to be her eyes and ears in the world. Nari wondered how many of them there were, all across the frozen forests, in the places where the world of people sometimes infringed upon the wilderness, and where the wilderness sometimes pushed back.

Now she ran through the cold and the dark, darting amongst the trees, making her own path. Winter might be frigid here, but to this new Nari, surrounded by the forest and the cracking snow, the glory of nature, this new freedom was all that mattered. All the life in the world depended on protecting the remaining wilderness from the spread of humankind, but there were more dangerous things than people. Sometimes, the spirits of the forest needed to protect the people from a far older malevolence, and thus maintain the balance of the world.

As she ran, hooves punching through frozen snowpack, Nari felt great purpose. She had been fleeing from obligation, seeking freedom, yet somehow she had finally found freedom in an obligation greater than she had ever known.

Free, determined, she burst from the trees and found herself running along open ground between the forest and the Road of Bones. Sunrise had yet to creep to the horizon but in this part of the world, morning arrived long before the night retreated. People would be up and traveling to work, hunters would be out, though even at the busiest part of the day there were few cars this time of year.

The sky had cleared and the stars glittered against the endless indigo of heaven.

She decided she would run till dawn.

Laughter touched her heart and she bounded across snow-packed permafrost, racing north. To her left, she spotted something moving on the road. A lone figure, a woman.

Nari knew her. She slowed and canted her head to one side, heavy antlers tugging at the muscles in her neck. Staring, she trotted several steps closer. Wary, she crept forward, hooves crunching loudly on ice, and studied the woman. Her memory had become strange, sensory, more attuned to scent than sight, and her mind had begun to lose the capacity to retrieve the names of things and of people, but after a few seconds she snatched it from her head.

Ludmilla.

In terror and desperation, they had left the woman dying in the road. There had been no chance of saving her, but Nari's heart had ached with guilt at the thought of having abandoned her. Now, as she took several steps further, climbing up on the snowbank beside the road, Nari realized she could see right through the old woman.

The ghost sang in a low, rasping voice, shaking a little cluster of bells as she walked. She paused, spoke a sentence or two of prayer, made the sign of the cross with her free hand, and then walked on. A dead woman, offering blessings for those who had died so many years before her.

Nari took another step on the snowbank. One hoof crunched

through the snow and she snorted loudly, shook her head, and backed away. When she looked up, she saw the ghost had paused to watch her.

Ludmilla smiled kindly and raised a trembling, spectral hand to wave.

Nari inclined her head in a many-antlered bow. She snorted again, turned, and darted off toward the trees. Toward new purpose.

Behind her, softly singing, the old ghost continued on with a purpose all her own.

Nari wondered if Ludmilla's new life had been a gift or a curse. Was she free now to do as her heart desired, or imprisoned in the path she had made for herself? As she reached the edge of the forest, Nari hesitated, wondering the same about her own path. This life . . . was it a gift, or a curse?

A chill went through her as she realized she had asked the same question in her old life. Gift or curse, the only way to discover the truth about life was to live it.

She stamped her front hooves, shook off the chill, and entered the forest.

Acknowledgments

The longer I'm at this writing gig, the more difficult it becomes to write these acknowledgment sections. Writing a novel is a long process and the author receives help in all sorts of ways, sometimes a vital bit of information or a supportive note or kind word when it's most needed. *Road of Bones* has its own life, has carved out its own piece of mine, but really every book is the culmination of everything that came before. So first, my thanks to all those who will go nameless here, and who have lent me their expertise or their love along the way.

I'm grateful as always to Connie, forever my best friend, my light and laughter, and to our children, Nicholas, Daniel, and Lily, who are now all grown and each of whom brings me joy every day. Thanks to my literary agent, Howard Morhaim, for his faith and keen eye, and to my manager, the indefatigable Pete Donaldson. I'm grateful to the team at St. Martin's, especially Sarah Bonamino, Allison Ziegler, and Cassidy Graham, and above all, to my editor, Michael Homler. Your passion for the stories I want to tell is such a gift. Profound thanks, also, to my Titan Books editor, Cath Trechman, and to the entire Titan team. Gratitude is due to my family, by blood and by marriage, especially my sister, Erin Golden, and my brother, Jamie Golden. Thanks to all of the friends who are there when I need a sounding board, a kick in the ass, or a good laugh, and who help keep me sane, including Tim Lebbon, Tom Sniegoski, Amber Benson, Jim

Moore, John McIlveen, Brian Keene, Bracken MacLeod, Rio Youers, and Mike Mignola. I'm incredibly fortunate to know that there are many others I could add to that list, so if you're reading this and thinking "Bastard, where's my name?" it's probably on this longer list. (Yes, Tony, that includes you.) I'd like to thank Bruce Springsteen for accompanying me on the journey of *Road of Bones*. I mean, I'd like to thank him, but I don't know him, so if you bump into him somewhere, pass it along, okay? And, of course, I'm grateful to each of the authors who agreed to give this novel a very early read, in particular, Stephen King. I suspect it was the serendipitous timing of a certain *New York Times* article about the real-life "road of bones" that prompted him to pick this book up from his presumably massive stack of didn't-ask-for-this-but-maybe-I'll-read-it books, and so I'm also grateful to the writer of that piece and the *Times* editor who said, "Print it." I'm humbled and thankful for Stephen King's kind words, and those of Paul Tremblay, Catherynne Valente, Stephen Graham Jones, Catriona Ward, and Josh Malerman.

Finally, my thanks to you, dear reader. I couldn't do it without you.

About the Author

Christopher Golden is the *New York Times*-bestselling author of *Ararat*, *Road of Bones*, *Snowblind*, and many other novels. With Mike Mignola, he is the co-creator of such comics series as *Baltimore*, *Lady Baltimore*, and *Joe Golem: Occult Detective*. Golden has edited and co-edited numerous anthologies, including *Seize the Night*, *The New Dead*, *Hex Life* and Shirley Jackson Award-winner *The Twisted Book of Shadows*. The author has been nominated ten times in eight different categories for the Bram Stoker Awards, and won twice. Golden is also a screenwriter and producer, as well as a writer of audio dramas and video games. He lives in Massachusetts.

Twitter: @ChristophGolden
Facebook: ChristopherGoldenAuthor
Instagram: christopher_golden